BROWSING COLLECTION
14-DAY CHECKOUT
No Holds • No Renewals

HUSH HARBOR

HUSH HARBOR

a novel

ANISE VANCE

HANOVER
SQUARE
PRESS

HANOVER
SQUARE
PRESS™

Recycling programs
for this product may
not exist in your area.

ISBN-13: 978-1-335-44952-8

Hush Harbor

Hanover Square Press
22 Adelaide St. West, 41st Floor
Toronto, Ontario M5H 4E3, Canada
HanoverSqPress.com
BookClubbish.com

Printed in U.S.A.

For Aggy, Richard and Hudson Vance.

For Grandma and Mamanjoon.

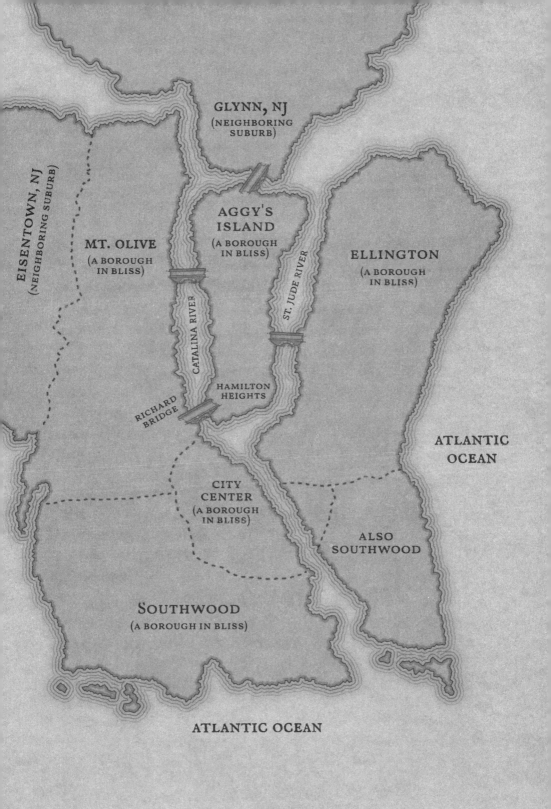

PART ONE

Malik

1

A SOLDIER APPROACHED THE CAR. The dog at his side raised its snout and snarled at the darkening purple sky. Malik put a hand on his chest expecting a ripple of fear. It did not come. Instead, his heart tightened at the thought of his grandfather, hundreds of miles away, alone, at home, dosing himself with anxiety pills because his only grandchild had set out for Bliss City that morning. By nightfall, that grandchild would be a traitor or a corpse or a member of the Hush Harbor resistance.

Malik had left a goodbye note. Should he have asked permission? Sat down and explained why he was joining what his grandfather called a moral circus? Malik knew the conversation would rapidly devolve. His grandfather would cite empty maxims about the arc of moral history and working with your enemies and forgiveness, forgiveness, forgiveness. Malik would listen with compassion, and his doubt would grow. He would question his decision. How could he not? Leaving would break his grandfather's heart.

No, Malik thought. It was better to simply disappear into the night with a duffel bag on his shoulder, a small notebook in his pocket and a bus ticket in his hand.

The soldier knocked on the driver's seat window. Malik noticed Zahra's knuckles turn white on the steering wheel. She rolled down her window, letting in the humid air. A raindrop landed on the windshield. Then another. The soldier glanced at the clouds and cursed before he handed Zahra her documents.

"Your license and registration checked out," he said.

"Like I told you," Zahra replied. "We're visiting our uncle. He's getting up there."

The soldier nodded and pursed his lips. "Don't do anything stupid."

"Of course."

"Five miles down this road, there's another checkpoint. And you're going to need special permissions to get past that one."

"Got it."

"How far in is your uncle?"

Zahra glanced at the GPS. "Just a couple of miles from here."

"Go straight there. No sightseeing."

"We understand."

"Okay."

The soldier backed away and they drove through the checkpoint. The rain grew heavy and encircled the car as the voice of the GPS spouted directions. Malik stole glances at Zahra. He tried to imagine what she was feeling. Was she tamping down her fear? Energized by her anger? He wondered if he should start a conversation, then considered her stiff-backed posture and thought better of it. Her attention stayed true to the road.

Two hours prior, she had picked him up at Philadelphia's Penn Station. He'd taken a mostly sleepless twelve-hour bus ride from Durham. Despite his exhaustion, he immediately recognized an evolution in his former college mentor. Once upon a time, she reminded him of a brown Medusa. Her hair, all bounce and curls, stormed around her shoulders. She led rallies with a bullhorn pinned to her lips and indignation bottled in her throat. While she was neither the most eloquent nor the most charismatic of Chapel Hill's campus leaders, Malik had envied her boldness, her unabashed expressions of rage. He also envied the bullhorn, so teasingly close to her lips.

She balanced her public persona with relentless compassion in her private life. She often pulled the freshmen radicals aside and asked after their families, their grades, their troubles. She remembered who read which poet and who loved what type of muffin and who needed an extra nudge to speak up. She bathed them in attention and they showered her in adoration, much of it unwanted. It took Malik a full eight months to accept that his crush would not be returned. Still, at the end of the school year, when she graduated, he was crestfallen.

Four years later, she'd barely greeted him when she picked him up. He had imagined her observing changes in his demeanor. In his physique. Still well shy of six feet tall, he had sprouted several inches from his freshman height. Never particularly athletic, he had taken on a gym habit over the last year. For the first time, his forearms showed veins and his chest was squared with muscle. He carried himself with the fresh confidence of someone newly attuned to the potential in his limbs. He had complemented his reconstructed body with a hairstyle that better suited his angular face. No longer did he wear the high-top box cut that reeked of *The Fresh Prince*. His buzzed hair grounded him, made him feel older. Mature, even. It prompted him to stop experimenting with facial hair and shave his patchy beard and undergrown mustache. In his thirties, maybe, he would try again.

To his great dismay, Zahra either dismissed or did not notice these changes.

He, on the other hand, immediately noted her hair. Pulled back tight in a ponytail. He could not recall seeing it like that in college.

They drove across Franklin Bridge in silence. His eyes darted from the dashboard to her face to the Delaware River beneath them. Hesitantly, he cleared his throat. She lifted two fingers off the steering wheel.

"We're not going to talk yet," she said.

He bristled at her command. Had he done something wrong? He pulled the small black notebook from his pocket and reviewed notes from their prior conversation. He had followed her instructions to the letter. They had met at the appointed time and place. He had brought nothing with him. He had told no one where he was going or why. Not even his grandfather.

He stuffed the notebook back in his pocket. Perhaps, he thought, her silence was an indictment of the Zahra that lived in his imagination. He had forgotten her flaws and kept only the hero's virtues. Maybe his initial impression of her, colored by a rush of freshman enthusiasm, was also to blame. Surely an eager-to-please eighteen-year-old was not the best judge of character.

Now, after passing through the checkpoint with its soldiers and dogs, he felt a mix of determination and anxiety. He attempted to direct his attention to the landscape but made out only the outline of a gas station through the sheets of rain.

"I can't believe you're actually here," Zahra said. "You're kind of an idiot, you know."

Malik turned to her, startled more at the sound of words than at their content.

"What?" he said.

"You probably shouldn't be here."

"What are you talking about?"

"You should be at home. Safe. With your family, your grandfather. Finishing your grad school applications."

He narrowed his eyes. "You're mad I'm not completing my applications?"

"You're supposed to be a historian. Not a freedom fighter. Or whatever we are."

"Aren't you supposed to be graduating law school right now?"

"It's not the same. I hate law school. You love history."

He paused for a beat. "Grad school or no grad school, you could also still be at home. Safe. With your family."

"My family—" She stopped herself and waved a hand dismissively. "The point is you shouldn't be here, but you came anyway, and…"

Heat rushed over his skin.

"You recruited me."

"I've recruited a lot of people."

"And I'm one of them."

"I have mixed feelings about that."

"We're literally going to Bliss right now. I'm going to fight."

A smile, bemused, flickered over her lips. "Do you know what you're fighting for?"

"Justice."

She rolled her eyes and he suddenly felt like a child. "Justice?"

"Yes," he said, loudly, in hopes volume might cover his creeping uncertainty. "Justice."

"The people you're going to meet are serious people. Don't embarrass yourself with clichés."

"It's true though."

"What's true is that white supremacy doesn't respond to reasonable appeals based on justice. It responds to threats."

Malik recalled saying almost the exact same thing to his grandfather. He scolded himself for declaring his fight in a way that was both true and too obvious. He would have to harness his tendency toward simplistic idealism. It smacked of naivete.

"You're right," he said, hoping the concession would shift the tone of their conversation. "And that's why I'm joining Hush Harbor."

"You're not understanding what I'm saying."

Annoyance ran through him. "Fine. Then say it in a way that I'll understand."

"Hush Harbor threw out its list of demands. It doesn't negotiate. Its only purpose is to uproot white supremacy wherever it exists and plant down something entirely different. You either do that by force or you die in the process. Maybe both. This isn't the kiddie version of revolution. This is an uprising. You and I and everyone there… Who knows if we come out."

Malik absorbed her meaning. He heard the guilt in her voice. That was it, then: the reason for her silence and her mixed feelings and her distanced posture. She was worried for him. He leaned back in his seat and scratched at a hole in the car roof's fabric. He wondered how to tell her that she was not among his motivations for joining the revolution. Instead he remembered his parents, how they were taken from him, and fury flared in his gut.

"You once said that to submit to oppression is worse than to perish in a hopeless cause. I believe that. Not because you said it, but because it's true."

"I said that?"

"In college. On a panel."

"I used to be pretty smart."

"It's easy to be smart in school."

She smiled and Malik recognized a warm glimmer of the Zahra he had known.

"I'm here because I want to be," he said. "Not because you started texting me."

She glanced at him from the corner of her eye.

"I didn't want to pull you into this," she said. "But they asked me to find someone for a particular job. I thought of you."

"They?"

Zahra turned off the ignition and Malik belatedly noticed they were parked in a suburban cul-de-sac. How long had they been still? He looked out the window, examining the modest homes through the rain. Malik's grandfather warned him about these kinds of places. *Don't go walking there*, he would say. *Don't even go out past dark. Don't become the next stand-your-ground debate.*

"Well, she. Not 'they,'" Zahra said. She pressed her palms

against her head, flattening her hair. She seemed suddenly distracted. "You'll find out soon enough. Stay focused on tonight."

Malik grabbed his duffel bag and followed her to the patio of a small blue house, just as a clap of thunder reached them. A middle-aged woman with squared shoulders appeared in the doorframe. Though she was just a few inches over five feet, Malik recognized strength bundled in her arms: a fighter or bodybuilder, or both. Not someone with whom to trade fists. He felt vaguely racist for thinking she was Chinese. She could just as well be Korean or Japanese or Vietnamese. He couldn't tell the difference. Was that bigoted? His anxiousness resurfaced and he took a step back.

"Zahra," the woman said. "Good to see you again."

"You, too."

The woman delivered Malik a blank stare.

"Call me Suzanne."

She waved them in impatiently and directed them to a small living room with family pictures on the walls.

"You're on time," she said. "Barely. We leave at last light. That's ten minutes from now. Snack bars are in the kitchen if you're hungry. Take no more than two." Her eyes settled on Malik. "You're not going to eat dinner tonight. If you were early, you could've joined me for pasta. I've got clothes for each of you upstairs. You'll need to change into them. Leave your old clothes here. Leave your bag, too. Leave everything. You understand?"

"What about my note—"

"Everything. No exceptions." She cracked her knuckles. "You need to go to the bathroom? Because if you do, now's the time. We're not going to stop for potty breaks."

Malik raised his hand.

"This isn't a classroom," Suzanne said.

"I have a question. You didn't let me finish last time. Why do we need new clothes?"

Zahra shot him a look. "You'll see in a minute."

Suzanne nodded. "Zahra, come with me. We've got a new protocol for you." She gestured at Malik and then at the stairs. "You, go get ready."

Ten minutes later, Malik idled on the porch wearing the clothes laid out for him. He had faithfully followed Suzanne's directions with one exception: he kept his notebook. He passed a hand over the embroidered garbage truck on the left side of his black shirt, above the initials GCC. He found no tags on the black pants and no insignia on the black sneakers. The notebook fit snugly into his back pocket.

Zahra emerged from the house with her head shaved clean. The sight of her hairless momentarily stunned him. She ran a hand down her skull.

"What happened?" Malik asked.

"She shaved it," Zahra said.

"Why?"

Zahra shrugged. "We'll find out soon."

"She didn't say anything?"

"No."

"Did you ask?"

"Malik."

"Did you?"

"What did we just talk about? When someone tells you to do something, you do it. Exactly the way they say. No questions."

Malik's spirit rebelled at that thought. Questions, polite and insistent, were the foremost expression of his identity. How could he, a Black scholar in the making, not query the world? He gestured at her car, parked down the street.

"You're just going to leave your car?"

Zahra shook her head. "It's Hush Harbor's car."

Suzanne pulled up in a green station wagon. A painted sign that read GCC ran across its side. As soon as they were seated, she pulled away from the curb. Malik, rather deliberately, asked another question.

"What's the plan?"

Suzanne made no sign she heard him. A minute passed. When she spoke, he could not tell if it was in response to him or her own initiative.

"The checkpoints are built on concentric circles radiating out of Bliss. Think of a dartboard. Aggy's Island is the bull's-eye. Make sense?"

Malik pictured a map of Bliss, New Jersey. Only two miles at its widest and four miles long, Aggy's Island reminded him of a miniature Manhattan: a Bliss City borough, one of five, entirely surrounded by water. The St. Jude River ran along its northern and eastern borders while the Catalina River bounded it to the west. As if squeezed, the island narrowed until it formed a tip at its southernmost edge. There, the Catalina flowed into the larger St. Jude. Hamilton Heights, once the largest housing project on Aggy's Island and now home to the Hush Harbor revolution, sat on a hill above the joining rivers.

"Yes," Malik said. "Makes sense."

Suzanne nodded and continued. "As the circles become smaller, the security gets tighter. You passed a checkpoint that granted you entry beyond the first circle. That one is just a formality. A warning fifty miles away from the city. Each successive circle is more difficult to penetrate than the last. You need special permissions to go in or out. Zahra, open the glove compartment. You'll find two IDs, one for each of you."

Zahra handed Malik a laminated blue slip, listing a series of attributes: name, age, weight, social security number, address. A fuzzy photo of someone who looked vaguely like him filled the corner. He noted a barcode and a series of numbers on the back.

"That's called your Blue ID. It gets you in. It gets you out. If an officer stops you and you can't produce it, you're subject to indefinite detention and interrogation. It's your only—and I mean only—protection tonight." She paused to underscore her meaning. "Do you understand?"

"I understand," Malik said.

"Good. Now look at the back of the ID. In the top right-hand corner, the GCC logo." He flipped over the card. It matched the logo from his uniform. "GCC stands for Green Collecting Cooperative. That's a garbage pickup company. There are still some people living in Bliss's outer boroughs and suburbs in addition to the National Guard and police forces that are essentially squatting there. They need their garbage hauled away. So, tonight, we're trash collectors."

"Why would we be picking up trash at night?" he asked.

"They limit the number of vehicles allowed on streets inside the circles. Those who have priority get the hours they want. Trash collectors do not have priority."

Flashing lights and a barricade appeared in front of them. Suzanne slowed the car. As they inched forward, several National Guard vehicles, with their lights on, came into view. They occupied the width of the road. Suzanne collected Malik's and Zahra's Blue IDs and rolled down her window as a round-faced soldier approached the car. Another circled it with a sniffing dog.

"IDs," he said, pushing back the hood of his raincoat.

Suzanne handed him their identification.

"You're GCC?"

"Yes."

He pointed his flashlight at Zahra and then at Malik. It momentarily blinded them.

"Open the trunk and the hood."

Suzanne popped them open. The soldier with the dog inspected them. He nodded at the round-faced soldier.

"Step outside. One at a time. Starting with the driver."

The soldier patted Suzanne down, then he called for Zahra, and then Malik. Malik discreetly slid his notebook from his back pocket before opening the door and placing his hands on top of the car. The soldier's hands hit his body roughly. They swept down his shoulders and his sides. When they got between his legs, shame shot through him.

"I'm not enjoying this any more than you are," the soldier said. Somehow, Malik knew differently. The lilt in the soldier's voice, the melody of power. The energy coming off his hands. Did he linger an extra second on his thigh? Malik told himself to remain still. He had practiced restraint his whole life, made an art of it. If Suzanne and Zahra could get through the soldier's invasive touch, so could he.

When Malik got back in the car, the soldier disappeared into one of the vehicles in front of them. Malik found his notebook and placed a palm over it. His shirt, now wet, clung to his torso. A minute stretched to ten. A different soldier, taller than the other two, returned and handed back the IDs.

"You've been here before," he said to Suzanne.

"Yes, sir," she said.

"You've got to go through three more checkpoints."

"I remember."

"You know how much time you got?"

"Yes."

"Six hours." The soldier glanced over his shoulder and pointed down the road, his lower arm blocking his mouth from the other soldiers' line of sight. His voice softened. "Don't take more than five. New orders are anyone suspicious is an enemy combatant. Fire at will. If they're confused about who you are or how long you've been out, they won't hesitate."

"We'll be back in time."

The soldier sniffed loudly, dropped his arm. Malik read the name sewn over his breast pocket: *P. Schwab*. Was he one of theirs? A Hush Harbor spy? Malik sat very still, as if the wrong movement might give Schwab away.

"Okay," Schwab said. He motioned at the cars. They drifted apart to make a small opening. "You can go."

Suzanne drove through the opening. A mile later, they stopped at a red light. Malik looked out the back window. The checkpoint had been swallowed by the storm. To his right, a mall sign advertised a handful of anchor stores: Gap, JCPenny, Macy's, Nordstrom. Through the rain, he noted boarded-up windows. A valiant parking lot light flickered, its bulb fighting the dark.

Eventually, they reached another checkpoint. They passed it only to repeat the process again. Fresh waves of humiliation flooded Malik at each pat-down. What gave them the right? A constitution drawn up by slaveholders and rapists and toothless thieves? With effort, he again distanced himself from his fury, assessed it intellectually. He reminded himself that Black people were murdered by the police before Obama took office and well after Trump left it. White violence transcended electoral politics. He brought to mind historical lessons he learned in college, whiteness as an ideology wed to capitalism, capitalism as the engine of the state. State authority as power predicated on violence. His emotions steadied as he sank into scholarly repose. When his list of evidence finally arrived at the current year, 2030, he was more certain of his decision to join Hush Harbor than ever before.

Ninety minutes after their six-hour window began, they passed a fifth checkpoint and turned two corners before arriving at a strip of warehouses. They drove to the end of the road and parked in a dirt lot filled with garbage trucks.

"Let's go," Suzanne said, leaving the car.

Malik clambered out, noting that the rain had finally eased to a drizzle. The sound of lapping waves reached him. He blinked and waited for his eyes to adjust to the dark. Less than fifty yards from where they stood, flat ground gave way to a steep bluff overlooking the St. Jude River. He watched it flow south before curling away. He considered its path and used it to pinpoint their location. They had parked just north of the city, across the river from the borough that was their destination: Aggy's Island. A cautious optimism settled over him. Hush Harbor lived at the southern tip of Aggy's Island. They were only a handful of miles and a river-crossing away.

Three sharp knocks on the garbage truck wrested him from city gazing. Figures emerged from behind the truck. He thought his imagination was playing tricks on him. Among the figures stood a thin Black man about Malik's height. A woman, not an inch taller than Zahra, stood next to him, her head also shaved. At passing glance, especially in the dark, the newcomers were passable replicas of him and Zahra. A third figure approached. She more than resembled Suzanne: she was her spitting image.

Malik leaned toward Zahra.

"Does Suzanne have a twin?"

"Quiet," Zahra said.

Suzanne and her apparent twin hugged briefly.

"They're ready," Suzanne said.

"Okay," said her twin.

"The ghosts have their papers?"

The two look-alikes flashed Blue IDs.

"They know their names?" said Suzanne.

"Ask them."

Suzanne questioned the look-alikes. Names, addresses, weights. They answered correctly.

"Okay." She pulled a pair of coats from the garbage truck and handed them to Malik and Zahra. "Wear these. And make sure you put the hoods on."

Malik followed the order, but the coat was heavy. It would only make their warm and humid night more difficult.

"Why do we need these?"

Suzanne pointed upward. "Surveillance. At night they spot you using thermal imaging. We have to mask your body's temperature. The coat's outer layer matches the temperature around you. The inner layer matches your own temperature. Touch your lower back."

Malik felt a hard square stitched into the coat.

"Is that a battery?"

Suzanne nodded.

"Does it actually work?"

"So far." Suzanne shrugged. "Or we've just been lucky."

Malik wondered many things: How did the coat sense hot and cold? How did it adjust its own temperature? And how had Hush Harbor acquired technology that must have been developed for or by the military? Before he could ask, Suzanne pointed to her twin, who had also put on a coat.

"Follow Myra. Good luck."

Myra walked toward the bluff. Malik and Zahra scampered after her. Behind them, Malik heard Suzanne and the look-alikes climb into a garbage truck and drive off. The truck became a hushed rumble when they reached the bluff's edge. Myra snapped her fingers for Malik's attention.

"This is the last time we speak till we get there. Pointing forward means go straight. Right means right, left means left. I point down, that means stop moving. I move my hand side to side, that means drop to the ground." She frowned, peered over the river. Night had fallen. "What do you think happens if the police catch us? We're worse than criminals. Worse than enemies. We're traitors." Her eyes locked on Malik's. "Follow every instruction exactly as given. Got it?"

"Got it," he said.

Myra started down the bluff. Malik took several deep breaths and followed. The mud slid beneath his feet and he slipped. His hands scraped against the ground. He managed to right his body and took his next strides carefully. Every so often, he looked up to see Zahra navigating the steep slope with small steps and arms stretched out for balance. He copied her approach.

At the bottom, Myra allowed them a moment to regain their

footing. He wiped his brow and the salt from his sweat mixed with cuts on his palm. His hand stung. He grimaced and set aside the pain. The St. Jude flowed against a sandy bank only a dozen yards away. He edged toward it before Myra snapped her fingers and pointed east and their trek began again.

The bank widened as they trudged through drizzle and mud. Its waves coiling, the St. Jude seemed more rope than water. He sensed anger in it and did not know whether to fear or welcome the emotion. They edged away from the river to the top of the sandy bank. Myra came to a sudden stop next to a patch of tall weeds.

"What's happening?"

"Quiet, Malik," Zahra said.

Myra rummaged through the weeds and plucked out a long metal rod with a hook on one end. She tapped the hook against the ground. It clinked. Metal on metal. A rusted manhole lay at their feet.

"Are we…"

Myra stared at Malik as though he were a child.

"When I pop the cover, you lift it off. Put it back down with one of its lips a couple of inches over the hole." She gestured for him and Zahra to stand on opposite sides of her. "On three."

She stuck the hook into the plate and hoisted it as Malik and Zahra searched for grip. They heaved the plate upward and set it down just as Myra instructed.

Myra retrieved a thumb-sized flashlight from her pocket and knelt. She bent an ear to the hole. Zahra followed suit and Malik mimicked them. He heard gentle sloshing.

"No," Myra said, hardly audible.

She pointed the light at the hole. An arm's length down: water. She leaned back on her heels and switched off the flashlight.

"Shit."

"Shit?" Malik said.

Myra and Zahra stood. They exchanged a tense glance. Malik scrambled to his feet.

"There's a backup plan," Malik said. "A different route?"

Myra nodded. She opened her mouth as if to speak, but then something caught her eye over Malik's shoulder. He turned and saw a speck of light bobbing on the St. Jude. He heard a faint buzz and the light doubled in size. He looked at Myra. Her hand moved side to side frantically. "Down," she ordered. "Police." She dropped to the ground. Zahra, too. He looked at the light and made out the outline of a Jet Ski. One? Two? He felt a hard tug on his pant leg and suddenly his limbs went to jelly.

"Get down," Zahra said, her voice a hiss.

He dropped, his heart hammering.

"Don't. Move," Zahra whispered.

He went still. The engine's buzz beat against his eardrum. Malik remembered Schwab's warning: orders to fire at will. Above him, fluorescent light drenched the bluff, then moved downward. He pressed himself against the earth, sensing the light skim the crown of his head. He thought, my grandfather was right. This was a mistake. In an instant, the light moved on, and darkness returned. The engines wailed away, but still he hesitated to move. He tried to breathe and found his lungs rattled but working. Slowly, he turned his chin and saw Zahra lying next to him.

"You're a fucking idiot," she said, under her breath. She pushed herself up and reluctantly lent him a hand.

Myra, already standing, gripped his shoulders. He recognized compassion, stern though it was, in her expression. His chin trembled. "We're okay. You're okay. Breathe." She held him for another moment as his feet steadied. When she turned, a pang of fear burst into his chest. He reminded himself that they had not actually been spotted. As they started walking, his limbs came back to solid form but his nerve endings tingled. He resolved not to be caught in a frozen panic again.

They trudged on. He glanced over his shoulder and could no longer make out the Jet Skis. Beneath them, the mud softened. They walked for another thirty minutes or so, until they reached a small cave at the base of the bluff. Myra turned on her flashlight to reveal a speedboat crammed inside. Hurriedly, she switched the light off and motioned for them to pull the boat. It scraped against rock as they dragged it free of the cave. Once on mud, it slid easily across the bank and into the river. Myra climbed in when they were thigh deep in the water. Zahra followed and Malik scrambled in last, cautious not to tip the boat. Myra checked her watch and gazed across the river. She took in a deep breath and pulled the engine cord. The boat came to life, zipping across the St. Jude more quietly than the Jet Skis. Water crashed over the stern, sloshing at their feet. The boat jostled so hard Malik thought it might capsize. Myra deftly moved the rudder and the vessel found its center.

As they approached shore, Malik expected docks to appear. Instead, he saw only another sandy bank leading to another steep bluff. He wondered if crossing in the most inhospitable location was a safety measure: sections of the river with piers that led to gentle ridges were likely heavily patrolled.

Myra cut off the engine a dozen yards from shore. Malik and Zahra followed her as she slipped into the St. Jude and grabbed hold of the boat. They guided it to the bank before Myra gestured toward the bluff. They left the boat behind a jut of rock, hidden from all but the most observant passersby.

They continued along the shore and soon a daze dropped over Malik. The lack of sleep and water and food. He stared at his feet and tried to focus on his breath.

"You okay?" Zahra whispered.

"Tired."

She pointed ahead at a concrete bridge that spanned the river and its shores. "Hush Harbor is on our side of Richard Bridge. City Center is on the other side."

Even in his exhaustion, Malik marveled at Bliss's landscape: bluffs rose sharply from the river's sandy banks, lending the city a romantic aura more akin to clifftops and lighthouses than industrial jungle. Richard Bridge ran from a bluff that marked the end of downtown to a bluff that marked the beginning of Aggy's Island. Close to the bridge's ends, steep staircases led down to the shore for pedestrians interested in fishing, boating or strolling along the water. Simpler times, Malik thought. Now the staircase represented the final leg of their journey through a conflict zone.

"Almost there," Zahra said. She squeezed his elbow and dropped behind him.

Malik imagined driving across Richard Bridge from City Center to Aggy's Island. The Hamilton Heights projects, home of the Hush Harbor revolution, was the first set of buildings just off to the right. In pictures, they struck him as a study in ambivalence, a cluster of dull brown structures unwilling to decide if they were intended for families or prisoners or the gloom of unkept promises. He tried to remember the maps. Hamilton Heights' nine buildings formed two letter *u*'s, with the smaller *u* nestled inside the larger one. Their flat ends, open, faced the river. Their shape reminded him of shells resting on a shore.

He returned his attention to their trek with renewed energy. As they approached the bridge, a fluorescent light flashed over the staircase. His heart quickened. Had Myra set her flashlight on it? He looked ahead to her. She did not move. She held nothing in her hands. His breath stilled.

Behind them, a buzz. He turned and caught a glimpse of a police boat, its docking lights washing over his face. The engine wailed and above it a bullhorn: "Don't move."

Zahra pulled on his arm and began to run. His legs jolted awake and he raced after her. He twisted an ankle in the sand and righted himself and sprinted harder. The bullhorn commanded them to stop. It warned of something he could not hear over his heartbeat. He caught Zahra and Myra just as they reached the staircase and dove onto its steps and three short blasts rang out. At their feet, a chunk of the staircase's concrete siding fell. Above them, dirt crumbled from the ridge as if a waterfall. No sign of the third bullet. They scrambled up the steps on all fours, Zahra in the lead. The bullhorn shouted more commands. Malik heard Myra grunt below him. He looked back. One of her legs pushed her up a step, the other lay limp.

"On my back," he whispered. She nodded. He sidled under her and she wrapped her arms around his chest.

"Quickly," she said.

He pushed an inch off his stomach and dragged them onto the next step. The engine grew louder as though the boat were coming to shore. He felt Myra tense each time her leg thumped against his. Her weight bore down on him. A bead of sweat dripped off his forehead. His lower back spasmed. Just as he thought his strength might wane, Myra flew off him. A second later, hands gripped his shoulders and pulled him over the last step and onto the bridge. He landed with his cheek to asphalt. The squeal of a tire shoving across pavement came from behind him. Footsteps worked around his sides.

"Gunshot wound," a voice said. "Her leg."

He raised his eyes. Two large figures lifted Myra and carried her along a slim pathway lined by disfigured vehicles. Zahra trailed them. They rounded a corner and disappeared from sight. His ragged breath stirred small stones on the ground. He rose to one knee and glanced behind him. An enormous motorcycle now covered the entryway to the staircase. He listened for the police speedboat's engine. In the distance, he heard a faint whir soften into silence. He stood slowly as though testing his own strength.

Dump trucks and rusted SUVs and discolored minivans surrounded him. Hush Harbor's makeshift barricade. He inched forward, right up against one of the trucks. He searched for an orienting sign. On his left, a beam of light cut through a crack between the truck and an RV. He peered through the crack and counted three more rows of vehicles. He leaned forward.

The crack ran through the barricade, a direct view across Richard Bridge. On the other end, a hundred yards away, a tall metal fence with razor wire warned the world from approaching. The government's barricade. A half-dozen watchhouses, made of glass and metal, were raised onto platforms behind the fence. Floodlights watched over the eerie structures and illuminated the bridge. He could see outlines of soldiers inside each watchhouse.

A pair of eyes blinked at him from the pickup truck's window. He stumbled back and caught himself against another car. The face, not much older than his, delivered a grim stare. The realization came quickly: Hush Harbor's own guards. The man looked at him and mouthed, *Go.* He sped down the passageway, alert to other eyes watching him. The trail between cars turned right and curled back on itself. At several junctures, it split. A string of red dots stained the path along which Myra had been carried. He followed the trickle of blood through the maze.

2

THE SCRATCHES ON THE ceiling were disconcerting. Malik hoped they were the remnants of a dream he could not remember. He blinked several times, but when he refocused, the three long lines remained. Were they evidence of desperate clawing? A fight or a madness or a nightmare? Regardless, how did they get on the ceiling?

He rotated to his side as pieces of the previous night floated back to him. His conversation with Zahra. The checkpoints and pat-downs and Jet Skis. The bridge with its watchhouses and soldiers. He wondered where Myra had been taken. He figured there must be a makeshift infirmary at Hush Harbor, some place where people heal.

The rest of the room was empty but for the mattress he lay on and a wooden chair and a bedside table. He registered a piece of paper, propped into a triangle, saluting him from the table. Hastily, he reached for it.

The note instructed him to attend a meeting in Morrison Hall at 1 p.m. He glanced at his watch. Five minutes. Less than a handful of hours at Hush Harbor and he had already fallen a step behind. He scrambled off the bed and squeezed on his shoes, grabbed his small notebook from the bedside table and jammed it in his pocket. He read the note again. It gave clear directions. Down the hall to the stairs, two flights to the ground floor, a right and then through the metal double doors. On the stairs, he noticed Myra's dried blood on a pant leg of his jeans. He caught himself against the banister and then kept moving. No time to think about clean clothes.

On the ground floor, he rounded a corner and then another, and soon realized he had gone too far. "Shit," he said, under his breath. He half jogged back down a long hallway and stopped when he heard voices behind a door. He looked at his watch and felt relief: a minute to spare. Just as he was about to open the door, a tautness in the conversation kept him from entering.

"That won't be the last time," said a man's voice.

"You keep saying that," a woman replied. "I'm well aware."

"They're firing at will."

"That was always their policy."

"They're getting more aggressive with it."

"What did you expect? The government to lay off?"

"They'll attack Hamilton Heights soon."

"So you say."

"You know I'm right."

"So what if you are? Are we supposed to shoot first?"

"If we know what they're going to do, then we have the right to stop them."

"Self-defense. We resist in self-defense. We agreed to that."

"That's suicide, Nova."

Malik stepped back. *The* Nova Prince? The other person, the man, must be her brother, Jeremiah. He chided himself for not instantly identifying the voices of the revolution's leaders. How had he not recognized their intonation, their cadence? He had studied their talks with the same tenacity he'd studied for final exams. The siblings shared an assertive speech pattern. Their sentences started fast and high and ended in low-pitched final-

ity. Even their questions sounded like declarations. From behind the door, Malik heard an edge in their voices he had not
registered before. He realized they were talking about Myra.
This could not possibly be the meeting he was supposed to attend. He glanced at a plastic sign next to the doorframe: it read
Room B1, not Morrison Hall. Thank God he had not entered.

Maybe, though, he could spare another moment listening in.
Hearing the revolution's innermost conversations was among his
chief desires. How did Nova and Jeremiah Prince come to their
decisions? What logic guided them? More to the point: How did
they think? He desperately wanted to learn at their feet.

Then, he considered the ramifications of being caught eaves-
dropping. The embarrassment. Overcoming his aching curiosity, he walked away and prayed they would not soon leave the
room and catch him slinking down the hall.

He retraced his steps and found a sign for Morrison Hall next to
double doors. Hurriedly, he entered and joined a circle of twenty
or so young people in various states of disrepair. They mumbled
in nervous conversation and kept their eyes to the entrance after
he passed through it. A mural reached from floor to ceiling on
the opposite wall. He was about to examine it more closely when
the door hinges squealed, and a lean woman entered. Thick braids
hung well past her shoulders. Two people followed behind her.
The room hushed. Collectively, they recognized her. Fidgeting
hands slowed to a still. Attentiveness, like a candle, lit.

Malik had seen her in interviews, quoted countless times on
social media. She was the topic of talk shows and blogs and his
own dinner table. On screens, her face exuded defiance. Sharp
angles and squints. In person, her features were softer. A tiny
scar on her left cheek, some gray hair at the roots of her braids.
Signs she was more human than symbol.

She took a seat and crossed her legs. A smile hovered over
her lips, that of a performer in complete command. As a stagehand in college, Malik had witnessed actors sweat and fidget

and vomit before taking the stage. Some contained their anxiety by running through lines, others jumped up and down or became overly verbose. Few were so certain of their gifts that they remained entirely calm. But those few were the reason Malik loved being a stagehand. Unseen, he could shape their worlds by rigging scenery or organizing props or gently offering bits of encouragement backstage. He never wanted the spotlight, afraid of what it might bare in him, but he did long to be part of the show. And he quickly learned that the only shows worth his time had a lead who knew her power. A lead like Nova.

Malik took out his notebook, eager to record her words.

"Good morning," she said. "Welcome." She went around the circle making sporadic eye contact, nodding as if she had known them all for years. Eager expressions replied yes, indeed, somehow she had.

"Strange. I don't mean to be self-deprecating, but how strange. That you were waiting to hear from me."

She paused.

Nova Prince's name was almost as well-known as the president's. They likely would have waited for hours or days to hear her speak. Malik, undoubtedly, would have. She was the face of a revolution.

She went on.

"Twelve months ago, I was a second-year law student who couldn't get called on in class. I used to spend countless hours studying, hoping to impress my peers and professors. Like many of you, I was highly idealistic. I was set on a career through which I could do the most public good. I thought I was going to be the next Thurgood Marshall or Bryan Stevenson or, with more than an ounce of luck, Sonia Sotomayor. But nagging questions refused to leave me. What history was the law coming from? What assumptions did it make about human nature? What powers confined it, subdued it, beat it down?

"The more I learned, the more I saw the law for what it was— the bruised pulp of what we once named justice.

"I started raising my hand in class more often. The professors entertained my questions at first. Then, they started to ignore me. Most of my fellow students did the same. I was the instigator. The radical. The person who would not just shut up and learn and content herself with the smallness of their arguments."

Nova lingered. She placed her fingers over her mouth and dropped her chin. A moment passed. Another. The air thickened. She lifted her head.

"I promise you, that will be the story of our country. There were 98 percent of us absorbed in our tiny debates. Feeding our inconsequential egos. Fixated on owning an acre of status or wealth or both. Lost in the trees.

"Then there were the few of us who saw neither the trees nor the forest. We saw the soil. We noticed that there was rot. We rubbed the dirt between our fingertips and knew it was poisoned. Beyond redemption.

"Remember, you are not here for incremental changes. You are not here to reform only one police department or to bring justice to only a handful of officers or to strip away only one set of bad policies. You are at Hush Harbor to build an entirely new society free from white supremacy. You are here for complete revolution."

The room remained silent, as though a prayer had been spoken. Maybe it had. Malik scribbled several of her key phrases in his notebook. *Lost in the trees. Beyond redemption. Complete revolution.* He scanned his cohort. Some were leaning forward, elbows resting on knees. Others held their breath.

His mind returned to the argument between Nova and Jeremiah. Yes, of course, they were there for revolution. But the more interesting question: *How* to revolt? Clearly, Hush Harbor went far beyond protests and lawsuits and riots. In a turn reminiscent of the Black Panther Party, they took up arms. They seized an entire borough of the city. Sitting in Morrison Hall, the illusion of stability reigned. But just hours ago he'd dropped against St. Jude's muddy banks for fear of a searching police light. He'd carted a bleeding person up a staircase while staring at soldiers eager to hear guns speak. He recognized a noose strung around Hush Harbor.

When Nova spoke again, her tone shifted from stirring to administrative.

"I'd like to meet each of you personally, and I will in the next few days. Right now, though, you need a true orientation. You'll meet with your facilitators upstairs in ten minutes. Until then, go to the bathroom or take a walk. Don't bother trying to text or call anyone." She took out her phone and waved it at the ceiling. "The government jammed most frequencies. Apparently, the revolution won't be posted."

The group laughed and slowly dispersed. Malik could tell that many desperately wanted to approach her. They stole glances before half-heartedly slouching away.

Malik hovered by the mural. It tugged at something in him. A memory or lost thought or buried feeling. An enormous blood orange sun, streaked with collaged glass, pulsed at the mural's center, kissing the horizon line. Light bounced off the glass, somehow both threatening and warm. Black cutouts of a girl and a boy sprinted across the horizon. The layered orange backlit the figures, emphasizing their bent knees and elbows and slightly raised chins, their moving joints. Were it not for the long strands of grass beneath their feet he might have thought they were created to live in the sun itself. Symbols painted in nearly transparent colors floated below the horizon. Stars, spirals, branches, turtles. They reminded Malik of figures sewn into cloth fabric sold at a Ghanaian store on his street. His grandfather bought a piece from the shop not long after Malik's parents were imprisoned. After hanging it in their living room, he gathered Malik onto his lap. No more than five at the time, Malik curled into his grandfather's chest, absorbing scents of cedarwood and patchouli.

"Do you know what those shapes mean?"

Malik's grandfather pointed to the symbols, three across, on the fabric. Malik shook his head.

"The first one, the one that looks like a heart with a circle inside, means hope. The cross with two extra lines on the bottom means bravery. The last one is the most important. What does it look like to you?"

Malik answered cautiously. "Like a smile. And then a wheel on top of it."

"Very good. A smile. It means love and harmony."

"What's harmony?"

"Harmony is like when you hear a song. There are many sounds but they all go together. They all make the song work." Malik's grandfather paused to kiss the top of the boy's head. "Why have I put these up?"

Malik searched for an answer. "They're pretty?"

"Yes. And what else?"

"They're important?"

"That's correct. Would you like to know why they are important?"

The boy nodded vigorously.

"You know what it feels like to be sad." His grandfather placed a hand on Malik's chest. It was large and warm and could catch a falling heart. "It's good to be sad when sad things happen. But did you know you can feel two things at the same time? Like when you eat ice cream too fast, you feel pain from the cold and happy because you're eating ice cream. Yes?"

"Yes."

"And so when you're sad, it's possible to feel hope at the same time. These symbols remind us of things that it is sometimes hard to feel." He paused a moment for Malik to digest. "Do you think that it's easy to do that? Feel hope when you're sad?"

"No."

"Why not?"

"When I'm sad, the sad is everywhere. But I'm not sad right now."

"No? What are you feeling now?"

"I'm…angry."

"Why?"

"I heard you. On the phone. It isn't fair. Mom and Dad aren't coming back."

Malik's grandfather drew in a long breath. He squeezed the boy closer to him. They remained silent for a minute. The boy put a hand on his grandfather's stubbly cheek. It was slightly damp. His stomach knotted. Had he done this to his grandfather? Made him cry?

"It's okay, Grandpa," Malik said quietly. "It's okay. I'm not really angry. It's okay."

The old man cleared his throat and set another kiss on Malik's head. He wiped the tears from his face. When he struggled to find words, Malik relieved him of the duty.

"Tell me about the middle one, Grandpa," Malik said. "The bravery one."

Malik saw the symbols every day for two decades. Some days he would think about their meaning, some days he would barely notice them. But they were always there. Reminders of his parents. Reminders of praiseworthy virtues. Mostly, though, reminders to check his anger lest it hurt those closest to him. How early he had learned that lesson, to robe fury in genial smiles and deflection. To present a contentedness bordering on naivete. As he grew older, he tucked his unruliest shoots of rage beneath his intellect. He noticed how much better the world treated him as a Smart Young Boy instead of an Angry Black Kid. He added this to a growing list of reasons to always remain calm. When he entered college, he found the classroom perfectly suited for his suppressed fury. There, he could launch attacks on injustice using academia's clinical language. His detachment was a virtue, his impassivity a power. After graduation, he decided to apply to doctoral programs in history. He envisioned a life of distinguished scholarship.

And, then, a revolution broke out.

Standing next to the mural, he rubbed his temples, wondering how long he had been lost in memory. Was he already late to the orientation? Just then, someone touched his forearm.

"You like the mural?"

He turned around to find Nova staring at him intently. He felt a flush of embarrassment.

"Yes," he said. "It reminds me of a lot."

"Me, too," Nova said.

Malik noticed how dark her irises were. She blinked and resettled her eyes on the painting. She crossed her arms as if to study it.

"Are you an artist?" she asked.

He coughed though he did not need to. An urge to say yes welled up inside of him.

"No. Not really."

"There are plenty of artists here. I'm sure someone would be happy to give you some pointers on painting. If you wanted, of course."

Painting? Malik thought. Here? Where did they get the materials? How did they have enough time to paint?

"It's important," she said. She addressed the words more to the mural than to him.

"What is?"

She shifted her feet. She planted them shoulders' width apart. He grew acutely aware of his limbs. "That you have something to root you. It's easy to forget yourself in our world."

He recognized her tonal shift. From friendly to pensive. It nudged him off-kilter. He tried to unravel her meaning. She glanced at her watch before he could ask more.

"It's time," she said. "Your orientation."

3

THE SKY OFFERED RUMORS of light. Puddles shrank slowly beneath the morning fog, dwindling remnants of a storm. Malik's footsteps patted out a soft rhythm on the concrete paths. In his first few days at Hush Harbor, he established only one habit: rise before the sun and walk.

Around him flower beds, tended to by the children as part of their education, ran down the walkways. Murals of Nat Turner and Marcus Garvey and a dozen other figures safeguarded the night and welcomed the day. Ladders leaned against walls, evidence of paintbrushes searching for more space. In between two buildings, a small field with makeshift soccer goals relaxed in the early morning cool. A single guard walking across the field on his hourly patrol disrupted its tranquility. A reminder that their peace was protected by the potential of violence.

Malik relished the predawn silence. A frenetic energy rolled over Hush Harbor once the sun rose. Worn-out cooks and cleaners set about preparing breakfast for hundreds of people. The night guards swapped patrols with their daytime brethren. Unable to keep their children inside, a few dozen haggard parents trickled out of buildings a little after seven. Then, the rest of Hush Harbor woke. Teachers scurried to makeshift classrooms, a couple of floors of empty apartments they had turned into a school. A separate group, dedicated to inventory of every conceivable material, started counting food, crayons, paper, guns, bullets. Maintenance crews walked the grounds and determined which field's grass needed to be cut and what lightbulbs needed to be changed and which rooms were ripe for repainting. A small set of farmers gathered around community gardens where they planted fruits and vegetables. Malik had envisioned a paramilitary campground where everyone carried a gun and no one attended to basic needs. Instead, he found an emergent society full of tasks and roles and relationships he had only begun to understand. The scholar in him desperately wanted to document this new world, to write its history even as it unfolded.

Market days, more than anything, surprised him. Every Tuesday and Friday, the complex's northern gate was lifted to the surrounding community. Malik had thought the rest of Aggy's Island would be vacated. Those who wished to join the uprising would have, and those who did not would have fled Bliss. But, of course, many stayed. Some had nowhere else to go. Some feared how the police, suspicious of anyone leaving Aggy's Island, might treat them. Some considered themselves part of the revolution but had no wish to reside in a dilapidated housing project when their own homes were close by.

On market days, tables lined the central courtyard and sweaty shoulders jammed against each other. Items were bartered without currency. A homemade chocolate bar for prayer beads. Two rolls of toilet paper for a half of a jar of shea butter. Basement-made beer for a used pair of jeans. Those who did not live at Hush Harbor made sure to visit the kitchens. There, they were given free rations for a few days. Bread, rice, beans. Vegetables, if there were enough. Rarely chicken or beef.

Malik had only seen two market days so far. On the first, he simply marveled at the spectacle. How did so many goods make their way to a militarized section of an already cordoned off island? More immediately, how did Hush Harbor manage the event's logistical complexity? He guessed over five hundred people from surrounding neighborhoods came in and out of Hamilton Heights that day. Soon, he discovered that a group of ten was dedicated to organizing market days. He wondered if the team was too small.

On his second market day, he recognized some of the children who passed through the gate. They also attended Hush Harbor's makeshift school. The realization made him feel silly. Of course a revolution so high-minded would not leave out neighboring children. He should have known.

Now, in the moments before daybreak, he indulged in quiet. He listened to his own choppy breath. He synced it with his walking pace, eased into a rhythm and found himself in one of the complex's small courtyards. Several paths cut through the courtyard's grass and divided it into six triangles that formed the points of a star. At its center, a bed of red roses, decorated by tiny bits of dew, caught what little light made it through the fog. On his second day, Zahra had explained that this was a memorial for Kemba Jefferson.

Malik approached the roses carefully. Fourteen feet by fourteen feet, Zahra had told him. The meaning was obvious. Kemba's age and the number of bullets that struck him. Malik recalled when the news first broke. The hashtag 14x14 flooded his feed. He scrolled through Instagram posts lamenting the death. Some called it a tragedy and left it at that, others decried the specific police officers responsible. The most radical took aim at the police force with terms like *white supremacy* and *mili-*

tarization. One of Malik's acquaintances surprised him with a post that empathized with the police officers. Malik unfollowed him and returned to the posts marked #14x14.

Over the next several weeks, the national media stuck with the story. Malik wondered why this shooting drew so much attention while a thousand others went unnoticed. Perhaps the 14x14 tag's catchiness propelled it to prominence. Malik could not figure why he, too, so steadfastly followed the drama. He watched as increasingly curious journalists flocked to Bliss City press conferences. Mayor Clarence Locke soothed concerns without entirely relieving them. His colleague, Chief of Police Rex Baker, attempted to quash controversy with a tone Malik found patronizing. Reporters pecked at his statements until little was left but the sense of a cover-up. Eventually, Mayor Locke would return to the podium in an effort to clean up the mess. Nevertheless, each press conference ended with journalists more energized than when they had arrived.

Soon, stories claiming Kemba resisted the police circulated online. Major newspapers tried to find sources and verify claims, though no validation came. The stories, however, continued to pop up on Twitter accounts and blogs. Malik slid down a rabbit hole, searched out details and found shifting narratives. He meticulously logged the discrepancies in his notebook. Did Kemba refuse to stop walking when told or did he stop? Was he wearing headphones or not? Did he reach for a gun? Did he shove one of the officers? Was it a punch? Were they even physically close enough for that? When Malik tuned back to network news, he saw speculation reported as fact.

Hunting for more information, he found Twitter accounts that belonged to people protesting outside of Bliss city hall. Pictures showed a hundred of them. He watched live streams of marching and quickly learned that a pair of siblings, Jeremiah and Nova Prince, led them. He read a list of their demands: atop it was a public trial of the two officers involved in Kemba Jefferson's death. Then came demands for inquiries into the operations of the police force, the court system and public school funding. Malik watched a YouTube video of the Prince siblings discussing the myriad ways in which white supremacy thrived in Bliss. They advocated for a full transformation in local and national government: resetting budgets, reinventing programming, realigning missions to meet the needs of the most vulnerable. Calm and resolute, their demeanor resonated with Malik as much as their messages. They spoke as though they were compassionate doctors outlining a critically injured patient's path to recovery. Intuitively, Malik trusted them. In the coming days, he noted the number of views on their video rise from hundreds to thousands to tens of thousands. The number of protestors rose alongside it.

When the media showed no signs of letting the story rest, Chief Baker announced an internal investigation led by the police force itself. Malik observed the number of protestors double. He sensed events would unfold quickly now. At press conferences, reporters aggressively questioned the validity of the local investigation. Soon, with the *New York Times* and the *Washington Post* calling his office, Mayor Locke asked the state government to intervene. The protestors were incensed as reporters outlined the many connections between local and state agencies: How could the state attorney general credibly investigate Bliss City when a quarter of her office once worked for it? The number of protestors doubled again. Finally, the mayor announced a grand jury.

Malik refused the cautious optimism others nurtured. Some pundits and allies envisioned well-trained minds bringing intellect and moral courage to an awful task. Surely, at some point during the deliberations, the seriousness of their duty would take hold of the jurors. Surely justice would be served. Malik recognized the fantasy. He would not be suckered into it. His own life testified to that dream's childishness.

As the case played out behind closed doors, he watched the protests change shape. Marches swelled to thousands of people. Yet despite their growing numbers, the protestors held fewer signs. They broke out into fewer chants. They walked longer distances. They stood for days at a time. With few exceptions, they wore all black. The network news regularly interviewed the police officers selected to cordon off streets and guard against hostile action. Several discussed how they were unnerved by the protestors' silence. The same broadcasts attempted to interview the protestors. Jeremiah and Nova Prince refused, and the rest of the protestors followed suit. Malik noted a shift in their tenor and stance. What was an outburst of indignation had simmered into its most essential fury.

One month after the grand jury was convened, the state prosecutor's office filed a press release. Officers John Marbury and Sylvia Sanders had been cleared of any wrongdoing. The jury decided that, in all likelihood, suicide by police had occurred. A single social media post in which Kemba detailed rationales for suicide was cited as evidence. Just like that, life was supposed to go on.

Despite expecting the verdict, Malik felt despair well inside of him. He went out for a walk, leaving his laptop and his phone in the living room. He spent the next hour meandering through downtown Durham. He caught sight of some old classmates and avoided them. He tried to think of nothing. Even in the brief moments he succeeded, he felt despondency beneath emptiness. Soon, he realized the futility of walking: hope would not be found around the next corner. Shoulders curled inward, he dragged himself back home.

In his living room, he hesitated to pick up his phone. How much more time could he spend letting the world claw at his skin? He allowed himself a single peek at his notifications. He saw a stream of tweets about a video leaked from the jury's deliberations. Instinctively, he clicked on a link. The video was neither too grainy nor too distanced.

A teenage boy with headphones on walks down a quiet street. Two officers, behind him, yell for him to stop. They yell some more. The teenager turns in the direction of the camera. Slight confusion rises on his face. He sees the officers. He appears to nod. He reaches into his pocket. Quickly, the officers raise their guns. In a blink, two shots. In a blink, several more. Four seconds and fourteen total. The boy is on the ground. Whispered screams of *Oh my God* come from above the camera. One of the officers walks, casually, toward the boy. He stands over him. Abruptly, the recording ends.

Malik watched the video dozens of times. He thanked fate for the truth. He thanked cell phones and their cameras and a neighbor wise enough to film from her window.

An hour later, Bliss's local paper reported on the first skirmish. Soon, a dozen separate brawls broke out. Malik scrambled across Instagram and Twitter and Facebook and network news to gather details. He pulled up a map of Bliss, a city he had never visited, to find reference points. On Aggy's Island, near Granby Street, a group of police officers left three Black men unconscious and bleeding. Two died within hours. On Tower Avenue, an officer peeled away from a fight after sustaining three broken ribs and a cracked collarbone. In City Center, over a dozen protestors were severely injured along with a few cops. Wave after wave of citizens met law enforcement at neighborhood lines, pushing them farther into affluent, white sections. Malik searched for and found online histories of the city. He began to understand the fault lines. The protestors traversed every imagined boundary—the train tracks, the highways, the St. Jude River.

The following morning, the police department erected barricades on each of four bridges connecting Aggy's Island, where the city's Black population was concentrated, to the rest of the city. One of those bridges led, almost directly, from City Center to a housing project called Hamilton Heights. There, Jeremiah and Nova Prince, along with dozens of others, announced the Hush Harbor movement. They also announced they were armed.

From the bed of roses where he now stood, Malik strained to see Richard Bridge. The bridge that led to City Center and its gleaming high-rises. The same bridge he and Zahra and Myra had climbed up only a handful of nights prior. Framed between Hamilton Heights buildings, it shimmered in the rising sun. The soldiers and their glass watchhouses stood at its far end. They sent a crackling light over Hush Harbor, as though tracing a path for bullets.

The impasse would not last.

Violence radiated off the bridge. Everything they did, they did in its shadow. His stomach twisted, but he had grown used to the sensation. He thought about saying a prayer for Kemba and then thought again. He could not recall how to pray. Or, more accurately, how he should feel when he prayed.

Malik stepped away from the memorial and saw Nova Prince walking toward him. An uncomfortable clamminess spread over his palms. She wore her signature gray pants and white blouse. He had never seen her in any other combination and, he thought, for good reason. They reflected consistency, reliability. He sensed something unshakable in her. It both comforted and intimidated him.

Maybe she, too, was just out on a morning walk. But then she smiled and waved, and a heady mix of consternation and excitement scrambled his thoughts. He didn't know where to put his hands. He tried his pockets and his hips and dangling them at his sides. Finally, he clasped them behind his back and summoned a calm exterior.

"Good morning," Nova said.

"Good morning."

"You're up early."

"I like the quiet."

"I'm sorry to disturb it."

"I didn't mean—"

"I know." She rubbed his arm reassuringly. "One of the things you lose here is the ability to chitchat."

"I was never very good at it."

"Excellent. Then I don't have to try." She patted her mouth with her fingertips several times. "You don't know it yet, but I owe you an explanation."

Malik's curiosity piqued. How could Nova Prince possibly owe him anything?

"Okay," he said. "How so?"

"A while back, I told Zahra to find me someone for a particular job. She found you."

On their journey from Philadelphia to Bliss, Zahra had indicated as much. But she never told him what role. Or why him. Though flattered, he set aside his gratification and adopted an inquisitive posture. He needed details before deciding if this was an honor or a joyless job or both.

"What's the role?"

Nova scratched her ear and looked to the side. "How much do you know about my brother?"

In a span of months, Jeremiah Prince had gone from eighth grade history teacher to a national figure. Along with the rest of the country, Malik knew the outlines of his life. He and Nova were born and raised on Aggy's Island, not too far from Hamilton Heights. From third grade on, they enrolled in programs for the gifted. Their parents did all they could to support their educations. They scrounged extra money for tutors and books, for summer schools and winter camps and trips to other cities.

The best universities in the country readily accepted Jeremiah.

He chose Dartmouth, thinking the peacefulness of a quiet town would do him good. Upon graduation, he pursued a master's in divinity from Harvard and followed it with a PhD in history from the University of North Carolina. Of all the paths in front of him, he selected the least lucrative and prestigious: teaching middle school history in his hometown. Less than two years into his career as a public servant, the thirty-one-year-old became the leader of a rebellion.

"Some," Malik said.

"Have you met him?"

Malik shook his head.

"He keeps himself busy," Nova said.

"I'm sure."

"Too busy. He's tired."

"Like burned-out?"

"Well beyond that."

"You want me to work with him, then? Like a kind of assistant?"

"I do."

The singular honor—working directly with Jeremiah Prince—thrilled Malik. Yet an undeniable wariness lurked in the corner of his gut. Surely, there were others at Hush Harbor perfectly capable of assisting Jeremiah.

"Why not someone else here?"

Tension ran across Nova's brow.

"He's friendly," she said. "He's warm. But he doesn't trust people easily. Frankly, he trusts almost no one. It'll be simpler to work with him if he can recognize something of himself in you."

"Something of himself? What does that mean, exactly?"

"You went to college at Chapel Hill. He was a doctoral student there. You were applying to PhD programs in history. He did his doctorate in history. You speak guardedly. He speaks as if the world depends on his words. You two are birds of a feather. I saw it when I sat in on your orientation sessions. I noticed how careful you are. How kind. How quiet, too. You ask questions and say little else. Yet, the members of your cohort are drawn to you. As though you were the only one holding a flashlight in a dark tunnel. That might as well be a description of Jeremiah."

Another surge of gratification swept through Malik. The thought that he could be similar to one of Hush Harbor's leaders was flattery in its highest form.

Nova crossed an arm over her chest and rubbed the side of her neck. "And besides, Zahra says that you're discreet. Trustworthy. Her opinions are as good as gold."

Unused to floods of compliments, Malik took a breath. He felt excitement tighten his chest.

"Okay," he said.

"Okay?"

"I'll do it."

Nova placed her hand on his forearm. She looked at him from a place far away. As if he were in a valley and she on a mountaintop. She gave his hand a light squeeze. In that moment, he felt as if she was a sister.

"Come with me."

Jeremiah's office knocked Malik off-balance. Books were piled into corners, some half-open. Light filtered through the sheer curtains hanging above stands with marked-up maps. Stacks of notebooks and loose paper rested precariously on the large desk at the room's center.

A giant whiteboard, filled to its edges, hung next to the door. Color-coded arrows pointed to dotted lines and dotted lines led to words no bigger than what Malik would write in his notebook.

Too many thoughts had been thought in the room.

Jeremiah raised his head slowly and strained to detach himself from his reading. A broad smile broke across his face when he took in Malik and Nova. He removed a pair of horn-rimmed glasses, slightly too large for his face, and approached them languidly as if relishing the build-up. He was several inches taller than Nova and just as lean.

Much to Malik's surprise, Jeremiah embraced him.

"You're the one my sister says will watch over me," he said. He tossed Nova a teasing glance. She rolled her eyes and sat in one of the chairs by the desk. Jeremiah and Malik followed.

"I'm not the easiest person to work with," Jeremiah said.

"He can handle it," Nova said.

Malik observed the nuances of their interaction. How many times had they danced this dance? Nova suggests, Jeremiah resists. Nova persists, Jeremiah relents.

"Nova says that I'll like you quite a bit." Softness in his tone, indicating the care with which he chose his words. Malik recognized that this was not a man who would waste time on unnecessary chatter.

"I hope so," Malik said.

"She says that I'll trust you."

"You will," Malik said. He believed it wholeheartedly.

Jeremiah rocked back in his chair. He exuded a sudden exhaustion. "My sister is a very good judge of character. Sometimes too good. But, in this case, it seems irrational to rely on her alone. After all, she's known you less than a week. How could she be reasonably certain that this is a good match?" He gestured at the space between them. "No. She couldn't. It seems, then, that we are all trusting in Zahra's word."

Malik weighed this and found it more than acceptable.

"Zahra is a good person to trust," he said.

"You're right," he said. "She is." He reached for a glass of water and took a sip. The glass shook ever so slightly in his hand. "Now what? Nova, what is this arrangement supposed to look like?"

"Malik can manage your schedule. He can move on to other things when he's more familiar."

"Fine," Jeremiah said. He pulled out a black notebook and placed it on the desk in front of Malik. "Here. You'll need something to take notes."

Malik pulled his notebook from his pocket.

"That's okay. I have my own."

Jeremiah smiled and tilted his head. "Good. Very good."

4

MALIK REVIEWED THE MORNING'S SCHEDULE. For the past week, he had sat in a creaky chair outside of Jeremiah's office watching a steady stream of grim-faced visitors come and go. They all quickly assessed him and accepted his vague role. Few engaged beyond the necessary formalities.

He thanked God for Nova. She routinely interrupted his loneliness, arriving early to meetings and idling with him. Often, she would pull a tangerine from a well-concealed pocket and share it with him. He ruminated on this and many other things about her. How many pockets did she actually have? What did her schedule look like? Why did she spend what must have been precious time chatting with him? Unprompted, she matched names to faces and explained the roles of the people who filled Jeremiah's schedule. He took detailed notes. The simple act of recording knowledge grounded him.

The day had only just begun and Malik already wished she would appear from the staircase. Instead, the office door opened.

"Malik," Jeremiah said. "Come in here."

Surprised, Malik stood up slowly. The request was out of pattern. He wondered if he should feel caution or apprehension or dread. None of those emotions came to him. Unexpectedly, a pulse of excitement ran through his chest. A change, almost any change, would be better than twiddling his thumbs at the door.

When he entered, Jeremiah gestured toward a chair and laid a manila folder on the middle of the desk. Late the previous night, he had instructed Malik to hold on to that same file. He said that someone would come to collect it.

After an hour, boredom overcame Malik. He opened the file, fully intending to take nothing more than a glance. It contained three pages of grid paper stapled together. At first, he thought the handwritten numbers were a sort of elaborate code. The stuff of revolutionary lore. On second appraisal, he discovered that they represented dollar amounts. Costs and expenses. He found himself both disappointed and startled at the file's mundane contents. He had given expenses at Hush Harbor no thought prior to that moment. But, of course, even the most basic of things required money.

Although Malik could not make out what each column represented—the headers were obscure abbreviations—he tallied the totals in his head. The mental exertion felt stimulating, and when he finished his calculations, he wished for more columns. A couple of his totals did not match the totals on the sheet, so he double-checked and found several more errors. Hesitant to interrupt Jeremiah with what may have been Jeremiah's own miscalculations, he scribbled a quick note, placed it on top of the papers, and slid the file under the door. When midnight arrived, and the mysterious someone had not materialized, he decided to call it a night.

Facing Jeremiah now, he regretted that decision. What if the person had shown up just a few minutes after he left?

"I know I shouldn't have been looking at it," Malik said.

Jeremiah waved him off. "It's good work."

Malik felt satisfied. Finally, he had contributed in a way other than shuttling people to meetings.

"I have more," Jeremiah said. "Work. If you're interested."

"I am."

Jeremiah nodded and slid the folder to the side. He spread a large, photocopied map of Bliss over the desk. A stamp at the bottom of the map read: *Prop. of Angelou Public Library.* Jeremiah rummaged through a drawer and came up with a Ziploc bag full of chess pieces. He took out four, placing one on each of the map's unruly corners. He held on to a fifth piece, a pawn, and gently rolled it between his fingers.

Malik studied the image. Its title read *Bliss City, 1910.* He noted the city's boroughs in relation to Aggy's Island: Ellington across the St. Jude River to the east, Mt. Olive across the Catalina River to the west. City Center directly south and the sprawling Southwood borough beneath City Center. The Atlantic Ocean cradled Ellington and Southwood, forming a reverse letter *L* on the city's eastern and southern shores. A red *O*, the size of a thumbnail, had been drawn on a spot in Southwood. Malik gestured at it.

"What's the *O*?"

Jeremiah shrugged off the question. "Never mind it for now. How much do you know about sewers?"

Malik shook his head. "Nothing."

Excitement glinted in Jeremiah's eyes. He adjusted his glasses. "Prior to the twentieth century, most cities were synonymous with cesspools. Garbage rotted on streets, human and animal waste piled up in alleys, disease festered and spread and killed innumerable people. The poor were the most affected, but the wealthy couldn't escape the filth, either. Then, a miracle for the rich—the streetcar. A means to travel far and easily. A wealthy gentleman could live in a distant neighborhood with his family and still commute downtown when business demanded his presence."

Jeremiah leaned over the map. He pointed to City Center and then traced a path northeast. His finger crossed into Ellington. "In Bliss's particular case, this is where the wealthy moved. Having learned a valuable lesson from City Center's lack of infrastructure, they paid local authorities to install several sewer lines in Elling-ton. And for a number of years, they lived quite contentedly in their stench-free borough. Then a terrible thing happened. Other people, not quite rich and not quite poor, followed them. The so-called middle class." A mischievous smile flickered over Jer-emiah's lips. As though he himself had sent the newly moneyed to disturb the landed gentry's peace. "Say you're a wealthy gentle-man from an old money family. What would you do if a growing and powerful group was encroaching on your private fiefdom?"

It took Malik a moment to realize the question was not rhe-torical. "I don't know. Set up some special rules around who could live where?"

"Very good idea. But this is the first decade of the 1900s. Zoning will not become a widely accepted city practice for an-other ten or twenty years. And you, terrified of the incoming neighbors, need an immediate response."

"Buy up all the property and refuse to sell?"

"Another good thought. The trouble is that this new money moves too quickly. They scout and buy and build faster than you can think. And even if you did purchase the surrounding land, how would you make any profit from it? By building units to rent to the very middle class you're trying to keep out."

Malik pressed his lips together. "Then I have to move again."

"Correct." Jeremiah's index finger circled Aggy's Island. "Its residents are mostly Black so you can easily displace them with a simple scheme—buy their homes from slumlords and raise the rent. The expense of building new houses—houses that befit your wealth and status—will be exorbitant. Transporting material to the island and puzzling out its terrain are expen-sive efforts. These costly problems are, however, good things. Natural market barriers that exclude the newly moneyed. Their pockets do not run quite that deep. There is only one linger-ing challenge."

Jeremiah paused. Malik stared at the map, searching for a clue. He rewound their conversation. The problem came to him slowly.

"No sewer system."

A broad smile rose on Jeremiah's face. Malik could not help but return it. Jeremiah leaned forward again and drew his index finger along the St. Jude and Catalina Rivers.

"The waste gets dumped straight into the rivers or stays on the island indefinitely. The stench is relentless. Disease is more rampant here than anywhere. But local authorities don't care about living conditions on an island of Black people. And it goes without saying that the people themselves have neither the power nor the money to successfully push for a real waste disposal system."

"But I do—" Malik shook his head, slightly embarrassed that he had so quickly inhabited the role of early twentieth-century gentleman. "I mean, Bliss's wealthy families do."

"Exactly."

Jeremiah drew his finger over a dotted line running east from the island's northern end through Ellington and into the Atlantic Ocean. Then pointed to another dotted line running down from the island's southern tip through City Center and then Southwood before, once again, arriving at the ocean.

"Sewer tunnels. Modeled after those constructed in nineteenth-century London." Jeremiah lowered his voice a touch. "Large enough for a person to walk through."

Malik eyed the path he and Zahra and Myra had taken to reach Hush Harbor. He tapped the spot at which the northern dotted line met Ellington's shore.

"When I was coming to Hush Harbor, we were supposed to take this tunnel?"

"Correct."

"It flooded. Does that always happen during storms?"

Jeremiah frowned.

"No."

He rolled the pawn slowly from finger to finger. He fixed on the map as though he might will it to shape-shift. He took off his glasses.

"World War I started before they finished construction. The project was abandoned in favor of more patriotic work. The local government either lost or never kept a record of the tunnels. They don't officially exist. Obviously, that's to our advantage. But if they don't exist, nobody maintains them. It's a small miracle they made it this long." He tapped the northern tunnel with his glasses. "Straws and camels. The night you arrived, the storm broke the tunnel's back."

Malik scanned Aggy's Island, searching borders he already knew. Rivers on all sides. Four bridges, each barricaded. Two sewer lines, one unpassable. Hush Harbor's isolation was an abstract idea when he watched the revolution from afar. Now the reality of it churned his stomach.

"Can you drain it?"

"Not without professional equipment. And weeks of labor. And the certainty of attracting attention."

Malik pointed at the southern sewer line. "So this is it? The only safe way in or out?"

Jeremiah tilted his head and laughed. He flicked the pawn into the air and caught it.

"Nothing we do here is safe. We have one tunnel now. That's more than anyone thinks we have." He lifted up the manila file that Malik had worked on the prior night. "Expenses for the things that come into Hush Harbor. If you'll be keeping track of these records, I'd like you to have an intimate appreciation for *how* our goods come in and out."

"Okay," Malik said, unsure of exactly what he meant, except that it somehow involved the tunnels.

Jeremiah cleared the map and returned the chess pieces to their bag. He kept the pawn, using it to gesture at several files stacked on the desk's corner.

"For the time being, could you check these for errors?"

"Of course."

"All by hand. Wrong computer in the wrong hands connecting to the wrong network could mean the end of us."

"Got it."

"Thank you."

Malik stood, hesitantly. He wanted to ask how they had discovered the unfinished sewer system and what they would do if the southern tunnel collapsed and where they found money for the goods Hush Harbor received. Instead, he watched as Jeremiah turned back to his reading, fingers fiddling with the chess piece.

"Do you play?" he blurted out.

Jeremiah looked up as though surprised there was another person in the room.

"I'm sorry?"

Malik gestured at Jeremiah's hand.

"Chess. My grandfather taught me. When I was a kid."

Jeremiah held the pawn between his index and middle fingers. He rolled it into the center of his palm as though cradling a small treasure.

"Old habits." He carefully set the pawn on the desk. His eyes lingered on it. A brief moment passed, and his focus returned to the notebook. "No."

"No?"

"I don't play much anymore."

Jeremiah smiled at him and offered nothing else. Malik sensed their conversation had reached its limit. He picked up the files he was supposed to review and backed out of the office, wrestling with his new unknowns.

"It feels longer than a month," Zahra said.

They sat outside on a bench, eating sandwiches for lunch.

"Feels like a year."

Malik thought of all he had learned since arriving. The logistics alone—hours spent coordinating the movement of food, toilet paper, toothpaste—took up the better part of his days. Then, he arranged schedules: which cooks would prepare which meals, which guard needed off of the nightshift, which smuggler was ready for what route. When he arrived at the budget, tallying expenses on grid paper, he wished for nothing more than a computer. How much easier would this be if it were not all done by hand?

Still, he relished the sense of utility he took from the work. He was at the core of the revolution—inching closer to its secrets. Just the prior night, he had noticed a small red *circle* on a map of Bliss pinned to Jeremiah's office wall. Same as the marking he spotted the day Jeremiah told him about the tunnels. This time, when he asked what it represented, Jeremiah hesitated but did not deflect.

"Originists."

"I'm sorry?"

"A white supremacist group."

"I haven't heard of them."

"No one has. That's their modus operandi."

Malik squinted at the *O*. It sat deep in Southwood, Bliss's southernmost borough. "We should be worried about them?"

"Yes. We should."

"Do we know what they have planned?" Malik regretted the question even as he spoke it. How would Hush Harbor possibly know what a white supremacist group was plotting?

"No." Jeremiah took his glasses off. "The Originists are not public information, even at Hush Harbor. Their existence is between us."

Malik considered the group and found them predictable. Of course white supremacists would come to Bliss to oppose Hush Harbor. Surely the revolutionaries would not be surprised by this? Why, then, the need for secrecy? He thought to ask and then decided against pushing his luck. One secret, the first Jeremiah had shared, was victory enough.

On the bench with Zahra, Malik filled with pride. He restrained the childish impulse to impress her with his newly learned and clandestine information.

"Some of the new recruits arrived last night," Zahra said.

"I heard."

Malik had compiled the expense sheet for their transit. Twelve arrived, all in pairs.

"Did I look the way they look?" he asked.

"Worse."

He smiled, happy that Zahra could find some humor in her work. Her role—smuggling people into Bliss—was among Hush Harbor's most difficult. Food and other goods were dropped off in discreet city locations by some process and people Jeremiah had steadfastly avoided describing. From those locations, Hush Harbor's smugglers picked up the goods, navigated backstreets and found the closest entrance to the one remaining tunnel. Heart-stopping work, but ultimately simple.

Zahra, on the other hand, smuggled recruits from points far outside of Bliss through half a dozen checkpoints, unpredictable patrol routes, and terrain defined by steep bluffs, muddy shores and a wide river. Her job came with hazards at every turn.

"You brought one in?"

"A few."

"Any close calls?"

"Always."

Malik recalled climbing the staircase to the bridge with Myra on his back. Thinking of that moment unnerved him. He often and inadvertently glanced at the bridge and the watchhouses while going about his tasks. Was it his imagination or did they move an inch forward every day?

"Did you ever check up on Myra? After that night?" he asked with a hint of shame.

"No."

"Neither did I." He fiddled with a piece of grass. "Isn't that weird?"

"In normal circumstances, yes. But here?" She twisted her lips. "In this place, everything and everyone has a function and each function needs to be performed for the whole society to develop. We can't get distracted."

"I wouldn't consider checking up on an injured person a distraction."

"This sounds harsh, but it is. We have work to do before we all end up catching it worse than she did. Remember what it felt like to carry her. It's a lesson."

There were, he thought, many such lessons to learn. Hush Harbor vibrated at a jarring frequency. How could it not? If Malik walked fifty yards south, he would spot government soldiers. If he eavesdropped on any cafeteria conversation, he would hear tales of trauma. Shootings and beatings and humiliation. If he dared probe their collective psyche, he would find the threat of violence humming beneath it. These people, his people, lived lives under siege well before Hush Harbor. And, now, at the center of a revolution, they clenched their teeth and gripped their sanity and remembered their purpose. To fight white supremacy. To nurture a new order. To do their job in the revolution.

"You look tired," she said.

"You, too."

"I am. Revolutions are exhausting things."

He thought of the accounting tasks he still had left. "Mundane, too."

"Until they're not."

And when would that be? What was their endgame? Jeremiah spoke of expanding their territory to include the rest of Aggy's Island, a task that required more recruits to secure their borders. Nova placed emphasis on shaping the revolution's culture and practices, grounding themselves in a communal approach to living, before extending their geographic boundaries. Both Prince siblings spoke about the necessity of survival, of building a new society, of autonomy and self-determination. Malik could not see a route toward true independence that did not involve battle.

"Until they're not," he said.

Zahra stood up and brushed off her pants. She watched a guard disappear around a corner.

"Be careful, Malik," she said.

The moon washed Hush Harbor in a powder white sheen. Jeremiah told Malik nothing other than to follow. Malik had not thought to ask where they were going and why. Usually, his questions would come unbidden. But over the past several weeks, he had sensed a delicate trust spool between him and Jeremiah. They found rhythm, a bond, in the quiet of their shared work. They spoke rarely and thought much and discovered resonance in that balance. Malik's questions seemed less than urgent now.

Together, they slipped between Hush Harbor's westernmost buildings, approaching a guard at a gate. His beard reminded Malik of Frederick Douglass. Jeremiah signaled and the guard leaned back on the gate. It gave precious few inches, and they squeezed through. The warm metal bars brushed Malik's chest. Moments after, he heard a lock fall into place.

They walked along Bliss's empty city streets, passing a stream of brick row houses and yards with gnarled trees. They walked by a small playground with green slides and yellow swings and blue monkey bars, all miserable and out of place in the vacant city. Had any of the children now at Hush Harbor visited the playground with the bright colors in their previous lives?

A minute later, they stood outside a row house with a dull red door and a knob painted black. Jeremiah pulled a key from his pocket and unlocked the door. Inside, Malik tasted dust. It grew syrupy as they moved to the back of the house. Jeremiah stopped and flipped on a light. They stood in a large kitchen with white cupboards and a stainless-steel sink. Jeremiah quickly pulled a small breakfast table from a corner revealing a hole in the floor big enough for a single person to slip through. A rope, tied to a large hook in the floor, coiled like a snake at the hole's edge.

Malik waited on Jeremiah, expecting something. An explanation, perhaps. Or just an acknowledgment. Jeremiah tossed the rope down the hole, used it to climb down. The rope went taut for a second and then Malik heard a thud. Yellow light dissipated the hole's darkness. Malik peered down and saw Jeremiah holding a flashlight. He kneeled and grabbed the rope before shimmying into the hole.

The ground sunk an inch when Malik landed. Somewhere between mud and dry dirt. Jeremiah led them through a low-slung tunnel. Malik stretched out his arms and tickled both walls. Small rocks and clumps of dirt fell at his touch. He felt fear in the enclosed space though he had never thought himself claustrophobic. He imagined he was a volunteer on the Underground Railroad or an Allied agent working against the German occupation, but neither image brought him comfort or bravery. Unexpectedly, a memory of his grandfather eating dinner came to him. Roasted chicken with Italian herbs. A side of greens with a mustard dressing dribbled on top. A piece of chocolate for dessert. He ate it slowly, as if it were the highest luxury. Homesickness panged in Malik like hunger.

Then, Jeremiah came to a stop. A rope dangled from a hole above them. Jeremiah grabbed it and tugged twice. The rope went taut in his hands.

"Ready," said a voice from above.

"Ready," Jeremiah replied. Someone pulled the rope up and Jeremiah along with it. Malik waited ten anxious seconds before the rope came down again.

"Do you have it?" the voice asked.

"Yes," Malik said.

A moment later Malik stood in a cavernous warehouse lit by

flashlights. A man in his early thirties stood with a woman decades older than him.

The woman eyed him. "Who is this?"

"This is Malik," Jeremiah said.

"Alright," the woman said, more question than affirmation.
She wiggled her jaw and the deep grooves lining her face trembled. How many years had poured into those grooves? They
were not wrinkles but riverbeds.

The man pushed up square glasses and said something inaudible.

"Say again, Jenkins," Jeremiah said. "Louder please."

Jenkins toggled his head between the floor and Jeremiah. He
reminded Malik of a skittish dog.

"I think the question Billie and I are asking is why is he here,"
Jenkins said. He stood still as a statue. Billie's round frame vibrated at a low frequency.

"He can help," Jeremiah said. "With the moving."

"He can help?" Jenkins said.

"I trust him."

"But we had a plan." Jenkins's voice went almost inaudible
again. Billie placed a gentle hand on Jenkins's back.

"Next time, tell us before you bring someone new," said
Billie. "He doesn't like surprises."

"Of course. You're right."

Malik strained and failed to see where the giant room ended.
Glancing over his shoulder, he could make out the outlines
of several enormous vehicles. GCC garbage trucks. For a split
second, he thought he was falling too far into memory. Was that
Zahra standing next to the trucks? Several figures waited there
in silence. One of them had Zahra's shape and height. Her posture, impossibly straight-backed, was too familiar. Of course,
he thought. She would be in the middle of whatever highly se-
cretive thing was happening.

"We will need significant amounts of time," Jenkins said.
"Perhaps a week."

"I know," Jeremiah said.

Jenkins clasped his hands. He reminded Malik of a professor standing in front of a whiteboard explaining a complex equation.

"The other thing," Billie said.

"Yes," said Jenkins. "The other thing. We will need to coordinate closely with someone on your end. I assume you do not wish to use one of the regular receivers."

"That's correct," Jeremiah said.

"Very good. This is another reason you have brought Malik." Jenkins stated it rhetorically. His earlier displeasure at Malik's presence had vanished, replaced by a rationality almost mathematical in its precision.

"You're sure?" Billie said.

"Like I said," Jeremiah said. "He's here to help."

"Alright," she said.

Jenkins placed his attention on Malik. "We are moving many large boxes. A fraction will go to Hush Harbor. Most will go to other cities. Those not intended for Hush Harbor are not currently your concern."

"What's in the boxes?" Malik asked.

Jenkins paused.

"If I'm moving them, I should know what's in them," Malik said.

"He's right," said Billie, her voice a low and impatient rumble.

"Very well," Jenkins said. "Equipment."

"Equipment?"

Jenkins flicked his hand as if the question was an insect he could swat away. "Explosives, guns, ammunition." He pointed to the three people next to the trucks. "Those assigned to help are there."

They approached before Malik had a moment to process.

"Ready?" Zahra said.

Angst flickered in his stomach. He brushed it aside.

"Yes."

5

MALIK SHUT HIS EYES and began counting down from one hundred. At eighty-eight, he was more awake than when he had started. He rolled to his side and cringed, his abs exacting payment for even the most basic movements.

His grandfather came to mind. The accountant would shake his head and sigh if he knew his grandson had become a manual laborer. *We didn't work the way we worked for our children to lead such lives.* The week of nighttime hauling through tunnels and alleyways was finally over. They had safely set down the last box in the last basement two hours prior.

Jenkins and Billie and Zahra and the others, whose names Malik was never told, had slipped out the northern gate. Jeremiah and Malik cut through several courtyards on their way to the Walker Building. Unexpectedly, Jeremiah paused in Morrison Hall. He'd pointed his flashlight at the base of the mural of the boy and girl running along the horizon. The figures seemed to wink in and out of reality. Behind them, the sun throbbed as though wishing it could gather substance and break away from the wall. At that late hour, with exhaustion vining through his limbs, Malik almost believed that it could.

"It's beautiful," he said.

Jeremiah's lips parted as if to say something. He gave a slight nod. Malik could not tell if it was meant for him or the mural or both. Malik watched him approach the mural. Jeremiah set his hand on the boy and then on the girl. Tenderly. As though the painting was the children's dream and his touch might wake them. He rested the side of his head against the wall and stayed like that for a moment. Malik dared not interrupt him. When he turned around, he looked sorrowful.

"Take tomorrow off, Malik." He tried a smile. It flickered out quickly. "We're all tired."

Now Malik tossed in bed, unable to sleep. Gingerly, his toes found the floor. He grimaced as he stood, calves throbbing. He grabbed his notebook, in case an epiphany happened upon him, and slipped outside.

Beneath the clouded moonlight, he stretched his aching muscles. He pulled a foot to his backside to elongate his thigh and twisted his torso side to side and then, straight-legged, reached to the ground. Still, unease lingered in his limbs.

He wished for a breeze and instead heard his grandfather's voice. *Search*. After he lost a game of Monopoly or was teased at school for performing too well or was sent adrift by memories of his whole family together, his grandfather would lay a large hand over his heart. He would look the boy in the eyes. *Breathe with me.* They would inhale together, exhale together. In time, Malik's lungs would bring calm to his mind. *Search*, his grandfather would say. *Tell me what you find.*

Invariably, Malik would lie. Bury any disruptive emotion. *I'm okay, Grandpa,* he would say. *I'm okay.*

He could see his grandfather clearly now. Long and oval, the old man's face had barely a wrinkle. Dark freckles dotted his broad nose and upper cheeks. Small indents lived above his nostrils, the result of wearing his reading glasses constantly. Memories of his grandfather carried a physical sensation of warmth.

Malik noticed his hand growing hot on his chest. His heart agitated against his rib cage. *Tell me what you find.*

"Why the hell am I here?" Malik said.

With no one there to hear, the words suspended themselves in front of him. For weeks, he had leaned on dispassionate logic: the injustices done to Kemba, and others like him, were emblematic of a corrupt system that needed complete overhaul. Hush Harbor was the center of a burgeoning revolution. And, so, he would serve Hush Harbor.

Now a different motivation played at the edge of his psyche. His parents. He rubbed his hands over his face, hastily brushing aside their memory. He pulled out his notebook and began to write down the questions on his mind.

Was Hush Harbor supposed to run like a monarchy with Jeremiah as king? Shouldn't power be diffuse?

Why had he spent the last week moving arms? Why did they need more weaponry?

Where did the other weapons go? The ones that did not come to Hush Harbor?

Why had Nova not helped move the boxes?

The act of writing brought order to his mind. Control. Composed again, he looked to his left and right. In the dark, it was difficult to make out the guards on their routes. At first, the sight of their guns had left him anxious. The theory of revolution was different than carrying it on your hip. The reality of violence troubled him, but this was what he'd signed up for. He was not ignorant: he knew revolutions were messy and rife with compromise. There was no utopia, no ideal justice. There was only this place and that place, and one had to be better than the other. Hush Harbor was the better place. Or, at the very least, held the promise of a better place. A decision, then: he would quit questioning his surroundings. Moving forward, he would let answers come to him.

He returned to bed and fell asleep, tolerably aware that he'd avoided the memories that had kept him up in the first place.

He slept through the day until a mean hunger woke him at dinnertime. In the cafeteria, he ate mushy peas and dry potatoes with a gusto they did not warrant. When the food settled, he took note of the room. A few tables away, a group of people around his age laughed boisterously at a joke he could not hear. Next to them, a twentysomething woman with blue beads at the ends of her braids delicately placed her hand on that of a young man with thin dreads and a scruffy beard. The man stopped his nervous chatter, smiled, lifted his thumb to rub hers. Throughout the cafeteria, forks and knives scraped against plates. Playful arguments rose above the din. He heard bits of sentences.

Best ever.

Do you remember?

Give you some context.

He realized just how alone he was. Except for the occasional meal with Zahra, he ate by himself. For the most part, he worked by himself. Lord knows, he slept by himself. Surprisingly, he did not ache for camaraderie. He was too tired for that luxurious pain. He wanted to read or sleep or both. But he sensed that tonight was not the night to remain alone. He wanted an escape from his thoughts, not more hours spent regulating his brain.

He placed his plate in a bin and made for the Ringgold Building on the southernmost edge of Hush Harbor. As he climbed the stairs, he reminded himself that Jeremiah had given him the time off. In fact, it was Jeremiah who, days ago, told him about Hush Harbor's makeshift bars and recommended a visit to Antonio's.

On the top floor, at the very end of the hall, he knocked on a door that looked like all the rest. A moment later, a smiling goateed man opened it.

"Antonio?" Malik asked.

"Yeah," Antonio said.

"I'm Malik," he said. "Someone recommended… You know what, never mind. I'm sorry to bother you."

Antonio stopped him before he could turn away.

"Malik?" Antonio laughed. "You're in the right spot. Jeremiah told me you might come around. Come in, come in."

They navigated around a couch and a few tables to a makeshift bar at the back of the living room. Malik nodded at the few people already there. Absently, they nodded back. He pulled himself onto a barstool and tentatively rested his elbows on the ledge. Behind it, Antonio poured a beer.

"You want some?" Antonio said.

"I'm not a big drinker."

"You know this is a bar?"

"I just needed to do something different."

Antonio poured him a glass of water. "I understand."

Malik studied the rack of bottles on display. "Smuggled?"

"Someone has to keep the troops happy." Antonio winked. He carefully dried a glass and set it alongside a row of other glasses. Several knocks came from the door, rescuing Malik from his desperate attempt to fish for an interesting topic of discussion.

Malik surveyed the room. Upon entering, he had not noticed a smaller back room—a bedroom in a prior life—just off of the living room. Curious, he slid from his stool to take a peek and found Zahra sitting at a corner table under a floor lamp. She sipped amber liquor from a short glass. Her lips parted slightly as though she were in deep contemplation. Just as he realized his eyes had lingered too long, she looked up. Her eyebrows knit in amused confusion and she mouthed his name and waved him over. He thought back to his college days, what he would have given to have a drink with her.

"You're here?" she said.

She wore a loose blouse cut off at the shoulders. He could not help but notice the collarbone hinting at her shirt line.

"I am."

"How?"

"I walked."

"Smart-ass."

"Jeremiah told me about it. I have the night off."

As she crossed and uncrossed her arms he sensed an uncertainty in her that he had never sensed before. She pointed at his glass.

"Water," he said. He wondered whether he should feel embarrassed about this. He found that, in front of Zahra, he was not. He pointed back at her drink.

"Whiskey. Neat." She raised three fingers. "Third one."

He nodded. Three, while drinking alone, seemed like a lot to him. But, then again, he barely knew Zahra outside of their narrow college and Hush Harbor worlds. She could have been a bartender on the weekends or a tasting expert or an avid fan of aged whiskey. How would he possibly know? Still, intuition told him something might be amiss.

"You doing okay?"

She smiled, nostalgia in her eyes. "Do you remember I used to do theater? In college?"

"I remember you in the ten-minute play festival."

Zahra tilted her head. A teasing grin crossed her lips. It occurred to Malik that she, too, would recall her performance in that festival demanded she wear nothing but underwear.

"Really?" she said.

"I mean—you were in a lot of things." His cheeks were suddenly hot.

"Uh-huh." A laugh barely suppressed. "Like?"

"Like…" Flustered, he needed a moment to recall working as a stagehand in a production she headlined. She commanded neither the stage nor the audience, but her commitment to the role drew stellar reviews from the *Daily Tar Heel*. At the time, he wondered if she might have a career in acting. "I worked on one of your productions. When you played Hester. *In the Blood*."

"My God, you're right. You were a stagehand?"

"Yeah."

"I totally forgot. I'm sorry."

"That's alright. I liked being behind the curtains. I didn't really want to be seen or remembered." He surprised himself with the openness of his reply.

"I'm the opposite," she said. "I loved the spotlight. The stage. The stakes. Sometimes I think maybe I joined the revolution because I wanted to be part of a drama."

Her honesty surprised him even more than his own. He considered that, perhaps, it was only the whiskey talking. Then again, nothing in her appearance signaled a clouded mind.

"I think that's okay," he said, venturing support. "You also want to help the world. I think it's okay to have more than one motive."

She smiled at him gratefully. "The worst part is sometimes I question whether anything good will come from this. You know, in law school, I interned with the mayor's office for a year? They offered me a job. I said no when Nova recruited me to Hush Harbor. I remember thinking why write reports that pushed for small policy reforms when I could be part of a much bigger transformation?"

"I didn't know you worked for the mayor. Or that you knew Nova in law school," he said. Somehow, he wasn't surprised. Though Nova was several years older than Zahra, they would have made a natural pairing. Incorruptible. Determined. He felt as if their friendship was a fact he should have anticipated.

"We became close at Livingston Law. She's why I'm here. She and…" Her eyes grew distant and her sentence trailed off. "Anyway, we all have our reasons."

Malik sensed her reluctance and set the conversation on a different course. He wanted to prolong their time together, not cut it short with unwelcome prying.

"How long have you been here?"

"Since the beginning."

He considered what an exhilarating experience it must have been. To be at Hush Harbor from its inception. To be privy to the thinking of its founders, to shape its nascent ways of life. What a grueling experience, too.

"Four months here is a long time," he said.

Zahra nodded. "The novelty has worn off. I miss my life before. All I see now is the work. An endless resistance." She paused. Her eyes darted around the room. They resettled on him. "What if someone wanted to leave? Would they be allowed? I mean, would that be too much of a risk?"

"You want to leave?"

She shook her head. "No. But that's not the point. If we aren't allowed to leave, what does that make this place?"

Malik felt the air around them tighten. Under the table, he coiled his hands together. Zahra drained the rest of her whiskey. He watched her lips linger on the glass. A moment later, he caught himself staring at the slope of her shoulder. He shook it off and tried to be a good friend. He, too, missed the outside world. He had not flipped through a Black studies journal or gotten lost in Wikipedia entries on ancient African kingdoms or joyfully imagined arguing with long-dead and racist authors since arriving at Hush Harbor. There was more meaning in his small rituals than he had previously known.

"You know, I thought that you might go into acting," he said.

"I thought so, too. Law school was just more practical."

"Do you miss the theater?"

Zahra's shoulders went slack. Nostalgia glinted in her eyes. "Yeah," she said. "A lot."

They spoke for an hour more. Zahra detailed her life's passion. Characters she kept with her long after her costumes were put away. Actors who became family off-stage. He observed her demeanor shift from dejection to engaging charm to somber introspection. She carefully described the thrilling nervousness of opening night and the sweet dismay that accompanied closing. She reiterated an earlier thought, bringing their conversation full circle. Malik heard sadness but, this time, only a little stress.

"I used to think about Hush Harbor in the same way," she said. "A grand drama."

Their knees touched and he noticed.

"And now?" he asked.

"And now I remember that some drama is best imagined, not lived." What felt like a minute passed and then, as if by magic, her muted expression lifted into a wide grin. "That's not my line. One of my directors said it. The cast was being particularly rowdy."

"I would've believed it was yours."

"You're kind. Thank you. For talking." Zahra picked at the corner of the table. "Maybe we can plan to talk more?"

They decided to take a walk together the next night. Away from an unwelcome audience.

It was ten o'clock, earlier than he thought. He decided to take a circuitous route back to his room.

A pleasant headiness consumed him as he considered his night. He had just spent the better part of the evening comforting his old crush. And, stunningly, it felt natural. He sensed a bond form between them, different from the relationship they previously had.

He slowed his pace to better enjoy the giddy sensation swimming through him and tried to restrain himself from thinking too far into the future, from obsessing over their planned walk. He focused instead on the way she had looked at him. Surprise in her oval eyes, maybe even a smidgen of delight.

In the central courtyard, he paused. Someone stood by the

bed of roses. He assumed the person was praying or meditating or lost in thought. He veered away to give the person some privacy. Out of the corner of his eye, he recognized the long ropes of hair, then he caught the figure waving.

"I thought you were avoiding me." Nova smiled.

"I'm sorry. I didn't know it was you."

"I meant over the last week."

"I was with—"

"I know."

"We were—"

"I was just teasing."

He sensed something other than playfulness in her tone. Not anger, either. She appraised him as an older sister would a brother.

"You seem okay."

"I am."

"You went out tonight?"

"Sort of a bar, I guess. Antonio's."

"I like that place."

"You've been?"

"At the beginning. I don't go anymore. You met some people?"

"A few."

"Good. Working with Jeremiah can be isolating."

"Yes. It can."

Nova said nothing in return. Feeling awkward in the silence, Malik studied the sky. No clouds. The stars, bright, formed constellations that he now wished he had learned.

Nova pointed her chin at the roses. "You know they tried to pay his relatives to keep the memorial service private."

"Who did?"

"The police chief."

"Baker?"

Nova nodded. "He was afraid it would cause a reaction. Like Emmett Till."

"It did."

"The reaction should have been bigger."

Malik puzzled through her statement. The memorial service was part of a chain of events that led to an armed rebellion. How much more of a reaction could there have been?

"Bigger?"

Nova rubbed her palm on her forehead.

"You should see something," she said. "If you're working with Jeremiah, you need a more complete understanding."

She took out her phone. She entered several passwords and pulled up an image. She handed the phone to Malik.

At first, Malik did not recognize anyone in the picture. Standing in a line, five men posed in tall white hats and white robes.

"I don't get it."

"The man all the way on the right."

The figure had a grin splashed across his face. A strange mixture of anger and glee. John Marbury.

"When was this taken?"

"A few months before Kemba died."

Malik's grip tightened. He pointed at the hat and robe.

"Is this KKK?"

"No. Wannabes."

"Are they associated with the Originists?"

Nova delivered him a surprised glance. "You know about the Originists?"

"Like you said, I work for Jeremiah."

She nodded and gestured at the picture. "These guys were just friends. No formal organization. Now, though, we think Marbury is holed up with the Originists. They gave him refuge."

Malik riffled through the names of news anchors and reporters and bloggers. He recalled his notes. Many of them mentioned the possibility of a direct connection between white nationalism and Kemba's death. To some, it was a far-fetched idea. To many others, it was a fact waiting validation. No one produced evidence. Had some editor squashed this particular part of the story months ago? How did the photo wind its way to Nova? And how long had she been carrying it, a grenade with a loose pin, jangling in her pocket?

As if reading his mind, Nova answered.

"We've had the picture for months."

"Why don't you make it public?"

"Jeremiah thinks the timing isn't right yet."

He absorbed the information. Confused, he flicked his gaze from Kemba's roses to the gray concrete pathways, to the crescent moon above. No answers came. "The timing isn't right?"

Nova turned to him and laid a hand over his heart as though it were a casual gesture. Her palm cooled his chest.

"If they all knew…" She came to a stop. He sensed that more words, desperate and agitated, shoved at her closed mouth. She refused them life.

She tapped two fingers on Malik's chest and released her touch. She took a few steps and then stopped abruptly and turned.

"Revolution and violence are not the same thing. Remember that."

She walked away, leaving Malik with only bright stars and swarming heat.

That night, Malik dreamed of a chameleon city. His mother held his right hand, his father held his left. His mother tucked a map into his pocket. Abruptly, his parents vanished. He turned in circles searching for them. He pulled out the map, hoping it held a clue. The map burst with color. Lines forked and fanned and broke again. He pointed his feet true north and walked until the city ended and a desert began. Beyond the sand, he saw the pinkish outlines of mountains. He walked into the desert.

The top of his skull began to burn. He heard fluttering overhead. Scores of laundry lines with small sheets of paper clipped to them flowed from the city to a mountain peak ahead. He squinted and thought they looked like flocks of migrating birds, lost and out of formation. He followed the lines until they hung at a point low enough for him to read one of the papers. *Soon soon.* Some laundry lines began to circle back toward the city. The papers they carried read: *How long.*

Malik woke from the dream several hours before dawn. His body felt hot and sticky with sweat. He threw off his shirt and lay back down and the same dream swallowed him whole. He woke in a sweat again. He wanted to stay awake but the dream had not left him. This time, he stood in it and did not move. From the desert, he watched the papers flutter to and from the mountain peak. The messages changed. *We promise*, came from the city. *Broken*, came back from the mountain. *Patience*, came from the city. *Crisis*, replied the mountain. *With you*, came from the city. The mountain peak answered, *On our own.*

6

ZAHRA AND MALIK ADMIRED a mural on the side of the Ring-gold Building. An image of a woman with shoulder-length dreadlocks and beaded earrings stood expectantly against a pattern of interlocking triangles.

"Do you know who that is?" Zahra asked.

"I assumed it was someone named Ringgold. Like James Baldwin on the side of the Baldwin Building and Kendrick on the side of the Lamar Building."

"Faith Ringgold. Come."

She interlaced their fingers. On this, their third late night walk, Malik already knew Zahra sometimes restrained her excitement for fear of losing her audience. When she set it free, it bubbled up quickly, pure and lighthearted. He had not anticipated this trait in her, so different from her usual serious demeanor. He cherished it. A secret part of her personality. He liked to think she shared it with him as one might a gift.

"Do you want to tell me about her?"

"Can I?"

"Please."

"I fell in love with her a few years ago. She was a painter and a quilter. When I look at her work, I feel like a dimension goes from blurry to clear." Zahra twisted her lips. After a moment, she continued. "Say you always inhale your food. Then, one day, someone puts you in a dark room and places something cool in your palm." Zahra held out her right hand, palm upward, and mimed placing an item in it. "The person tells you to take a hundred deep breaths. You do. Then, they tell you to take a small bite." She pretended to take a nibble. "The taste overwhelms you. Sweet and creamy and bitter like nothing you've had before. You take another bite and swish it around your mouth." She drew her tongue around her mouth. "It takes you a moment to realize you're eating chocolate. You wonder if its flavors, its textures, its power had always been there." Zahra swallowed the last of the imaginary chocolate. "That's what Faith's work does for me. It makes me encounter the familiar in unexpected ways."

Malik looked at the mural and tried to imagine a quilt affecting him the way Ringgold's work affected Zahra. Had any art, ever, impacted him so deeply? The mural in Morrison Hall came to mind. Maybe, he thought, he should visit it. He leaned closer to her. She laid her head on his shoulder and sighed.

Malik considered the obvious fact that someone at some point must have painted Ringgold on the building.

"Who painted it?" he asked.

"Nova."

"Really?"

"You don't know? She did most of the murals here."

"By herself?"

"People help out, but she directs them." She nodded at Ringgold. "I helped with this one. She got me into painting in law school. It's almost a religious thing for her."

Malik gazed at the mural with new appreciation. He felt the mood turn intimate and he searched for something personal to share with Zahra. Oddly, he only surfaced moments with Jeremiah. He thought of the way they worked together. They stayed silent and concentrated on the tasks at hand. There was both practicality and choice in wordlessness. Their determined focus bonded them. Could work be considered a form of intimacy? He thought that, yes, it could. He concluded it best to avoid spilling details of one intimacy into another. That decision made, he returned to the moment, to Zahra, with little to say.

He let his eyes drift away from the painting, to the lapping waves of the St. Jude and the bridge with its barricades. In the dark and at a distance, they appeared only as specks. Still, he could have sworn the soldiers were staring at him. If given the chance, how quickly would they pull their triggers? What consequences would they face for ending a life? He knew the answer. None at all. Anger slithered across his gut. He felt a storm in him. He squeezed Zahra's hand and she squeezed back. He let the tempest stir.

He searched for some clarity in the midst of fury. He found only a single question: When would people in uniforms stop taking Black lives?

"My parents," he said. "I lost them when I was a kid."

"Lost them?" Zahra asked. She rubbed his arm. "They passed away?"

He shook his head. How much detail to give about a history he had never spoken out loud? Should he start with the debilitating bouts of pain his mother endured, pain for which disbelieving doctors prescribed only ibuprofen and rest? Or the day his parents—churchgoers, teetotalers—decided his mother's suffering demanded real relief? A discreet cousin slipped them an address far enough away that no one in Durham would discover they were buying pot. Several counties north, in Virginia, they found a freshly painted white cottage with a small garden of roses out front. A middle-aged white woman wearing a reindeer Christmas sweater greeted them at the front door. Later, the town's local paper would claim that the dealers were difficult to catch precisely because of that cottage and the roses and the sweater: they operated within a picture of civility.

If Malik's parents had arrived an hour earlier, the transaction would have occurred without interruption. An hour later and they would have driven away from a cottage surrounded by barricade tape. Instead, they stood at the dining room table, trading cash for weed, at the precise moment the county sheriff's deputies had planned to raid the house.

In the coming weeks, a young district prosecutor hungry for a big win, and the one-man newspaper shop that reported on local gossip, carefully constructed a narrative: local marijuana growers, encouraged by out-of-town distributors, had set up a regional drug ring that stretched all the way to Durham and beyond. Never mind that the growers claimed not to know the out-of-towners, and the out-of-towners claimed never to have visited the town before. Never mind that a drug operation of that magnitude would require significantly more marijuana be grown. And never mind that the sheriff's deputies found no astonishing heap of cash, no evidence of an enormous profit to match the enormous accusation. The felony charge remained: drug distribution and sale across state lines. Possible penalties included life in prison.

An all-white jury skated by arguments in favor of Malik's parents. They listened, intently, to the prosecutor's rebuttals: the drug dealers would never snitch on each other, the weed farms were distributed across counties, the money was hidden. The dealers were caught in the act. Cash changing hands, plans being hatched. What else would those out-of-towners be doing there? If they just wanted to buy an ounce for themselves, wouldn't they just stick to Durham?

Two years later, after the guilty verdict and the initial shock and the waves of disbelief, an unusually attentive prison doctor noted the frequent bouts of pain Malik's mother suffered. Pain so severe, she told him, that she had once sought to relieve it with an illegal drug, the pot that landed her in prison. The doctor asked if she also experienced swollen feet and frequent fatigue. A few tests later, he diagnosed her with sickle cell anemia.

Next to Zahra, Malik's chin trembled. He wanted to tell her the whole history but only a few words trickled out. "They were put away. Twenty-year sentences. They're still there, in prison."

He remembered the visits. The impossibility of his mom and dad living in a place other than their home. His tiny sweater itched. He wanted to rip it off and scream and punch and kick everyone in the room. They made it real, those people. They made it okay that his parents had been taken. He refused to speak for days after each visit. He refused to speak about his parents' loss at all.

He ran a knuckle under his eyes. It came away wet. He stared straight ahead.

"Malik," Zahra said. "I'm so sorry."

Before he could respond, a light flashed in the distance.

"Do you—"

"Yeah," she said.

They skirted past the Ringgold Building toward the edge of the bluff. The light, bobbing on the St. Jude, advanced from the left. He made out the hull of a police deck boat bobbing in the river. Three people rode in it, a driver and two gunmen kneeling against a side fitted with long-barreled rifles. A bullhorn sounded and one of the police officers, shouting through a megaphone, directed orders at a small speedboat beneath the bridge: "Don't move."

The speedboat ignored the command and sped to shore. The same path Malik and Zahra and Myra had taken to reach Hush Harbor. Except tonight's speedboat crossed the river much too close to the bridge.

The bullhorn blared again: "Don't move. We will shoot."

The speedboat kept its pace and the police advanced steadily, their rifles raised. Dread, like a heavy rain, broke over the river.

Malik stuck out a hand and Zahra whispered *no no no* and a dozen shots rang out and three people leaped into the water and it was impossible to tell what bullet went where.

Malik's hand trembled. The deck boat cut toward the speedboat, now sputtering aimlessly. The gunmen hauled in a limp body. They spotted another person swimming to shore and approached, guns trained. The body slowly rose with hands held high and waded back in the water and climbed into the deck boat. One gunman kept his weapon aimed at the two prisoners, Hush Harbor revolutionaries, while the other helped the driver search for the third. After several minutes, they fired the boat's engine and sped away. The third revolutionary was probably dead.

7

THAT NIGHT, HE WOKE half a dozen times in a coil of fury. At one point, as he attempted to fall back to sleep, he slipped into memory. His parents' ten-year anniversary party. He hastily undid the top button on a scratchy white collared shirt. Mud seeped through cracks in a makeshift dance floor on a garden patio. At four years old, he was attempting to dance the electric slide. His mom, lovely in an olive dress, kissed his cheek and picked him up and said, "Ready?" He nodded and she spun him more times than he could count. He laughed and instinctively stuck a hand in his mouth, an unbroken habit from his toddler years. She set him down and his legs wobbled and he found joy in that, too. "Electric Slide" changed over to "Signed, Sealed, Delivered" by Stevie Wonder and they sang along.

When the song ended, Malik's father joined them and tucked one arm under the child's backside and wrapped the other around his wife. Malik rested between their shoulders, playing with his father's slim olive tie. They smelled of rosemary and shea butter and sweat. He loved that smell. The deejay played another Stevie Wonder song. "You Are the Sunshine of My Life." His

parents sang it to him. Each of them kissed his cheeks in time
to the music. He nestled between them. Together, they swayed.

A weight landed softly on his chest and he came back into the
present. He looked around and was surprised to find he was in
Zahra's room. He lifted her arm from his chest and gently laid it
across her. He extricated his legs from hers, and reached over her
to open the window. It was raining, and a few warm drops landed
on the edge of the bed. Crisp air floated through the room.

He waited for Zahra to sink back into deep sleep. Her lips
parted and she rolled onto her side, her face toward the window. After a minute, he knew she would not wake. He wanted
to switch on the light and count the dark freckles beneath her
shoulder blades. He made out her silhouette beneath the sheet.
She was both shorter and curvier than she appeared clothed. He
wondered what she had learned about his body that surprised her.

Was he falling in love with her? Infatuation, surely. Her imagination gifted him relief from his own thoughts. And, at least
tonight, they satisfied one another's yearning for touch and care.
Something more textured than lust stirred in him. Not quite
love, but the adoration that foretold it.

This other thing he felt, this newly released fury, sat right
next to the adoration. It was warm and alive and stronger than
he could have imagined. Energized, he slipped off the mattress
and sat at Zahra's desk. He picked up a book on top of a neat
pile next to the reading lamp. He flipped to a tagged page and
started to skim a highlighted poem. *Blackbirding on the Hudson*
by Yusef Komunyakaa. He listened to the sounds of drizzle out
the window, imagined rain falling on the St. Jude. More water
to wash away the dead. He kept reading the poem and found
himself fixed on an image: a Black child disappearing unexpectedly. *Between a laugh & / a cry.*

He had no questions about what happened on the river only
hours prior. Neither did Zahra. They knew murder when they
saw it. In the morning, they would tell Nova or Jeremiah about

the police and the speedboat. But first they needed a reminder that they themselves still lived. In fear, in grief, in horror. But alive nonetheless. They kissed softly then heatedly and desperately and wretchedly. Together, they coped.

He returned to the poem and read from the top. Midway through, he paused at another image: memories of suffering dormant in blood, memories coming alive in the small hours. He drew his fingertips over the page. Zahra snored softly. The sun would soon climb over the river to relieve the moon. For the moment, however, he settled into the past. He remembered his childhood. Emptied of his mother and father. He thought of how they were taken. Casually. *Between a laugh & / a cry.* Fury stirred. Somewhere in him, a voice. Remember your mother, your father? Remember Kemba Jefferson? Remember that nameless one you saw murdered on the St. Jude?

How many more have there been? In 1619, the first slave ship landed; 1619, and Black bodies still less than.

The blood remembers the first voyage.

His fury fixed to bone. He suddenly realized there would be no turning back for him. No second thoughts. No hesitations. No moral quibbles over what it might take to be free. No questions on violence. He knew why he was there.

What was justice, he thought, if not a pretty word for retribution.

PART TWO

Quinn

8

THE TREADMILL WHIRRED BENEATH her as she breathed heavily. A strand of hair escaped her cap and dangled in front of her eye. Her hair had thinned from stress over the last few months, transformed from blond and straight to pale and wispy. She snuck the strand behind her ear and focused on the cadence of her run.

At mile four, she arrived at a memory: she saw herself in college, on a run with her roommate, Nova. Midway through, they paused on a hill that overlooked Bliss. Quinn slowly caught her breath. Nova, on the other hand, never seemed to tire. They watched the horizon turn pink over the St. Jude's waves. Fog began lifting off the river. Quinn mustered courage.

"I wanted to say…"

"I know, Quinn," Nova said. "You've said it already."

"I think I should say it again."

"Alright."

"I'm sorry. I am."

"It's okay."

All those years ago, Quinn had waited for the tension between them to lift, but it held firm. How much time and groveling before Nova truly forgave her? Three weeks and a dozen apologies and countless strained moments later, and still nothing. Even their weekly run together, a Thursday morning tradition, had become painfully awkward. Their friendship had never suffered a test so severe.

"You've got to forgive me, Nova."

"I just said it's okay."

"That's not the same thing."

"It's close enough."

"I thought I was doing the right thing."

She recalled finding the slips of paper under the door of their dorm room. Even then she was surprised by the care taken in delivering the hateful notes: three in all, they had been typed out, cut into tidy rectangles, and neatly folded. *Affirmative action bitch. Two-dollar ghetto whore. This isn't your school, nigger.*

Quinn had anticipated blowback to Nova's editorial in their college paper. In it, Nova vehemently defended the school's new admissions policies, which had sharply increased acceptance rates for people of color. Quinn had not, however, expected the backlash to include racism so blatant—and at their front door. Angry, she shoved open the door, but the hallway was empty. Where was the racist asshole? Did he slip the notes under their door in the middle of the night and slink away? Like a real-life internet troll. He needed to be found. Punished. With no further thought, Quinn marched to the resident assistant's room to demand justice.

Three weeks later, at the top of the hill overlooking Bliss, Quinn crossed her arms and drove her fingernails into her bicep.

"I was trying to protect you," she said. "I know it might have been easier to sweep it under the rug."

"God," said Nova.

"Telling someone was the right thing to do."

"Let's just drop it."

Nova knelt down to tighten her shoelaces and signal the conversation's end. Quinn's fingernails dug further into her bicep.

"Nova, we had to say something."

Nova rose slowly. She splayed her fingers and closed them into a fist.

"Who the hell is *we*? The complaint is filed with my name as the victim. The school forced me to go to counseling. The campus police interviewed me for hours. Whoever wrote the notes was coming for me."

"That's why I reported it—to protect you."

"Fuck, Quinn. Seriously?"

"Yes, seriously."

Nova rubbed her temples in exasperation. "Why do I have to explain this to you?"

"Explain what?"

"The only thing I had was a choice—how to respond. Report or not report. Burn the notes or keep them as evidence. Hole away in my room or yell what happened from the rooftop or do something in the middle. Doesn't matter. The choice was supposed to be mine. You took that away from me."

Quinn's stomach dropped. Instantly, she knew her friend was right. She reddened with shame and berated herself for her blindness. Why had she acted so impulsively when she found the notes? And how had she not realized the reason for Nova's anger sooner? She wondered how many similar mistakes she had made in her life. How many she would make in the future.

"I'm so stupid," she said.

Nova tilted her head and considered. "Yes."

"I'm sorry. For reporting it." Quinn sensed the tension between them loosen. She knew forgiveness, or at least the beginnings of it, came in that slackening. Still, she drew inward, embarrassed with herself. She ground the sole of her shoe into the dirt and wondered if she could burrow into the earth. "And I'm sorry that you had to explain it to me."

She ached to hear *I forgive you*, but knew better than to expect it. Resolution would not be so tidy, so instant.

"Come on," Nova said. "We've got to finish the run."

She squeezed Quinn's arm and started down the trail. Quinn watched her go, marveling at her grace. She touched the spot Nova had squeezed. A weight lifted from her chest. Their friendship would survive.

Quinn jolted into the present. She slowed the pace on her treadmill to a walk, legs wobbly from the five-mile workout. The college memory lingered at the edge of her consciousness, but she tried to remain present. She was the senior aide to the mayor of Bliss. Nova was one of Hush Harbor's leaders. They had not spoken since the rebellion began five months ago.

She stepped off the treadmill and checked her watch: six thirty on a Thursday morning. Whether she and Nova were together or apart, she never skipped their weekly runs.

Thirty minutes later, she showered, made coffee, and blended a banana and dark chocolate protein powder with cashew milk. Squeezed into her breakfast nook, she read a thick report, completed a month before Kemba Jefferson was murdered, that was titled "Police Misconduct in Bliss: Analysis and Paths Forward." She had spent a year writing it alongside Zahra, a preternaturally capable legal intern Nova had recommended. She knew every word of it. Every fact, every insight, every jarring chart. And yet she could not bring herself to put the haunting thing on a shelf.

Initially, she had harbored little hope the report would be anything other than a meaningless exercise in bureaucratic oversight. Prying relevant information out of the police department was a tall order. Then, after a couple of months, she noticed Zahra calling the first-year officers by their nicknames. She overheard her asking after a lieutenant's children and bantering with the police department's data analysts. She watched her shape-shift, finding the precise personality needed to cajole and assuage defensive officers. Outside of police headquarters, after observing Zahra mollify a particularly thin-skinned sergeant, Quinn could not help but marvel.

"You're incredibly good at this."

"This?"

"They like you. All of the officers. Everyone who works at the police department." Quinn pursed her lips. "It's more than that. They trust you."

"You say that like it's a miracle."

"It is."

"It's not so hard to connect with people." Zahra grinned and shrugged her shoulders. "I used to be an actor. They're an audience."

"Plenty of actors are obnoxious offstage."

"Let's pray you never meet me offstage."

Quinn laughed and found that she, too, liked Zahra quite a bit. For all her camouflaging, she never lied or politicked with the truth or played dumb. Quinn determined to place a little faith in her.

In the following months, she saw that faith richly rewarded. Trickles of useful information flowed through Zahra and into the report. Data that was once scrubbed to within an inch of pointlessness now came in raw. Documents missing from internal investigations were miraculously found. Zahra spent weeks distilling the information into insightful visuals. Like the table on page seventy-two: officers with both unusually high use of force rates and frequent mentions in internal investigations. Quinn thumbed to it. Two dozen names in alphabetical order. Smack in the center: John Marbury.

She could not quite place the feeling hissing through her. Disbelief? Guilt? Anger? She decided, months ago, not to waste time dwelling on it. Naming the emotion would change nothing. Instead, she told her speaker to play NPR and channeled the station's unwavering dispassion.

Asha Patel calmly delivered the obligatory West Coast Disaster Recovery update. The better part of Southern California remained uninhabitable. Asha reminded listeners that it would for decades. The camps remained stressed well beyond their breaking points. A United Nations disaster relief expert dispensed a winning quote in his Mexico City accent: *When we realize that the West Coast of the United States is among the biggest recipients of international aid, we begin to understand the scale of the devastation.* Asha deftly flipped to a seismologist. The scientist, her voice gravel and coffee, spoke now familiar geological terms. Full-margin rupture. Subduction zone. Cascadia. Asha translated into simpler language: along the West Coast, one tectonic plate had been thrust under another for millennia. The pressure of the converging plates caused earthquakes at various points along their fault line. Scientists had warned of the pressure building, of a bigger earthquake, one that could destroy the West Coast. And, finally, that earthquake happened.

Asha recited the questions asked of scientific experts daily. How likely was another earthquake off the West Coast? How much more damage would it cause? The seismologist stalled. Then, she, too, found a winning quote: *There are no guarantees in this world. The ground beneath us is shifting at all times.* Asha narrowed the segment's focus to the multigenerational Berry family. The grandparents lived in Seattle. The parents and their two children lived in Oakland. Both cities were rubble. Quinn ignored the rest of the segment, unwilling to learn the Berry family's fate.

She refocused when Asha spun up incomprehensible numbers on the economic depression. Unemployment rates in the thirties. GDPs and crop prices and stock markets in historic free fall. Asha introduced a Duke economist who specialized in recovering nations. She searched him for hope like a pickpocket examines a tourist. *We think this is the bottom of the fall but you never know until you start climbing up.* Asha moved on. She detailed incidents in Houston, Chicago and Philadelphia. Brawls outside of city halls and county services buildings. The lines for food banks, housing shelters and social services were growing longer. Asha played audio clips of the West Coast migrants involved in the skirmishes. *We used to have houses, now we fight for tents.* Asha promised there would be a lengthy feature on suffering farm families and the agricultural sector the next day. Food shortage, she said, is an ongoing crisis. With melancholy, Quinn recalled blending almonds into her smoothies. Then, she chided herself for mourning her personal and tiny loss. She knew there were more important issues. What were the thousands formerly working in the California almond industry doing now?

Asha arrived at Bliss.

"We are entering the uprising's sixth month," she said. "The situation remains tense yet stable."

Before Asha spoke again, Quinn asked her speaker to turn off. She took in her empty apartment and imagined Hush Harbor. Home to both Nova and Zahra. She wondered what they looked like now.

Quinn's doorbell rang. She prepared her briefcase and opened the door and nodded at her bodyguard. As usual, Earl pressed a finger to his lips. He pointed at the hallway ceilings as if to say, *Who knows who is listening.* As they walked from her apartment to the elevator, Quinn listened to Earl's dress shoes click against the tile floor. They took the elevator to the underground garage where a Range Rover was waiting for them. Earl took the front, Quinn the back.

From the driver's seat, Earl tossed Quinn a wrapped-up bacon, egg and cheese sandwich on a biscuit. The buttery scent of it danced around her nostrils. She took a large bite as Earl unwrapped his own sandwich and pressed a button to open the garage door. They emerged onto a soundless city street. She thought of what the scene might be like if so many had not already fled Bliss, the taxis that would be swerving between lanes, the dog walkers pulling the leashes of barking German shepherds. She imagined the lines outside Jubilee Coffee on the corner. She blinked again and the images went away. Sooner or later, she knew, she would have to get used to the vacancy.

Quinn thanked Earl for the sandwich and asked about his wife, Margaret.

"She's bored," Earl replied. "She hates the suburbs. Wants to move back to the city."

"I can understand that."

"Also, worried."

"About you?"

Earl laughed. "Wives of thirty years don't worry about their husbands. About you."

"I'll be fine."

"I keep telling her."

Quinn sighed at the sweetness of Margaret's concern. "Tell her I'll come visit sometime soon."

"She knows it's not the right time."

"Still. I'll try."

"I'll tell her."

Quinn rolled down her window and Earl chided her.

"You know you shouldn't be opening windows."

"There's no danger when there's no people."

"That's when there's the most danger."

Quinn kept her window open and they said nothing more about it. She watched her borough, Ellington, pass by. Shiny apartment buildings interrupted row houses. Occasionally, a single-family home jumped into view. They passed through her childhood neighborhood, and her skin crawled at the sight of her former house. The giant structure, three stories high and white stucco, imposed its hollow grandiosity on the street. She thought of her father and sent a bitter laugh at the house, hoping termites were gnawing through its foundation.

They crossed into City Center. Maybe she could ask Earl to turn back. Maybe they could drive to her apartment and she could gather her things and they could pick up Margaret and they could set a compass elsewhere. Leave whatever tragedy they were living. Leave Bliss altogether.

Instead, she said nothing. When she next looked out the window, city hall came into view.

Mayor Locke wore his best suit. He sat by a water fountain in the city hall courtyard. How many staged photos had Quinn seen of politicians in contemplation on a bench by that water fountain? Now the sight of Mayor Locke sitting there struck her as wretched.

Quinn noticed the sun reflecting off his head as she sat down next to him. He hardly moved.

"Praying?"

The mayor shook his head. "I don't anymore."

"Why? It might help," Quinn said, only half-joking.

"He doesn't listen."

"God?"

"Yes."

"I hope you're wrong."

"I'm not."

In the water's reflection, she searched for signs of his former vitality.

"What does your Imam say?"

"He left."

"Suburbs?"

"Lebanon."

"Do you still go to mosque?"

"For the chanting."

During their campaign, the mayor's strict adherence to Islam's prayer times had surprised her. She knew few politicians devoted to religion behind closed doors. On a rare night without rallies or donor dinners, he'd invited his campaign staff to his home. Quinn sequestered him in a corner of the living room, peppering him with questions on faith. He answered patiently, his measured baritone a bell. She pulled a small notebook from her purse and jotted down some of the things he said. He chuckled.

"Am I old enough to have wisdom worth writing down?" he asked.

Emboldened by his cheeriness, she angled her questions more directly.

"You said that we all have faith. That's not right. What about atheists and agnostics?"

"Faith isn't about religion or God. It's about belief in something fundamental. Sometimes that belief is blind, sometimes it's reasoned, and most of the time it's a little bit of both."

Other staff members joined them. Locke carried on as if he were in a private conversation.

"Take a physicist. To believe in her work, she must believe that there is order in the universe. Any scientist worth her salt would readily concede that human experience of the universe accounts for the smallest fraction of possible experience. How, then, can we prove that the physical world is indeed ordered? It is a fundamental assumption, an article of faith, even if we don't recognize it as such.

"Take a true skeptic. He does not trust religion or science. Naturally, he does not trust politicians." Quinn smiled self-consciously and noticed Locke's listeners, now almost a dozen, did the same. "He cannot see how human beings, severely limited in their physical and mental capacities, could build systems of knowledge based on the interpretation of their senses. Yet even this skeptic, so wary of epistemological leaps, has his assumptions. He believes that all human beings have his approximate physical and mental limitations. More importantly, he believes that the collective, through collaboration, cannot overcome individual limitations. His faith is in himself."

Quinn spun her pen around her thumb. "That sounds like an attack on individualism."

"It does," said Locke. He shrugged. "It is."

"Your namesake would be ashamed."

"My namesake is Alain, not John."

"Really?"

Unlike most politicians, Locke rarely spoke about his upbringing. Quinn traced a vague outline in her mind. Born on Aggy's Island. Parents unable or unfit or un-wanting. Shuttled between aunts and uncles and grandparents. Excelled in school and in sports and then in the marines. Chose his own name. Clarence Washington became Clarence Locke. And Clarence Locke became Bliss's first Black mayor in decades.

He took a sip of iced water. "Really," he said.

Sitting beside the pool now, Quinn scarcely believed the shell next to her once lived as Clarence Locke. She stared at their reflections again.

"I'm late?" he said.

"Yes."

"I give the staff trouble."

"A lot."

"I told them to look for other jobs."

"They would never do that."

"I know."

"They're loyal."

"They found faith in the wrong place."

"They found faith in you."

"Like I said."

Quinn wanted to say he was a person worth following. Time dressed him in the wrong moment and that was not his fault. She tried to predict the effect of her words. She saw more harm than good. They said nothing for a long while.

"You should leave as well," he said.

Quinn pushed her tongue against her teeth. When had his advice crossed from caring to patronizing?

"I can see the front page now," she said. "'Mayor's Senior Aide Abandons City in Crisis.'"

Locke flicked his hand.

"The media writes bad fiction."

"The truth in it is still true."

"You're not abandoning me if I tell you to go."

Quinn thought about all the ways Locke was brilliant and all the ways powerful men were blind.

"It's not about you. It's about Bliss. I'm not leaving my city." The sun danced in the fountain. "The governor's update started thirty minutes ago."

She stood and walked into the building. Locke came a minute later.

From across the conference room table, Governor Luna Santos sized up the mayor's staff, the police chief and his staff. Representatives from the National Guard and FEMA, and a token one from the Office of the President. She squinted at the portraits over Quinn's left shoulder and mouthed the words on the plaque: *The Honorable Mayor Kelsey Riley*. Quinn registered the disgust on the governor's face.

The presenter, an engineer bemoaning neglected sewer maintenance, finished speaking. With a nod, Locke passed Quinn permission to move the meeting forward.

She peered at the agenda and cleared her throat. "Next, please open your packets to the table on page seven. The weekly maintenance schedule for our water treatment plants. The cells in red are those tasks for which we are not currently staffed. You will see that nearly half of the cells are red. Our current employees can't cover those shifts indefinitely. Soon, red cells will mean missed tasks. And as missed tasks pile on missed tasks, the quality of our water drops. You see where I'm going here?"

Collectively, the room nodded.

"How long?" Santos said.

"That's hard to say."

"Your best guess."

"A few months. If we push our people to an extreme."

"How difficult is it to train new staff?"

"Training isn't the most significant problem." Quinn opened her mouth as if to start a second sentence and then hesitated. Santos finished the thought for her.

"The question is how do we get new people to work for Bliss. When even the old ones, like much of the water staff, fled once our current crisis began."

"That's right."

"What about neighboring towns? They can't send over spare help?"

"We've borrowed the people we can borrow. As you know well, Mrs. Governor, the West Coast disaster has caused a labor shortage in the whole country, including us."

"Just to be clear, is this water scenario an if or a when?" Santos asked.

"I very much hope I'm wrong, but I believe it is a when."

The room tensed. Santos swiveled in her chair. Locke remained still.

"We'll have to start notifying residents," Quinn said. "In case we can't find a solution. And we'll need to form a task force to—"

"Or." Police Chief Baker interrupted Quinn. He elongated his *o*'s and growled his *r*'s. "Or, we could just shut off the rebellion's water now." Baker crossed his arms and leaned back into a stab of sunlight. It showed bits of hair gel melting off his head. A thousand tiny spikes of hair, once firmly held by the product, drooped.

"We've had this conversation," Quinn said. She let a second tick. "Chief."

"Worth having again."

"I should mention that we can't get close enough to the Hamilton Heights building complex to cut off their water. But that's not what you meant."

"No. It's not."

"You want to shut off the water, period. To the entire city." Baker uncrossed his arms and placed two fists on the table.

"You got strangers in your house." Baker opened his palms as though extending an invitation to imagine. "Three choices. Number one. Do nothing and hope that they leave. Never works. Number two. Come in guns blazing. Effective. Messy. Fine for a man like me, but I can understand that it presents problems for politicians." He glanced at Locke. "Number three. Strangle them. No food in. No water. Pressure builds. Bodies got to survive. Even the dumb ones come out with their hands up."

"It's not the worst idea," said a large man across from Baker.

"It may be the inevitable strategy," said a woman with a pixie cut.

"There are still innocent people living in the city who want to continue living in the city," said Quinn. "They need water."

Baker shook his head.

"They should leave. What are they doing? Watching their city die. They leave, we take care of the problem. They come back to a safe city."

"Some of those people are children. There are also kids at Hamilton Heights." Quinn spun her pen around her thumb in an effort to distract herself from the angry throb in her gut.

"The rebels' problem."

"Children are our responsibility." She spun the pen faster.

"Rebels are using them. Human shields."

"That doesn't mean we have to be the bullets."

"This isn't playtime, Quinn."

"I know." Her voice went tight and low.

"There's nothing pretty in war."

"War?"

"What do you think this is?"

"A crisis."

"Bullshit word."

"They're not shooting at us."

"So?"

"It's not a war."

"They're holding you hostage."

The pen slipped off Quinn's thumb and slapped the table. "Us."

Baker bunched his lips and crossed his arms and the room understood that Quinn had prevailed.

"Thank you for the discussion," said Locke. His first words since the meeting opened rang with authority. It pleased and startled Quinn to hear this old version of him. He peered down the table and addressed the president's representative.

"Correct me if this statement is inaccurate. While both the president and I have declared a state of emergency, the president has not yet indicated his desire to actually use his emergency authorities."

"That is correct, sir," said the president's representative.

"Mrs. Governor," Locke said, "your office has been unwavering in its support of the Bliss local government. Are there any emergency powers your office wishes to declare at this time?"

"I continue to believe that the local authorities understand the situation far better than the state or federal government."

Quinn marveled at how easily the buck passed from president to governor to mayor. Perhaps Santos spoke some truth and Bliss was best positioned to respond. Perhaps shrewd politicians tossed around no-win responsibilities in high-stakes games of hot potato. And, perhaps, focused on rebuilding the West Coast and resuscitating the economy, the Bliss crisis had become the country's middle child: an urgent afterthought.

"Well, then," Locke said. His gaze circled the room. Another image of wilderness came to Quinn. A lion surveying the horizon for challengers. Curious.

"My decision today is the same as it was last month, which was the same as it was the month prior, which was the same as it was when our current crisis began. The water stays on." He turned to Quinn. "We need to figure out how to keep it clean. Get the Water Services Department employees back. Whatever it takes."

"Yes, sir," said Quinn. "I'll try."

Quinn watched Baker slowly pump his jaw. He noticed her and stopped and smirked.

"What's next?" Locke said.

An hour later, they took a picture for the media and broke for lunch.

In the mayor's office, Santos showed Quinn a wallet-sized photo album of her children. "This is the way my grandmother used to do it," she said to Quinn. "I like that the pictures take up physical space. It makes the memories real."

"I understand," Quinn said, and she did. She scooched her sofa chair closer to Santos. Locke, absorbed in his own thoughts, quietly ate his sandwich on the couch opposite them.

Santos flipped through pictures of birthday parties with two-year-olds covered in cake and soccer games with preteens sprinting after loose balls and a quinceañera featuring a dark-haired girl in a pink dress grinning wide.

"My daughter. Sofía. She made me promise I would tell people the braces are off now," Santos said.

"Braces can mean a lot at that age."

Santos chuckled a rich velvet blanket, warm and textured and large enough to cover a body. "Don't get me started."

She turned to graduation photos of her twin boys. "You see this one has a little mole on his neck? That's Santi. The other one is Javi. Don't judge me. Their full names are Santiago and

Javier. They just decided to make them rhyme when they were two years old. Conspirators from the beginning."

Santos pointed at the album's final and empty slipcover. "This is for Sofía when she graduates." She made the symbol for the cross and winked at Quinn. "One more year."

Santos turned and placed the album in her purse.

"Do you want children?"

The question struck Quinn as natural. More like a favorite aunt extending a conversation than a nosy neighbor pushing into her business. She decided to reply openly.

"I think I'd like a husband first."

"I can help with that. I'm a master matchmaker. I have a list of names." Santos paused and her mouth dropped into a frown. Her forehead wrinkled. "Unless you don't like brown people."

Barely a second passed before she threw her head back and laughed. Quinn joined in nervously. Santos winked at her and then glanced at her watch. She rolled her shoulders back.

"Are you ready?" Santos said to Locke.

"I'm ready," he said.

"Quinn, you said you have something for me?"

Quinn pulled a set of manila folders from her briefcase and handed them out.

"Take a few minutes."

The bullet points at the top of the page contained all the key information.

Almost one hundred white supremacists came to Bliss in the last month.

Their total number now stood at several hundred.

They came in through checkpoints manned by the police department.

They came in armed.

"The Originists." Santos said the name as though running her tongue over cracked glass. "Marbury's group."

"Yes. Sort of."

"He's not with the Originists? They sheltered him, correct?"

"Yes. But our latest information suggests a split. Marbury formed his own Originist cell."

"Why?"

"Apparently, he wanted to be more...aggressive."

"How many? With Marbury."

"At least a couple of dozen."

"The original cell is still somewhere in Southwood?"

"Yes."

"Where's Marbury's group?"

"We don't know."

Santos's expression went blank.

"What do they have planned?"

"Some sort of assault. But I should emphasize that our sources aren't exactly reliable—the handful of Originist recruits we've caught entering Bliss. They don't know the details of what's happening. They have different allegiances and stories and opinions. There's only one common thread—Marbury and his people split and are plotting an attack."

Quinn pictured Marbury, a pudgy man with short-cropped red hair and an enormous smile. How could this be a person capable of killing Kemba? A sudden burst of sadness filled her. She tightened her torso, found the contours of the emotion as though it were a solid thing. She imagined squishing it to the size of a thumbnail and flicking it away. She returned to the conversation.

"They're still coming through the police-controlled check-points?" said Santos.

"That's right."

"Not the National Guard checkpoints?"

"No."

"Who's involved on the police side?"

"We can't say for sure."

"Baker?"

"We don't know that."

"But it must be somebody high up."

"I think so."

"This is coordinated."

"Yes. Clearly."

"You trust your source? Not the Originist recruits, but the one that gave you the information in this." Santos picked up the manila file.

"I trust him."

Quinn smiled instinctively. How many sides did Peter Schwab convince daily? She had not seen her former bodyguard turned soldier turned informant for several months. Still, she knew his loyalties. They belonged to her.

"Just to be clear," Santos said. "You don't know for sure how high this goes."

"That's correct."

"Your thoughts, then."

"On what?"

"Baker."

"I'd be lying if I said I didn't suspect him. But, then again, he's not a white supremacist. Just a hardline law-and-order cop. Why would he let in more disorder?"

Santos closed her folder and rubbed two fingers on her temple.

"Clarence," she said.

"Yes," said Locke.

"Is Baker involved?"

"Yes."

"Are you sure?"

"I am."

"How?"

"I know him."

Their eyes met and Santos nodded.

"Why?"

"Chaos."

"Say more."

"He needs a different situation."

"Even more, Clarence."

"He needs violence to prove that more violence is necessary. Hush Harbor uses force only in self-defense."

Santos pressed her index finger against her thumb. "The nationalists attack, the rebels defend, Baker intervenes."

"Exactly."

Quinn fought the urge to shift in her seat. She suddenly wanted, desperately, to run away.

"You need to take control of this," Santos said. A blade shimmered in her voice. Locke received her words with the calm of a person who had thought the same thing a hundred times over.

A knock interrupted. From behind the door, a faceless voice called them.

"I'm so sorry," it said. "But we're ten minutes past time. Everyone is waiting in the conference room."

They threw out their sandwich wrappers and gathered their folders.

Hours later, Quinn watched the delegations trudge out of city hall from her office window. She turned away and drew an idle finger across her bookshelf, pausing at a spiral-bound document: a second copy of the report she and Zahra had produced. Maybe she should throw it out. The copy at home, too. Perhaps then it would stop guilting her.

She recalled the last time she read the document in its entirety. A year ago, on a chilly Sunday, she and Zahra sat at her breakfast nook and pored over it. They ate through an assortment of Mexican food from Quinn's favorite taco truck while noting misspellings and grammatical errors. They reached the report's conclusion just as Zahra finally reached for the *maduros*.

"Do you have ice cream?"

Quinn pointed at the fridge without looking away from her laptop. "The freezer."

Zahra returned with a container of Ben & Jerry's vanilla bean. She dunked a *maduro* in it. Quinn's attention swung between the report and Zahra's creation.

"Is that good?"

"Try it."

"You're kind of messing with a whole cuisine."

Zahra snorted. "My dad is Mexican. My mom is Black American. My bloodline can be mixed, but my food has to be segregated?"

Quinn dipped her *maduro* into the ice cream.

"Oh," she said, between bites. "It *is* good."

Zahra nodded as though she were an evangelist watching a friend's conversion. Then she gestured at the screen.

"Have you shown it to the mayor yet?"

"Haven't had the chance."

"You should find one. We're way past the first draft. It looks ready to me."

Quinn spun a pen on her thumb. She agreed with Zahra. They had scrubbed the report to within an inch of its life. Its narrative and numbers guided the reader to an irrefutable conclusion: the city had done nothing to address a disturbing pattern of police misconduct.

Quinn scrolled to the appendix. She still marveled at the information Zahra had coaxed out of the police department. What magic tricks had she used? Sitting across from the intern—at home and on a weekend and with a meal to share—Quinn wondered if Zahra had used the same tricks on her. She felt like a close friend, someone with whom trust came easy.

"I'm not sure we're there yet," Quinn said.

"Do you have edits? I can take a look."

"No. The report itself is good. Really good. But..." Quinn thought of the report's political consequences and sensed her concerns were better left tucked away. She shook her head. "Never mind. I think I just need to read through it again."

Now, alone in her office, she heard a low rumbling from the Riley Conference Room. She walked down the hall to find Locke placing a packet of Clorox sheets on the table. He moved chairs to the walls, plugged in a vacuum. Quinn's heart swelled. Locke had nothing to gain from cleaning the room. No article in the paper, no social media post, no approval rating bump. Just a clean space. Like the Water Services Department, the custodial team was significantly understaffed. Their tasks still needed to be done. Quinn joined her boss. She opened the packet of Clorox sheets and wiped the table up and down, always in the same pattern so no lines would show.

Minutes later, Quinn and Earl walked a block down from city hall and around the corner. They stopped outside an unpainted door with a crooked sign that read The Veto.

"The reporter is waiting in there," Earl said.

Quinn entered alone. An Irish fiddle came through the speakers, weaving melancholy through the bar. She noted the unoccupied tables. She glanced at the walls, filled with pictures of politicians and sports figures and celebrities. Her eye caught on one of the mayor when he was a candidate. She smiled widely beside him and Kyle, the bar's owner. The bar echoed with optimistic and boisterous clatter that night. Several glasses broke. A chair, too. Quinn apologized on behalf of the mayor's supporters and Kyle waved her off. *Only one thing bothers me,* he'd said. *And if you all are planning on winning this thing, you better know it.* He pointed at the rule emblazoned in red paint behind the bar. What's Said Here Stays Unsaid Elsewhere.

Now, Quinn wondered how often things were said there at all. A few old men with baseball caps pulled low sipped on beer the color of mustard. Kyle spotted her. He cleaned glasses that

appeared already clean. She knew he would look no more unless approached. If one did not want to be seen at The Veto,
one was not seen.

Quinn made her way to the back-corner booth and slid in.
She took in the slim woman across from her. Asha Patel pushed
her jet-black hair behind her ears. Quinn had expected a wrinkled forehead, maybe a gray hair or two. She chided herself for
feeling surprised.

"You came," Asha said.

"You insisted."

"I did. Still. I'm surprised."

"I like you. Or something approximating that."

"You don't know me."

"I know the sound of your voice."

"So do a lot of people."

"I like the way you tell stories."

"That means very little."

Quinn thought of Nova, how she'd once listed the differences
between *Native Son* and *Invisible Man* to her through a mouthful of pad Thai. Nova buried deep in her seat mumbling Danez
Smith poems at a screening of a prison documentary. Nova ig-
noring motion sickness to read *Burnt Shadows* on a bus to New
York. What was the insight she drew from that book? There
are no small corners?

Quinn settled into the booth. "How we tell stories means
everything."

Asha leaned back and crossed her arms. She studied Quinn
and Quinn enjoyed the attention.

"I grew up in Trenton," Asha said.

"I'm sorry."

Asha smiled. "It's not so far from Bliss. I remember your dad."

"He told stories for a living."

"He was a good politician."

"Yes."

"People loved him."

"They still do."

"He did a lot for the city."

"He did a lot for some parts of the city," Quinn replied. Asha pulled back, evaluated. A tiny space opened in their conversation. The possibility of honesty.

"I never liked him," Asha said.

"That's reasonable."

"Something about the way he talked."

"His tone."

"Sounded like cigars."

"He didn't smoke."

"Like cigars and back rooms and old leather couches."

"I know what you mean."

"His sound flipped during campaign seasons. Cigarettes and cafeterias and metal chairs."

"He was more chameleon than people think."

"It worked."

"He kept getting elected."

"I mean, he turned Bliss around. I admired him for that."

Asha's praise jangled in Quinn's ears. Asha Patel, Quinn's Asha Patel, should not admire Kelsey Riley. The voice that needled the truth out of scoundrels should not say gracious things about her father. Quinn considered the empty bar and the empty city outside its door. Home to ghosts and liars and myths.

"This is why I came," Asha said.

She handed Quinn her phone and earbuds. Quinn listened to the recording twice over.

"How did you get this?" she asked, returning the phone to Asha.

"Doesn't matter."

"I think it does."

"Do you have a comment?"

"No."

"Nothing?"

"It's not much in reality."

"But politically."

"I have no comment."

"Locke is already halfway out. Approval ratings in the tank. Allies distancing themselves. A restless city council that wants someone more…decisive."

"I'm aware."

"This recording will finish it. Give me a comment. Some context. Maybe it will soften the blow."

"Like I said. I have no comment."

Beneath the table, Quinn rubbed her palm over her knee. She recalled the many ways she had protected Locke: constantly spinning narratives to his advantage, habitually deflecting blame from him to his nearest rival, carefully tailoring his policies to a city where politics was more butchery than thoughtful dialogue. She had done her job and done it well time and time again. But even she could not save him from the recording.

Asha twisted sideways. She steeled her gaze. "Maybe you want the blow to land."

"What?"

"Maybe whoever wants Locke out promised you a promotion."

"I'm already a senior aide."

"Something like chief of staff sounds better."

"That's a shitty theory."

"Is it?"

Quinn rolled her eyes. Suspecting her, Locke's closest aide, of stabbing him in the back was like thinking Hamlet killed the king. She would have to disabuse Asha of that preposterous notion.

"Who'd you get the recording from?" Quinn asked.

"I don't give up sources."

"Baker."

Asha's face stayed still. "Anonymous."

"It was him."

"He's a likely candidate."

"He's the only candidate."

"Him and you."

"I didn't give you the recording."

"But your voice is on it. How do I know you're not working with Rex? Ousting Locke together?"

Quinn almost laughed. The idea of her working alongside Baker was farcical. Did Asha think she was that ambitious? That she would throw in her lot with an amoral narcissist hell-bent on power for power's sake?

"Absurd," Quinn said.

"Wasn't Baker a friend of your father's?"

"So?"

"A friend of the whole family, then."

"Ha."

"Like an uncle."

Quinn assessed Asha again. She admired her even more now. Her relentlessness. How she changed tack. How she pursued her story. Quinn knew nothing but the truth would satisfy this reporter. She locked on Asha's eyes.

"My father loved his work," Quinn said. "He believed in it with everything he had. That's not just something people say in speeches. It's true. Every night he would sit at the dinner table and tell me and my mom about how government was changing the city. The lives he was affecting. I'm sure you remember that he was a big man. Six-four and wide. When he spoke, his whole body trembled. Mighty. Righteous. People loved him because he stood up for them. He was everybody's best friend.

"After dinner, he would work for hours. I'd go to sleep and he'd still be there. Maybe once a week, before my mother died, I would hear several thumps coming from my parents' bedroom. Brief and methodical. One-two-three, one-two-three. Almost like a waltz.

"The next day my father would seem more relaxed than usual. He'd drink an extra cup of coffee, eat some pastry for breakfast. My mother would wince when I hugged her."

As Asha tensed, the wrinkles around the edge of her face revealed her age. She held Quinn's gaze, and a strange gravity hung between them.

"I'm sorry," Asha said, and Quinn blushed, recognizing her overshare. Quinn rummaged through her wallet and laid fifty dollars on the table, though neither of them had ordered a drink.

"I hated my father," she added. "His friends were not mine."

She left without pausing to see Asha's expression. She found Earl at the door and they made for city hall.

Quinn got back to her office to find Baker hovering over her desk. He had often crossed her mind in the months she and Zahra investigated police misconduct. Back then, he'd made little attempt to hide his displeasure. He took every opportunity to discredit their work with a torrent of anger and misinformation and rationalizations. Steadily, her hope for change eroded under his incessant bluster. As their report reached its final draft, and she waffled over its release, she'd turned to Zahra for fresh perspective and, with any luck, a dose of optimism.

"What do you think of Baker?"

They had sat across from each other in a dingy conference room tucked into a dingier corner of city hall. Mostly silent, they thumbed through loose-leaf drafts of the report. Two empty boxes and half a dozen stacks of paper, their source material, lined the table.

"Chief Baker?"

"Yes."

"Handsome."

Quinn cackled and almost threw her pen at Zahra. "Seriously."

Zahra played with the top of her ear.

"In college, I performed in a lot of terrible plays with shitty directors. Our theater department only had one true icon—Professor July Little. She was this small lady with cat-eye sunglasses and frizzy white hair and leather boots that came up to her knees. She spoke faster than anyone I knew and threw shade at legendary male playwrights. I thought we'd get along great. So, during my junior year, when I was cast in one of her plays, I was thrilled. It was my chance to work with the great July Little. But what do they say? Careful what you wish for?" Zahra drummed her fingers on a stack of paper. "Her arrogance overshadowed the play. It didn't matter if a scene failed or an audience left underwhelmed or the actors complained. She would not entertain the possibility that any part of the world she had built on stage wasn't working. She *could* not entertain it. I started to miss the shitty directors. Yes, Little's productions were slick. Technically sound. But they were also hollow. Projections of a singular style instead of a composition in service of the narrative. As someone who believed in the power of theater to effect change, she was dangerous to me. A person who worked for her own ego. For her own stature." Zahra's eyes narrowed. "Baker reminds me of July Little."

Now, at her office door, with Baker a dozen feet away, Quinn wished Zahra were with her. She needed someone whose instincts she trusted. She worried that her own, rattled and worn, would soon betray her.

She coughed. Baker turned and showed his palms in feigned apology.

"I'm sorry," he said. "I think offices are fascinating. A window into the soul. I couldn't help myself."

Quinn rounded her desk. Standing across from him, she noted

a slight hook at the end of his nose. Like some species of bird meant to peck and peck and peck.

"Well," she said. "What did you find?"

"Excuse me?"

"In this office. This window into my soul. What did you find?"

Baker bobbed his head. "Can I be honest?"

"Please."

Quinn gestured at a chair. They both sat. Baker leaned back and set his hands behind his head. He drew in a long breath and squinted.

"This office surprised me. There's almost nothing in here. Just a desk and a couple of chairs and the bookshelf. No stacks. No plants. It's almost like no one works here. Until you showed up, I thought I was in the wrong place."

"What were you expecting?"

"Usually, people have pictures. Of family and friends. Even a pet. Sometimes, they have art. You strike me as the type to have a painting on the wall. Maybe a memento from a trip to Mexico or Europe." He drew his hand across the room. "But you have nothing. It's all very strange."

Quinn caught his subtext and couldn't let it go unchecked.

"Very strange," she said. "For a woman."

Baker tilted his head. "I wasn't going there. But now that you mention it, yes. Very strange especially for a woman."

"There are stranger things," Quinn said. She readied her parry. "For example. Do you have many women serving as captains over in the police department?"

"We do a fine job with all of that."

"I could pull up the numbers."

"That's not necessary."

"But if you did such a fine job with it?"

"All I was trying to say is that I would've guessed you had

some pictures in your office. Considering where you work, I'd expect at least a photo of your father."

"You'd expect that."

Baker pulled at a slab of loose skin beneath his chin. "You know, he would have wanted this mess over with."

"Everybody wants this over with."

"Yes. But he would do what it takes."

"And what is that?"

"We gotta put them down. Bliss is going to explode. It's not just the rebels. It's also the supremacists. They're streaming into the city."

"You mean, somebody is letting them in."

Baker put his hands up and clicked his tongue. "Oh c'mon," he said. "You're talking conspiracy theories. Careful. You never know who's listening." He circled a finger in the air and grinned. Was that how he had made the recording? Bugging city hall? He settled his hands on his lap. "Nobody is letting anyone come into Bliss. Least of all me. But, for the sake of argument, let's say we've got a decent number of supremacists that have found their way here. Hundreds growing into thousands. How long before they decide to take on the rebellion? How many lives would be lost then? You think they're here for shits and giggles?"

"I think we need to handle the situation with care."

Baker grunted and leaned forward. "I like Clarence. No joke. I voted for him. But he has no idea what to do in this kind of scenario."

"You're making it worse. Tighten the checkpoints. Stop letting them in."

He shook his head. "Doesn't matter what I do or what you do. It's going to get bad. If your father were alive—"

"My father is not alive."

"But if he were—"

"Thank God he's not. May he rot in hell."

Baker recoiled. Quinn watched him register her seriousness. His features scrunched inward and then slowly opened in a laugh.

"May he rot in hell," he said. He laughed some more. "I thought he was an asshole, too. But you gotta buddy up to the boss. He spent all his time telling stories about himself. Never let anyone else talk. To tell you the truth, no one who worked with him liked him."

"I can believe that."

Baker rubbed his knees. He stood and rapped his knuckles on the desk. "This whole conversation was enlightening," he said. "This thing only ends the hard way. I'm praying for your boss."

Later that evening, having learned all she could about water treatment plants, Quinn left city hall and climbed into the Range Rover's back seat. Earl started the ignition and they slipped into the night.

Quinn's mind ventured from schedules and hiring and chlorine treatment to places it should not go. She attempted to distract herself by gazing out the window, but the lightless city offered her nothing. Her mind scratched at a four-day-old memory of Clarence Locke at his desk, examining a postcard with rowboats on it. He slid the postcard across the table to Quinn. It read, *No*. How many rejections was this now? Six? Seven? Quinn saw hope drain from his body. He slumped in his chair. Soft as a lullaby, he said, "These fucking animals won't even talk to me."

She had forgotten about this until she heard the words on Asha's recording. Instantly, the public's reaction played out in front of her. She knew some people would protest Locke's characterization of the rebels as animals. Some would hate that he attempted dialogue with them. Still others would despise his inability to bring Jeremiah Prince to the table. But everyone would hear the defeat in his voice. And defeat, Quinn knew, was unforgivable. The recording would end his already tenuous political career.

In the car, Quinn rubbed her thighs and rolled down a window. One thing at a time, she told herself.

Earl reached back and handed Quinn a red slip of paper containing an address. She recognized the street name from campaigning in Mt. Olive, Bliss's westernmost borough.

"This is her?"

"It's her."

"Sanders? Officer Sylvia Sanders? Who shot Kemba?"

"Her."

She looked down at the paper. Months of searching in the palm of her hand.

"How?" she asked.

"I got someone."

"You got someone?"

"A mole."

"Of course you do." Quinn shook her head in admiration.

"You see the times?"

Quinn looked at the paper and noticed *fridays midnight to three* written beneath the address.

"I see," she said.

"Only those times. You understand?"

"I understand."

Quinn wondered at Earl and her luck. He appeared in her life a week before her mother passed. A wide-faced man with a soft voice who sat next to her at the hospital and handed her a box of crayons. Seven years old, she could not bear that kindness. She cried while clinging to her seat. He knelt in front of her and said that it was okay to cry, that it was good. That sad things happened and that, one day, happy things would happen, too. He said that he could sit with her as long as she liked. The words felt like a river gracing dry land.

A week after her mother passed, she found herself in Earl's kitchen with a short, square woman.

"This is Mrs. Margaret," Earl said. "She's my wife."

Quinn said hello. Margaret motioned for her to sit at the table and she did. "Let's play a game," Margaret said. Quinn braced herself for a feelings wheel or pictures of sad-looking animals. Child therapists, she already knew, popped up everywhere. Instead, the woman handed out colored cards. "Have you ever played UNO?"

She passed the afternoon shouting "UNO" with Margaret. Earl baked cookies and refilled glasses of milk. He jumped into several hands and almost won one. Quinn, though, took most of the games.

When evening came, they ate popcorn and chicken tenders and watched old animated movies. In between *Moana* and *Mulan*, Quinn showed Margaret crayon pictures she had drawn of her mother. Margaret put an arm around Quinn's shoulders and stroked her hair.

"These are beautiful," Margaret said.

After a moment, Quinn said, "I'm running out of crayons."

"We've got some more here. Would you like to draw a little tomorrow?"

Quinn nestled against Margaret. The moment marked a new chapter in her childhood. She would spend afternoons and evenings at Margaret and Earl's, drawing and reading and playing. When she was older, she would do homework and help with dinner. She learned how to chop garlic from Earl and which recipes preferred coconut oil to olive from Margaret. Children from the neighborhood dropped by daily. Quinn learned their favorite foods and what to expect from whom. Nova helped with the dishes and Malcolm never made a mess. Remy rarely spoke and Kimara was quick to laugh. Margaret and Earl, with Quinn assisting, always cooked an extra portion or two in case someone wanted to stay for dinner.

In middle school, Nova took up photography when she found Earl's old camera on a bookshelf. Quinn volunteered to be her first subject and the pair spent weeks exploring lighting and angles and focus. Two years later, Quinn decided she would join the Speech and Debate Club after listening to Margaret's "Great Speakers" playlist on YouTube. Nova, already the club president, squeezed Quinn tight after her announcement. Together, the friends talked about which teachers gave out too much homework and, in so doing, left little time for more important afterschool interests. When Malcolm was not around, and sooner than either Margaret or Earl would have liked, they talked about their favorite boys. Nova dipped in and out of crushes, continuously disappointed with the immaturity of boys. But Quinn's admiration was not easily earned or lost. It took six months for her feelings toward Malcolm to emerge after he and his family moved to New York. She dared not tell anyone about her next crush, Remy, for fear that giving her feelings voice would once again trap her in yearslong adoration.

Eventually, the friends entered high school and fought calculus and, with Margaret's help, won. Earl assigned them chapters of *A People's History of the United States* as they waded through school textbooks. One day, Quinn wrote down a list of colleges on a notepad in the kitchen. She asked Earl and Margaret what they thought.

"I think your life is too important to be defined by a brand name," Margaret said.

"And, also, we're excited for you," said Earl.

Quinn wrote her college application essay on the couple. She had learned that, despite all indications, they were neither angels nor saints. One of Kelsey Riley's aides recommended them to the mayor who, with his wife's illness and imminent death, needed additional childcare. Reflecting on it as a high school senior, Quinn was sure that her father simply liked the optics. He would send his daughter to a Black neighborhood on

Aggy's Island to be cared for by a Black former teacher, Margaret, and a Black former cop, Earl. Earl and Margaret would use the great sum he paid them to subsidize their after-school program, which counted five children, several years apart in age, as its first students: Quinn, Nova, Malcolm, Remy and Kimara. In one fell swoop, Riley would become both an unassailable integrationist and a local philanthropist.

But Quinn wrote none of this in her essay. She wrote about the UNO card, a green reverse, that Margaret and Earl slipped into her backpack when she entered middle school. On the top, they had written their cell phone numbers. On the bottom, a note. *Find the right direction. We love you.*

Sitting in the Range Rover, Quinn dug through her purse. She unearthed a Ziploc bag with the tattered UNO card inside. She removed the card, placed it between her palms and brought her fingers to her lips as though in prayer. She thought of rights and wrongs and how when she turned enough times they pointed the same way. She hoped there was a God and hoped even harder that God had a plan. She put the card back in the Ziploc along with the red slip of paper.

"We're here," Earl said. He parked along a row of townhomes.

"How long do I have?"

"Two hours."

"Earl."

"Yeah."

"Thank you."

"Just be back here on time."

"No. I mean. Thank you."

Earl looked into his rearview mirror. He attempted a smile, but it was rimmed with sadness.

"Go on," he said.

Quinn approached a row house with a dull blue door and a gold knob. She tapped on the door, nerves fluttering. She looked

down the street and saw no cars. The door creaked open. She
slid into the relief of walls. She reached for Jeremiah and found
him and he kissed her with a fury that burned her lips.

   Jeremiah smelled of coffee. Quinn drew her hand over the
little curls of hair that dotted his chest. He snored gently then
harshly and then gently again. She scratched his chest and hoped
he would wake. She poked his skin with a long fingernail. He
stirred.
   "That hurt," he said.
   "Good."
   "Good?"
   "No sleeping."
   "Ever?"
   "While we're here."
She kissed him and wrapped her leg around his. She laid her
head half on his shoulder and half on his chest. Her lungs fell
as his rose and their breath found tempo. A sweet syncopation.
She wanted Jeremiah to turn the lamp off. She pressed her eyes
against his chest to evade the little light it gave. They could es-
cape here, she thought. If only they did not move. If only they
shut off the light and made home in their rhythm.
   "Remy," she said.
   "Yeah."
   "How many lives do you think we have?"
Jeremiah rubbed her back.
   "Three," he said.
   "Three?"
   "One before the revolution. One during. One after."
   "After."
   "After."
   "I'm not sure there's an after."
   "Neither am I."
They stayed silent a moment. Quinn had trouble imagining

the future. She turned her mind to the past. Margaret teasing her about the mayor's election win, just two years ago: "Do I have to call you Ms. Senior-Aide-to-the-Mayor now?" Earl joining in: "I believe the appropriate title is Madam Senior Aide." Margaret laughing, Quinn blushing.

In the kitchen, someone chopping tomatoes. Margaret saying, "Do you remember Remy? From the after-school program?" Quinn remembering Nova's brother, a boy too shy to speak, for whom she once nurtured a crush. Had he grown into this man with horn-rimmed glasses and a sharp jawline? "He's back home now. Took a job teaching history to middle schoolers, God give him strength. Go on now, Quinn, help with that salad." Remy scooching to make space for her. His fingers directing delicate, sharp cuts and the tomato falling into neat cubes. Him saying, "It's really good to see you."

Now, lying in bed next to Jeremiah, she gently tucked the memory away.

"I liked the before," she said.

"Me, too," he said. "Parts of it."

She curled into him.

"How are you?" he said.

"I'm okay."

"Yeah?"

"No. But, yeah. How are you?"

"The same."

"How's Nova?" A tremor snuck into Quinn's voice. For as long as she could remember, she and Nova had relied on each other for direction. They had chosen to attend Livingston College together. There, Nova was the first of Quinn's friends to suggest she pursue politics full-time. Quinn advised Nova to apply to law school. Once at Livingston Law, Nova grounded Quinn in the legal structures that reproduced racial oppression, including the vagaries around police brutality. When Quinn struggled to conceptualize her report on police misconduct,

Nova connected her with a fellow law student, Zahra. For over two decades, Quinn and Nova had been one another's compass at every baffling juncture. And, now, in the most volatile period of their lives, they were worlds apart.

"I miss her," she said.

"I'm sure she misses you, too."

"It's getting harder. To be apart."

"I can imagine."

"How is she?"

"Strong. Hopeful."

"As always."

"You'll see her again."

"I know."

She wanted to say that sometimes knowing and hoping were synonymous. Sometimes they were just called faith. She thought of Locke. How belief crumbled. Her heart tightened with guilt.

"There's a new recruit," Jeremiah said.

"There always are."

"Nova assigned him to me."

"To you?"

"To help me."

"With what?"

"Everything. Logistics, accounting, scheduling."

"Is he good at it?"

"Very."

"And you trust him?"

"I think so."

She trailed a finger down his side and reflected on how rarely he placed confidence in anyone. She could hardly blame him, especially now. In the midst of an insurgency, misplaced faith could prove catastrophic. Whoever the recruit was, she hoped he was worthy of Jeremiah's trust.

"Good," she said. "I'm glad."

"He's like me."

"How?"

"Focused. Very."

"He'll do well, then."

"I'm worried for him."

"Why?"

"Too much focus can take a person to the edge."

"We're already there."

"That's true."

"You can't worry about everyone."

Jeremiah pulled the sheets up. She inhaled deeply and caught the scent of detergent, then smiled thinking of him doing laundry for their safe house bed. She would have liked to do laundry with him. They would throw their clothes and towels and sheets into a giant pile, strip and toss what they were wearing on the pile as well. They would spend a day working through it all, washing and drying and folding and stacking. Placing clean things where they ought to be. And while loads were spinning in the machines, they would walk about naked. They would say nothing, and make love, and shower for no reason but to feel streams of water flow from shoulder to stomach to thigh.

Quinn kissed Jeremiah lightly. "I met with a reporter today," she said. "Asha Patel."

"*The* Asha Patel?"

"Yeah."

"Really?" He leaned up on an elbow.

"She's younger than I thought."

"How young?"

"Mid to late thirties."

"Not much older than us. Why did you meet?"

"She's running a story," Quinn said. "It'll bury Locke."

He sank back into the bed. They knew this moment would come. The grace period Locke's indecision had granted them would inevitably close.

"When?"

"Soon."

"You're sure? The story will sink him?"

"I'm sure."

"He's a good man."

"He is."

"Especially for a politician."

"That's why I worked for him."

"You holding up okay?"

"No."

"I'm sorry."

"It's alright. I'm trying not to…"

"Not to what?"

"Feel."

"I understand."

A long pause ensued. Quinn turned to logistics.

"We have to think about what's next. Without an elected mayor, the city council will appoint whoever they want as an emergency head. And after watching Locke flounder, they want a strongman."

"Baker."

"Baker." Anxiety slipped into her voice. "You need to act, Jeremiah. Do something."

Jeremiah bristled. "I act."

"Not aggressively enough. You know, you were right. About Baker and the police. They're letting in the Originists."

Jeremiah rubbed his eyes and sighed. He was tired of seeing reality clearly and not doing anything about it. Quinn was correct. He needed to do *something*.

"Nova is holding everything back."

"Still on the self-defense thing?"

"She'll never change her mind. I know her."

"You brought in the guns?"

"I did."

"Does she know?"

"Probably. But not from me."

"Then you're prepared."

"For what?"

"To make a move. With or without her."

Guilt swarmed Quinn. The idea of keeping Nova out of the loop bothered her far more than she could say. She wished she could speak to her. Hear her out. But neither time nor circumstance allowed that luxury. They needed to do what was necessary. Friendship, even a friendship like theirs, could not stand in the way of survival.

Quinn's alarm sounded. She rolled over and reached for the bedside table. Her phone's screen flashed five minutes. It began ticking the seconds down. In her purse, she found the Ziploc bag with the UNO card and the red slip of paper. She placed the slip of paper on the table. Rolling back to Jeremiah, she laid her head on his chest.

"Marbury formed his own cell. He's coming."

Jeremiah's body tensed. Quinn closed her eyes. In the handful of minutes they had left, she dreamed a time when they could be soft. She could not tell if that time was in the past or in the future or not in time at all.

"We found Sanders. The address and time are on the red paper on the table. You find Sanders, you find Marbury. You find Marbury, you can do some justice."

An hour later, Quinn opened the door to her apartment and bypassed the light switches. She made her way to the bedroom. She changed into an old T-shirt and a pair of shorts. She used the bathroom and brushed her teeth and took out her contacts. She put the toilet cover down and sat. Her hand trembled. She knew, now, she could not stop these nightly panic attacks.

Her brain began to spin, kicking up old memories. In the weeks before Kemba's murder, she had idled over her and Zahra's report. How many times had she lied to Zahra about it?

She had plenty of chances to show the mayor drafts of their work. She recalled her excuses. More time-sensitive matters needed the mayor's attention. The report needed more edits. More data. She steadfastly avoided voicing the truth: she did not want the mayor, still newly in power, to rock the boat. She wanted his career to survive, for her career to survive. So, she let the report languish, vowing instead to show it to him at a more opportune moment. Then two police officers murdered Kemba Jefferson. One of those officers, John Marbury, had been named in the report. Recommendation Number Four haunted her. *Immediate suspension of officers with unusually high use of force rates.*

She tried to stop her hand from trembling. She muttered the words Nova had said to her during their only college fight. *The choice was supposed to be mine. You took that away from me.* Had she done that again? Had she taken the choice to act away from Locke? From the city?

Had she cost Kemba his life?

The panic attack bloomed. Her rib cage tightened and her vision clouded. She dropped to the floor and the tiles bruised her knees. An urge to scream. She tried to shove the sound down but could not hold it. It rose through her chest, and tore up her neck, and splintered her mouth, and echoed on the bathroom tile. She screamed till her throat went raw.

9

THE NEXT MORNING, QUINN SAT at her breakfast nook with her smoothie on her left and her coffee on her right. She took a sip of each while staring at the report on police misconduct. Resisting the urge to open it, she wondered if Zahra was happy with the choice she had made. Their final conversation, a day after Hush Harbor announced itself, came as little surprise. Of course Zahra would spurn the city's job offer to join the revolution instead. Her scruples would permit nothing less than a full commitment to justice. Quinn told her good luck and clenched her cell phone when they hung up. Both then and now, she hoped Zahra knew they were on the same side.

Quinn stretched her neck and asked her speaker to play NPR. David Liu introduced himself and explained that Asha Patel was out on assignment. Quinn let him deliver the news while she leaned against her bay windows and checked her body. She felt fine, her anxiety now manageable. She slipped off her flats and pulled up her legs and sat cross-legged. The cool morning sun poured through the windows and over her face. She thought, for a moment, that maybe this was the beginning of prayer.

She waited. No inspiration came. No voices, no angels, no

miracles. She uncrossed her legs and shook her head. Prayer? Did she even remember who she was? She had never truly believed in God.

A sudden despair encircled her. What could she count on?

Her family? She almost laughed.

The mayor? A shell of himself.

Her career? Gone with Locke.

Jeremiah? At Hush Harbor.

Nova? At Hush Harbor.

She hesitated.

Yes, she thought. At Hush Harbor. The place for which she had been scheming and lying and risking her life. In a matter of days, when Asha broke her story, she would be ushered out of city hall with Locke. The physical distance between her and the revolution would no longer serve a purpose. Her mind snapped in alignment with her heart. She exhaled.

She stood and walked to her bedroom. In the closet, she found a small gym bag. She packed it with clothing and toiletries and placed it back in the closet. She laid her baseball hat on top. Tonight, she promised herself. She checked her watch. A dozen hours until dark.

PART THREE

Jeremiah

10

JEREMIAH PRESSED INTO THE CROWD. He paused as two children licking ice pops walked by. On his left, a couple examined vintage jewelry laid on a stand. On his right, a grandmother bartered for a box of cookies.

Remarkable, he thought. How Hush Harbor transformed on market day.

He relished the movement of bustling bodies. Slivers of space opened and closed in the crowd like portals to other dimensions. The rush of anonymity enveloped him. No one had time to recognize Jeremiah Prince when there were goods to be bartered. Important calculations to make. How many bars of soap for hair conditioner? How many for coffee? How many for chocolate? He watched a young man with a giant pot accept a paintbrush in exchange for a cup of tea. The tea seller dropped the paintbrush into a box. Another item, mostly useless, that could be hawked at the right moment to the right person.

Jeremiah spotted Malik scribbling in his notebook at the courtyard's center. There, the crowd was thin enough for him to stand without being bumped.

"Malik," he said.

Malik's pen paused. He looked at Jeremiah, then squinted at something over Jeremiah's shoulder.

"Do you…"

"Do I?"

Malik pursed his lips. "Never mind." He forced a smile and waved the tip of his pen at the market day commotion. "It's incredible."

"Market day?"

"It's a whole other… I don't know what the most precise word is."

Jeremiah filled with an unusual sense of pride. Hush Harbor more than survived. It was flourishing.

"Culture? Trade?" Jeremiah said. "Society?"

"Yes. Society."

Jeremiah gestured at the notebook. "You're studying it?"

"Is that alright?"

"Of course. Anything interesting?"

"The logistics, obviously, are complex. But the relationships are the most fascinating part."

"Relationships between…?"

"Sellers and buyers." Malik glanced over Jeremiah's shoulder again and tightened his jaw. With effort, he pulled his gaze to a table with a young couple selling cucumbers. "Take them. They sell the exact same produce for a startling range of prices. They exchanged a cucumber for a jar of coffee beans. Then, on their next trade, they gave one away for free. I tried to figure out their pricing scheme, but it made no sense. So, I started paying attention to their conversations. They talk to their customers for a good few minutes before every trade. I can't hear exactly what they're saying but I think they're figuring out what people can afford. They adjust their prices to match."

Jeremiah recognized the practice, common among market day sellers.

"Did you notice anyone give the sellers anything for free?"

"Someone dropped off a box of herbs. A delayed payment?"

"Exactly."

"It's like a neighborhood exchange. Except on a much larger scale."

Jeremiah considered the analogy. "It is like that. The key is trust. In a neighborhood, you trust people because they live right next to you. It's trust by proximity. Here, that trust is built on a shared set of ideals." He considered another less utopian reason. He nodded toward Hush Harbor's southern edge where the bridge was manned by soldiers. "It's also forged under pressure. We face a common threat."

Malik's eyebrows furrowed. He stared at something behind Jeremiah. His next words came softly.

"I just don't recognize…"

Jeremiah had no time to react when Malik dropped the notebook and pulled him close. "Run," Malik said, before pushing him away. Jeremiah tripped and hit the ground, headfirst and hard. His vision blurred. He heard several thuds behind him and Malik yelling, "Run, run, run!" to the crowd. He felt the ground come alive as dozens and then hundreds raced away. He covered his head. Feet came perilously close to trampling him. The crowd's center emptied. Several guards pinned down a squirming man. Malik straddled him and tore at his shirt. He pulled at something on the man's chest and the man shrieked when duct tape ripped hair and patches of skin from his body. Malik jumped up with a box in his hand. He turned south and sprinted. The air behind him singed. The slowest moving parts of the crowd, those who had not yet found safety, stared. He ran faster. He made it to the Ringgold Building and kept going toward the river. In one fluid movement, his arm pulled back and then launched forward. His body came off the earth as if he'd leaped off a high dive. The box soared into the sky. It spun, hanging above the river. An instant that stretched time. Then, the box exploded in a bloom of fire and a crack rattled the atmosphere and the orange light mushroomed up and Jeremiah wondered if anyone ever had a better view of a bomb.

The nurse pressed a swab of alcohol to Jeremiah's forehead. It stung and he pulled away. He peered at the two rows of beds running from one end of Hurston Hall to the other. Sheets neatly tucked beneath corners. An open closet revealed shelves of medical equipment. Stacks of emergency kits leaned against a wall. The infirmary reminded him of makeshift World War II military hospitals.

Malik idled at the far end of the Hall. Jeremiah thought to send him away but knew the young man would go only as far as the opposite side of the door. He replayed the sight of Malik ripping the box from the bomber's chest and hurling it into the sky. The act was nothing short of heroic. And yet, there Malik stood. As if nothing at all had happened.

Jeremiah adjusted his glasses, which, miraculously, had escaped uncracked. He looked at Malik again. Was that worry sown into the young man's expression? He could not tell.

"Stay still," Nova said. Begrudgingly, he obeyed and the nurse applied alcohol to his cuts.

"Does he have a concussion?" Nova asked.

"I'm fine," he said.

"I wasn't talking to you."

"Probably," the nurse said. "But I have a feeling he won't admit to the symptoms."

The nurse cleaned his forehead one last time. Jeremiah thought her last dab unnecessarily hard.

"I don't have any symptoms. I'm seeing clearly. I'm thinking clearly. My head doesn't hurt. I'm fine."

Nova ignored him and turned to the nurse. "Thank you," she said. "Do you mind if we have the room?"

"Not at all." The nurse quickly cleared away the cotton swabs and bottle of alcohol. As she exited, Jeremiah watched Malik open the door for her. Small and daily courtesies, far more than the occasional grand gesture, impressed him. He observed that Malik lived a life of small courtesies. His eyes welled. He blinked rapidly and the tears fell back. He could not let Nova see them: she would say unusual emotional displays were a sign of concussion.

"You should rest," Nova said.

"Have you talked to him?"

"Listen to me. You need to rest."

Instinctively, Jeremiah dropped his features into stern blankness. A big brother cautioning his little sister. Nova sucked her teeth but said nothing more. He wondered how these sibling tricks still worked.

"Have you talked to the bomber?" Jeremiah asked.

"Briefly."

"And?"

"He's not saying much."

"He said who sent him?"

"That's the only thing he says."

"He's an Originist?"

"Yes."

"Which cell?"

"Marbury's."

He looked off to the side. He ground his teeth.

"Dammit, Nova." He spoke the words as if she were the disappointment.

"You're upset with me?" Her voice spiked with incredulity.

"I told you this would happen."

"You told me white nationalists would send us a suicide bomber?"

"I told you Marbury formed his own cell."

"And I heard you."

"I told you he's a threat and the government's a threat. They're both coming for us."

"And I said that was obvious."

"You said we shouldn't attack."

"I was right."

"You're kidding me."

"How many times do we have to go over this? We're free-dom fighters. That separates us from them. We fight *only* in self-defense."

"You're saying that even after this bombing?"

"Especially after the bombing."

"It could've killed hundreds of people. Children."

"I understand that."

"Do you?"

"You don't give up principles under duress. Like a coward."

They both froze. She looked down. She splayed her fingers. Strain rode up his shoulders. He noticed his hold on the mattress's edge, then unlocked it. Heat rushed down his face.

"Like a coward," he said, his voice cool.

"I shouldn't have said—"

"That's okay."

"I didn't mean—"

"Yes, you did."

She took a long breath and raised her head and adjusted the hair tie holding her braids.

"This isn't the right time for this conversation."

"We'll never have a right time, Nova." He said it sadly and knew it to be true.

"You have a concussion."

"So you say."

"I'll check on you later tonight."

"Fine."

"I need to go talk to our people. Everyone is terrified about what just happened. I need to calm them."

"Go."

"You rest."

She made her way down a row of beds. Malik opened the door for her.

"Nova," Jeremiah called.

She paused.

"I'm done waiting for you," he said.

From that distance, he could not make out her reaction. He listened for the patter of her footfalls as she walked away.

The guards tied the bomber's ankles and wrists to a chair before letting Jeremiah see him. His body remained limp and his eyes stayed closed. The guards asked, several times, if Jeremiah would like one of them to stay in the room. Jeremiah politely declined. He only intended to have a brief conversation. Poke a little. Maybe he'd get lucky and the bomber would slip. Jeremiah wanted just one piece of information: John Marbury's location.

Jeremiah took a seat across from the bomber and studied him. Early twenties. Almost handsome. The face of a former high school athlete who tried rugby in college. Angled and broad. A little stubble. Tanned, in the manner of white people who hiked. Jeremiah imagined the bomber shotgunning beer on a fraternity lawn. The image made sense; the one in front of him did not.

One of the bomber's eyelids fluttered open. He cackled and tilted his head to the ceiling. He hummed a lullaby Jeremiah could not quite place. When he finished, he lowered his chin and glared.

"Jeremiah Prince," he said. "Unbelievable."

"What's your name?"

The bomber balked and shifted his head sideways.

"It's not a trick question," Jeremiah said. "We already have you imprisoned. I just want to know what to call you."

The bomber sniffed. "Samuel. You can call me Samuel."

Jeremiah recognized the lie and thought it silly. What difference did it make if he was Samuel or Bill or Daniel? No matter the name, the boy had attempted to bomb them. Jeremiah wondered if he could make him feel remorse. To break him down to a core humanity. How long would it take? What would it prove? Maybe it couldn't be done. What would be proven then?

"Okay, Samuel," Jeremiah said. "You almost killed hundreds of people today."

"You got lucky."

"Yes. We did."

"No. You. Specifically."

"How so?"

Samuel tongued his upper lip.

"Your boy with the notebook. He spied me following you. Kept checking me out like I was his type."

Jeremiah curled his toes. He took a moment to suppress his unease.

"I'm not surprised. You don't exactly fit in."

Samuel grimaced. "I should've set it off right away. But I saw the big fish. I'd be a legend if I took you down." He cocked his head and smirked. "Guess you'll be someone else's prize."

Jeremiah let Samuel's words slide by. He centered on his own aims. He kept silent until the moment reached calm. Then, he found his angle.

"You must feel…strange."

Samuel flicked his gaze to and away from Jeremiah. Quick enough for Jeremiah to know he'd hit a truth. He went on.

"You must feel disappointment. Rage. Confusion, even." He let Samuel stew. A handful of seconds floated by. "Nothing in your plan prepared you to be alive."

"You don't know anything about me."

Jeremiah could tell Samuel did not quite believe his own statement.

"What I know is that you planned to do something you thought was heroic. Then, you failed. And now you're wondering why you feel a hint of relief."

Samuel tried to laugh and sputtered instead.

"Are you my fucking psychologist?"

"I'm someone who understands your dilemma."

"You're a bullshitter," he said. Then, quietly enough he might have said it to himself, "You don't know shit."

Jeremiah watched him go inward. His face fell into a sad repose.

"Tell me why you joined the Originists."

At the mention of the group, Samuel's body hardened. He gathered up a defiant expression.

"I'm not telling you jack."

"That's fine."

"We know what you want."

"I'm sure you believe that."

"We know the real facts about you. You're trying to find John and anyone who thinks like him and eliminate them. Then you'll go after any white person who tells the truth about you. But we're going to stop you. We're going to stop you before you destroy our country."

"That's my plan? Murder?"

"Don't try playing mind games with me. I know you. We know you. Better than you know yourself."

"I see."

"I'm never giving up my people. And I'll never tell you where John is. You can torture me all you want."

Jeremiah perked up. The boy had made a mistake: in his youthful bluster, he had admitted to knowing John Marbury's location. But Jeremiah also registered determination in Samuel's voice. Delusion, too. A terrifying combination. He lifted his glasses off the ridge of his nose and rubbed the corners of his eyes. His head throbbed from the bombing. He sensed Samuel's conviction would give way eventually. The boy held a fragile faith. Still, he had the advantage of youth. His energy would take time to dissipate. Weeks or months. Unless, of course, more advanced methods were used. Jeremiah swatted away the idea. There were still lines he would not cross.

"We don't torture here," he said. "You don't have to worry about that."

Samuel cackled again. "Bullshit, you bullshitter."

Jeremiah considered if Samuel was, in a sense, correct. He looked around the empty room. One window, one mattress, two chairs. Food would be slipped in three times a day. The only visitors would be him and Nova. Their only interest would be information. Samuel would sit or stand or lie alone for days on end. Nothing but his own brain to assure him he was, indeed, real. Eventually, he would collapse into insanity.

Jeremiah thought to give the boy one last chance to save himself.

"Where's John Marbury?" he asked.

"Go to hell," Samuel said.

11

JEREMIAH BENT HIS HEAD and felt a light wind kiss his neck. He felt nauseous, and his brain thrummed against his skull. For a moment he forgot where he was. He waited out the mental spasm, a symptom of the concussion. Slowly, as though he were a child, he tested himself on the fundamentals of his reality. Kemba's killers, what were their names? John Marbury and Sylvia Sanders. And what were they doing now? Marbury had sheltered with the Originists and then, apparently, formed his own cell. Sanders lived under government protection. And where was he, Jeremiah? In the backyard of the safe house in which Sanders lived. Most importantly: Why was he there?

His brain jammed again. He fiddled with it like a sticky gearshift, then backed off and let it find its own speed. He needed to find Marbury for two reasons. Justice for Kemba's death had not yet been done. The Originists were an intolerable threat to Hush Harbor.

Jeremiah stared at the house in front of him. Marbury's former police partner was the best bet for information on his whereabouts. If he spoke with Sanders, maybe he would sniff Marbury's trail.

Fatigue swallowed him. The most basic mental processing
had become an enormous exertion. He realized that tonight his
mind would drift into the past. He accepted this and a memory
enfolded him: sixteen years old, standing on the banks of the
St. Jude with Nova. A quiet spot down the stairs on Richard
Bridge. Away from the city's noise.

"Do you know why it's called Aggy's Island?" Nova had asked.

"You've been at the library."

"Duh."

Jeremiah had smiled. In elementary school, he and Nova had
begun competing over who read more. The Angelou Public Library became their battleground. The librarians set aside books
they thought the siblings might find interesting. Jeremiah often
read on the floor, and Nova read by the large picture windows,
curling into a sun-washed red couch. The competition carried on through their middle school years and into high school.
Lately, the siblings had obsessed over Bliss history. One of the
librarians took note and showed them a large file cabinet labeled
"Aggy's Island: Records" at the back of the library. Stuffed with
maps and pamphlets and photocopied handwritten accounts, the
cabinet transformed their world.

"Tell me," Jeremiah said. "Why's it called Aggy's Island?"

Nova stretched her hands.

"There's this legend. About a man named Hudson. He was
born into slavery. When he was ten or eleven, his slave master
died. The slave master's property was split up among his children. Hudson ended up in one of the Carolinas, apart from his
family. A decade passed, maybe more, and Hudson grew into a
giant. Seven foot, muscle strapped. And hell-bent on freedom.
One night, deep in winter, when the best hunting dog was down
with fever, Hudson slipped into the dark. A two-day blizzard hit
during his escape. Call it divine intervention. No slave hunting
party would set out in that weather. Too easy to die.

"A year later, a seven-foot Black man appears on the swampy, mosquito-infested, no-good island between the Catalina and St. Jude Rivers. Technically, the island is part of Bliss City, but there are only two kinds of people living on it—criminals and the fatally sick. The government built a hospital on one end, a prison on the other. Hudson doesn't know or doesn't care. He builds a cabin. He starts fishing. He befriends a curious abolitionist and sells his catch for reading lessons. One day, he sticks up a sign outside his home. Aggy's Island. He shows the abolitionist to make sure he spelled it right.

"The abolitionist asks, 'Who's Aggy?'"

"Hudson says, 'My mother.'"

"The abolitionist says, 'Your mother?'"

"Hudson says, 'So she knows where to find me.'"

An ache found Jeremiah's chest. He wondered if Aggy ever found Hudson. Maybe they had reunited and lived together in freedom. Could he not hope, a little bit? Could he not imagine some small justice?

"The abolitionist wrote a pamphlet," Nova continued. "He claimed Hudson was the embodiment of America's pioneering spirit and proof that the Negro feels just like the white man feels. The locals mocked the story for a while. Who would put up a sign so his mother could find him, a mother who was likely dead and, if not, in slavery somewhere down South? Ironically, their mockery gave the name a foothold. Soon, Aggy's Island was all anyone would call it."

"You read the pamphlet?"

"And the pamphlets responding to it."

Jeremiah wrapped an arm around his sister. He tried to find words to express his gratitude. The island, their home, had histories knotty enough never to appear in textbooks.

"Thank you. For telling me that."

She laid her head on his shoulder. "We live on an island of ghosts."

He nodded slowly. He liked the idea of Hudson and Aggy

as ghosts. Guardians, even. He thought to offer Nova a story
in return.

"And an island of tunnels."

She glanced up at him. "Tunnels?"

"You're not the only one digging through that cabinet." She
punched his stomach playfully. He coughed in faux pain and
laughed. "There's a map you should see."

Now, at the safe house, Jeremiah saw a shadow pass over the
back door. He blinked back into the present and took a long
breath. The earth beneath him wobbled, or had the tremble
come from his legs? He waited for his feet to steady. When they
finally did, he made for the house and climbed three stairs onto
the wide deck. The doorknob turned without fuss. A young
woman stood waiting in a dark kitchen.

"Amelia?" Jeremiah said.

"Yes."

"I'm Jeremiah."

They shook hands. An insurance commercial jingle echoed
from a TV down the hall. The young woman straightened her
back and drew herself up to full height. Jeremiah noticed she
was as tall as he was.

"She's here?" Jeremiah said.

Amelia gestured toward the hallway. "Up front. In the living room."

"She's awake?"

"She doesn't sleep much."

Jeremiah imagined a bug-eyed woman heavy with delusion.

"She's odd," Amelia said.

"What do you mean?"

"Her social skills."

"They've deteriorated?"

"Sort of. They've adapted. To her current circumstances."

"How careful do I need to be?"

"She's not dangerous. Just strange."

"Okay." Jeremiah rubbed the back of his neck. "You know what you need to do?"

"There's a car?"

"On Anderson. Two streets west. A black Impala."

"I'll find it."

"When this is over, I'll come to you."

"Okay."

"You might go to Hush Harbor with me tonight. You might come back here. I don't know how this will end."

"That's fine with me."

Jeremiah sensed that this was true.

"Thank you, Amelia."

"For what?"

"This."

She shook her head. "I play my role."

Jeremiah imagined a world where her role did not involve midnight meetings and deception. He took a moment to wish that world for her, then stepped to the side. She passed in front of him and disappeared into the backyard.

Jeremiah stood in the kitchen and listened to the television. Mumbles and dramatic music and more mumbles. He found the noise almost pleasant. He bowed his head and whispered, "Give me strength. Let me do justice." He sensed Hudson and Aggy close by.

His mind tugged him into memory again, this time to his first day teaching middle school history in Bliss. A thin boy had arrived five minutes early. The boy's backpack, stuffed to its breaking point, rode on him like a turtle shell.

"Good morning," Jeremiah said.

"Good morning," the boy said.

"I'm Mr. Prince. I'll be your history teacher."

"Okay."

The boy walked past Jeremiah. He sat at a desk opposite the

door and beneath the windows. He took a pencil and notebook from his backpack and laid them on the desk.

"I'm Kemba. I'm new."

Jeremiah registered a hint of apology in Kemba's tone. As if being new was a personal failing.

A group of students entered with their backpacks slung over one shoulder and voices pitched high. Many excitedly searched the room for friends they had not seen since the prior year. Jeremiah overheard snippets of conversation. *Did you see how tall Marcus got? Did you see Monica's braids? Did you know they're dating now?*

Jeremiah quieted the room. He introduced himself. He took attendance, matching faces to names he had already memorized.

"How many of you like history as a subject?" he asked.

Less than half of the class raised their hands.

"Why do you like it?"

Several students raised their hands again.

"I like learning about why things are the way they are," said Alicia, with the set of brightly colored pens.

"I like the stories about war," said Michael, with the high-top fade.

"I just knew you wanted me to say I like it," said Javon, with a broad smile and a habit of tapping his pencil on his desk. The room laughed. Jeremiah did, too.

"I do want you to enjoy learning about history," Jeremiah said. "But I want you to know why you're learning about it. I've done my job if you can intelligently respond to two complicated questions. Those two questions are more important than any homework assignment or quiz or test you take in this or any other history class."

On each side of the room, Jeremiah had hung a large sheet of poster paper. He walked to one and wrote, *How Are You a Part of History?* He walked to the other and wrote, *How Can You Help Change the Future?* He handed out pads of sticky notes.

"Write your answers on these. Write as many as you want. Stick them up when you're ready."

Squares of yellow and green and blue and pink assembled on the posters like a piece of modernist art. Surprised, Jeremiah leaned against the chalkboard. His students required little encouragement. He waited for the class to settle before beginning a discussion on what they wrote. Forty-five minutes later, Jeremiah gave them their first homework assignment: write a one-paragraph history of their mother or father.

When class ended, the room emptied quickly. Kemba, alone, remained. He put away his pencil and notebook. With a slight strain, he shouldered his backpack and stood. He approached Jeremiah.

"I have a question about the homework assignment."

"Okay."

"Do we have to use a parent?"

"I guess not. You can use an older sibling or grandparent if you want."

"I mean, do we have to use someone who we're related to?"

Jeremiah paused and studied Kemba. His face, long and oval, carried no tension. His eyelids drooped. But his eyes betrayed unease. They scurried from side to side as if expecting a disruption. Jeremiah tried to find a word for what he saw in them: fear and anxiety and determination in equal measures. He realized he had left Kemba's question unanswered for a dozen seconds.

"Who are you thinking of writing about?"

"I don't know if it's okay."

"Tell me and we'll think about it together."

"He's not even human."

"Then we'll have to think hard."

Kemba curled his thumbs underneath his shoulder straps. "Have you heard of the Redwall series?"

"I don't think so."

Kemba explained that Redwall Abbey, the centerpiece of the

Redwall novels, was home to animals of all kind. A place they could find friendship and family. The animals did, however, face threats from evil enemies. They fought dozens of battles and sometimes triumphed and sometimes lost loved ones. They always protected Redwall.

"Which character do you want to write about?" Jeremiah said.

"Martin the Warrior."

"Why?"

"He was brave even though he was a mouse. He knew how to fight."

"From what you've said, a lot of the characters at Redwall were brave warriors. Why Martin in particular?"

Kemba looked at his feet and Jeremiah noticed the boy was slightly pigeon-toed. Kemba spoke to the floor.

"He did great things even though he didn't get to know his parents."

Jeremiah shooed away obvious questions. The boy's backpack seemed somehow heavier. Jeremiah wanted to tell him he could leave some things in the classroom. He would watch over them while Kemba went about his day.

"I think you should write about Martin. I'd like to read about him."

Kemba mumbled "thank you" and picked his feet off the ground and trudged toward the door. He crouched a little and drew his elbows in. He reminded Jeremiah of an infantryman rounding a corner into an unknown alley.

"Kemba?"

The boy looked over his shoulder.

"Do you know how to play chess?"

Kemba shook his head.

"Do you want to learn?"

Kemba shrugged.

"If you want, come at lunch. We'll play."

Kemba nodded and Jeremiah spent recess searching class-rooms for a chessboard.

Over the next several weeks, Jeremiah and Kemba spent lunchtimes playing chess. Jeremiah was careful to pack an extra granola bar each day, in case Kemba was unable to bring his own snack. "Here," Jeremiah would say, almost gruffly. "You can't play on an empty stomach. I want a challenger, not a pushover."

Eventually, Kemba gained friends with whom he could eat. He and Jeremiah moved their games to after-school hours. They played in silence. Occasionally, Jeremiah showed Kemba where in a sequence of moves he miscalculated or how to better parry an attack. Kemba took in the lessons quickly. He rarely made the same mistake twice.

One afternoon in October, Jeremiah and Kemba were locked in a competitive game. With his next move, Jeremiah trapped Kemba's knight. Kemba quickly deployed a bishop in support. The error bothered Jeremiah. Kemba was too good to make such simple mistakes. He should have let the knight go and used his move to prepare a new gambit. Jeremiah pressed his queen for-ward, readying the capture of both knight and bishop.

"I didn't grow up here," Kemba said. "On Aggy's Island."

The words, spoken softly, interrupted Jeremiah's focus. He often thought about Kemba's life outside of school. Where did he live? With whom? In which room did Kemba complete his homework? Did he have quiet?

Jeremiah had carefully avoided those sorts of questions. He knew trust between him and Kemba would be built with pa-tience.

"Where did you grow up?"

"Everywhere. Trenton, Camden. Even New York."

Kemba advanced a pawn to protect his bishop. Jeremiah stopped himself from shaking his head. He sent his own bishop flying across the board and sat the piece behind Kemba's de-fense. The game had only a handful of moves left.

"When did you come to Bliss?"

"I think, about three years ago. I came because my aunt said I could live with her."

Jeremiah was relieved to hear Kemba lived with family. "That's a good reason."

Kemba moved his trapped knight, ensnaring it further. Jeremiah recognized the effort of a desperate player. He captured the knight with a mere pawn. In rapid succession, Kemba took the pawn with his bishop and Jeremiah took the bishop with his queen.

"It only lasted two months."

"What did?"

"Me staying with my aunt."

"What happened?"

"She wasn't ready. She had her own problems."

Jeremiah wished he could say many things. That Kemba and his life were not problems. That a child should not have to bounce between homes. Jeremiah knew Kemba did not want him to know everything. He wondered if the boy also wished to protect the people in his past from judgment. To let them live in his memory, if nowhere else, cloaked in compassion.

"Who do you live with now?"

"Foster family. They're kinda nice."

Kemba played his remaining knight. He landed it in a spot that, only a move prior, had been in direct control of Jeremiah's queen. Jeremiah moved his queen back. Kemba shot his last bishop into the space now cleared of pieces by their back-and-forth.

"Check," Kemba said.

Jeremiah moved his king one position to the right. Kemba slid a rook in the same direction.

"Check."

Jeremiah had no choice but to place his queen in front of the king. Kemba took the queen.

"Checkmate."

Jeremiah stared at the board for a full minute. He savored the shock. Never had he been so happy at defeat. He looked at Kemba with pride. The boy's face remained placid.

"Well done," Jeremiah said. "Very well done. This deserves a celebration. On me. What do you think?"

Kemba smiled and his happiness lifted Jeremiah's mood even higher.

"Let's go get something to eat," Jeremiah said.

They went to a Sichuan hole-in-the-wall. They ordered more dishes than was reasonable and tested their mettle against *koush-ouji* chicken and *dan dan* noodles. Kemba coughed through his first forkfuls. He gathered himself with generous gulps of water. Then he took smaller bites in rapid succession, licking the broth from his lips.

Now, more than a year later, Jeremiah could still taste the chili oil. Slowly, he came out of the memory and into the dark kitchen with a renewed anger.

With no more thought, he walked down the hall and pushed open the living room door. Sylvia Sanders sat in a dining room chair pulled close to the television. She kept her eyes fixed on the screen. A newscast finished a segment on the restructuring of the United Nations, given the United States' inability to provide financial support. Jeremiah studied Sylvia. He had expected sweatpants and a belly and raggedy hair. The woman in front of him retightened her jet-black ponytail and sat so upright that wrinkles dared not line her white oxford shirt. Her hands gripped her knees with the intensity of a hunted animal. Jeremiah wondered how many hours a day she used to spend at the gym.

The broadcast went to commercials. Sylvia hit mute on the remote. She turned her attention to Jeremiah and smiled as if they had met before.

"Finally," she said. "You missed the breaking news."

"I'm sorry?" he asked, immediately regretting the question. Her nonchalance had put him on the back foot.

"The recording of Locke."

He struggled for a response that would change the conversation's direction and found his mind an unwilling partner. "What about it?" he asked.

"The leak must've been Rex."

"Why do you say that?"

"The simplest answer is usually the right one. He wants power. Always did."

"Some people are like that."

"Some people."

He sensed she meant him.

"I don't hunt for power," he said.

"Yes, you do. You created a rebellion."

"You sparked it."

Her mouth tightened. She turned off the television, clutched the armrests and drew herself inward.

"Is this a dream?" she said.

A pulse ran through his brain and he wondered the same thing. Their exchange had already swum away from him.

"It should be," he said.

"But it's not?"

"No."

"I haven't had a good dream in months."

"Neither have I."

She pointed at her head. "They give me pills to help."

"Do they?"

"Do they what?"

"Help."

"Not even a little."

"But you still take them?"

She shook her head. "I couldn't exercise. They made me nauseous."

"The side effects always get you."

"Have you ever taken antidepressants?"

"No."

"Would you?"

"If a doctor said I needed them?"

"Yeah."

"If I have delusions, I'd like them to be my own. Not something caused by a pill."

She wrinkled her brow. "There's virtue in that."

"There is."

"What do you do, then?"

He squinted.

"For the not good dreams," she said.

He took his glasses off and rubbed his eyes. Why was he talking about nightmares and antidepressants with this stranger? Exhaustion weighed on him. A throb took hold of his head. Why was he there again? For information? All he truly wanted was to sneak a message to Quinn and find a bed and lie in it with her for a time too long to measure. The scent at the nape of her neck lingered in his nostrils. Rose water. He imagined it as a wisp of cloud gradually growing until it covered his body and lifted him out of this house and into the sky. He ran a hand down his jacket, hoping to find a strand of Quinn's hair. Just some reminder that this man who slipped into living rooms was not all he was. It occurred to Jeremiah that Quinn and Sylvia were around the same age.

"I talk to friends," he said.

"That's the difference, then."

"Friends?"

"You have them." She peered over his shoulder. "Amelia?"

"She's gone."

"For how long?"

"Depends."

Sylvia's expression clouded over. "She's my best guard. She

watches the news with me. You know the others won't? We even cooked together once or twice. She never says much. I try to talk to her. I think she's the quiet type. That's why we never have long conversations. That's why I haven't gotten to know her. She's shy. Yes, that's why."

Jeremiah realized that Sylvia had stopped addressing him, muttering only to herself.

"But she doesn't pretend that I'm just a job like the other guards do. She knows I'm a real living thing. A human being. I think maybe people have forgotten that. I know, I know. I know what I did. But still, Amelia is kind to me. She has manners. Grace."

Sylvia's mouth kept moving. No sound emerged. She stood as though a tightened coil in her legs released. She looked Jeremiah in the eye.

"My name is Sylvester Sanders. It's good to meet you."

"Jeremiah Prince." Jeremiah wondered if he would have taken the handshake she almost offered. He imagined not. "Sylvester?"

"Yes."

"Not Sylvia?"

"Sylvester is my real name."

For the first time in many weeks, Jeremiah felt surprise. He studied Bliss's politics with a meticulousness bordering on insanity. How could a name so easily evade him?

"I didn't know that."

"My parents named me after my grandfather. He died two weeks before I was born. They figured I could just go by Sylvia."

"Which you did."

"Yes."

"But not anymore?"

"The media, the narratives—they made me look like something I'm not. They made Sylvia into a monster."

Jeremiah's belly lurched in disgust. The media alone was not responsible for her fate. She participated. Still, he tried to understand her aim.

"The world doesn't know about Sylvester," he said.

"She's mine." Sylvia beamed.

"You know, I used to teach history."

Jeremiah thought of textbook editors stitching together narratives. Pasts too complex to ever explain fully. Nova once told him that she painted to complement formal histories: her art compelled viewers to *feel* the past and, in so doing, chart a different future. Fragments of her latest mural came to him. He saw it by chance the night he and Malik finished transporting arms, and immediately recognized his sister's craft. While he knew her art spoke to many people, he sensed this piece carried a meaning designed for him. Why had she not told him about it? Or maybe she had said something? Did he forget? Worse still, did he fail to hear in the first place?

He tried to remember the mural. He set pieces he could recall together. The orange sun. Cutout figures of a girl and a boy running from one end of the horizon to the other. The sense of wind at their backs. The soil, a deep and earthy brown. Symbols, like roots, beneath the soil.

Sylvia swayed side to side.

"None of us can outrun the past," he said. She stopped moving.

"You don't know that."

"I do."

"Everyone says Officer Sylvia Sanders. Never Sylvester."

"It doesn't matter."

"Yes it does." Her voice rose in pitch. "Yes it does."

"A name won't change who you are, Sylvia."

"I'm not Sylvia."

"Even if names did have that power, someone will write a biography. They'll trace every detail of your life. How your parents met. Where you went to school. Your first car. Your greatest romance. They'll write more of your history than you can remember."

"They won't find the name. They won't—"

"Of course they will." Jeremiah spoke it softly. He spoke it with the assuredness of someone who knows how blades should sing when sunk into hearts. "They'll look up your birth certificate. They'll see it on your death certificate. They'll sow it into your story—she was a strange one from the beginning. It's all in her names. We thought she was a Sylvia, but really she was a girl named Sylvester. Of course she turned out so brutal. Of course she's different from our daughters."

Blood drained from Sylvia's face. A milk white gave way to pinkish undertones. She reminded Jeremiah of a scarecrow. Trim yet bloated. Standing but not quite alive.

She blinked several times in rapid succession.

"It's okay," she said. "Not everyone will understand."

She waved a hand in front of her face as though shooing away a fruit fly. She grinned. Jeremiah recognized her delirium.

"Come," she said. "I've been a terrible host. I haven't even offered you anything."

Guardedly, Jeremiah followed her to the kitchen. She switched on a coffee maker. She found cookies and arranged them on a plate. The scent of stale coffee grounds filled the room. Unexpectedly, it brought Jeremiah to his childhood. There had always been coffee in his family's apartment. As soon as he could reach across the kitchen countertops, he learned to set the pot. He learned many household chores that young. How to sweep the floor. How to take out the trash. How to put leftovers in the microwave for whichever parent returned from whatever nightshift first.

On many nights, he guided Nova through her bedtime routine. They brushed their teeth together. Each used the bathroom and changed into pajamas. They said a prayer or two. Nova would fall asleep in his bed. Using all his strength, he would carry her across the handful of feet to her bed. She would wake in the middle of the night, thinking she heard a monster when one or the other parent arrived home. He would climb into her bed, rub her back, tell her everything was okay. She would drift asleep clinging to his neck and chewing her upper lip to keep fear at bay. He would lie awake for several minutes wondering what monsters looked like. With little light, what was the difference between him and them? If he got up to use the bathroom and Nova's eyes half opened, would she mistake him for one? He tried not to move too fast for fear his sister might wake and think him something other than what he was.

"Here," Sylvia said. She handed him a cup of coffee. He almost refused. How could he accept anything from the hands of Sylvia Sanders, a murderer? Then, he remembered his purpose. He needed her to tell him where Marbury was. He swallowed his pride and accepted the offering. He smelled it. It was not bitter. He took a sip. She offered him a cookie.

"No. I'm okay."

"I made them earlier today."

He relented and took one and bit into it. He found it overly sweet. Sylvia moved to the sink. She spoke over the sound of dish washing.

"Baking is one of the ways I stop myself from going crazy," she said.

Too late, he thought.

She went on. "Baking and exercise and reading and the news. At least an hour of each in a cycle. Sometimes, if I feel good, I'll just sit for a bit between my activities. I'll let time pass. I feel like I'm a housewife in the 1950s. Except without kids and a husband and this is not my house. Do I have it better or worse than those women?"

Sylvia laughed bitterly. She cut off the faucet and squeezed soapy water out of the sponge. She looked at the back door with the ache of those who are trapped.

"I know what's happening to me," she said. "I'm a cop. I know what this kind of isolation does to a brain."

"This isn't really isolation."

"Still."

"This isn't even a punishment."

"It feels like one."

"They put you here for your safety."

"I know."

"You deserve far worse."

Sylvia gripped the countertop edge. Her knuckles turned red. She stared at Jeremiah. For the first time, he saw clarity in her gaze.

"Did I say I'm innocent?" she said. "I've been here, Jeremiah. Waiting, waiting, waiting. For you. For your sister. For the mayor. For someone to come and hand me my sentence. But who comes to visit instead? Who comes? He's why you're visiting me, too."

Jeremiah set his cup down. He tilted his chin up. The room collapsed inward.

"You find me, you find him," she said. "Right?"

"Where is he, Sylvia?"

"I don't know."

"Where's John Marbury?"

"I don't know."

"You're lying."

"I'm not."

"Are you one of them?"

"No."

Jeremiah sensed her dishonesty. He lowered his chin and tapped his fingers on the countertop. He wanted her to stew in her own deceit. When, finally, he broke the silence, he spoke with the calm of a prosecutor sure of the truth.

"Why does he come visit you?"

"He wants me to join him."

"Why won't you?"

"I told you. I'm not one of them."

"You told him that?"

"Yes."

"But he still comes."

"He doesn't believe me."

"Why?"

"I pulled a trigger just like he did."

Jeremiah's chest tightened. He focused on his heart in an attempt to keep from imagining Kemba's murder, a moment he had visited all too often. He counted its beats and waited for them to slow from a sprint to a run, to a jog. He returned to the conversation with a steady pulse.

"Then why would I think you aren't like him?"

"I shot for different reasons."

"How so?"

"I felt fear. He had hate."

"Naive."

"It's true."

"Sometimes fear and hate are the same thing."

"They were different that night."

"Not by much."

"Even so."

"A bullet is a bullet is a bullet."

"I wish I could take mine back."

Jeremiah dug his fingernails into his palm. Hearing regret from a murderer disgusted him. What did her wishes matter? Her sins had long since been committed, her principles long since vacated. Still, knowing he could use her guilt to his advantage, he determined to push further.

"Do you wish it for Kemba or do you wish it for you?"

Sylvia's jaw trembled and she swallowed hard.

"For him. Mostly."

"And also for you."

"I'm not a saint."

"Clearly." Jeremiah said the word with derision. "Where's John Marbury?"

"I don't know."

Jeremiah sipped his coffee. Sylvia was frail, perhaps. Off-balance, absolutely. Eager to atone? Yes. He wrapped his hands around the cup. Its remaining heat warmed his palms.

"Do you have chairs on the back porch?" he asked.

"You want to sit outside?"

"Yes."

Sylvia left the kitchen and came back with two folding chairs. On the porch, she set them a few feet apart. She waited for Jeremiah to sit before she did the same. Jeremiah crossed his legs. A rickety floorboard complained.

He sensed Sylvia was only a nudge away from doing what he would ask. How could he bring her to his side? How could he convince her of the rightness of Hush Harbor? No, he thought. He needed to reach beyond simple rights and wrongs. His case was not an argument. He needed to tell her a story. He looked her in the eyes.

"My father was a small man who looked large. He had a thick beard that he often forgot to trim. As a child, I would climb onto his lap and try to fit my whole hand in it. He would open his eyes wide and say, 'I think there is a mouse in my beard,' and I would jump off his lap and he would chase me. Sometimes my sister would leave her crayons and chase after my father and all three of us would run around the living room in a tiny circle. I remember thinking my dad's laugh was the size of summer. Long and warm. The thing you miss as soon as the cold sets in.

"On Sunday mornings, he would take me and Nova out for a drive so my mom could get a few extra hours of sleep. She worked nights as a nurse's assistant. On those drives, I remember watching high-rises turn into suburban homes and suburbia become flat, empty land. Then, as if from a picture book, farms. My father would pull into one with a little store next to the barn and a few picnic benches next to the store. A large blue sign hung above the store's doorframe. Billie's.

"My father would buy cheese, salami, bread, olive oil. Billie often threw in a bar of chocolate. She rarely said anything other than hello and goodbye. But we hugged her when we arrived and hugged her when we left. Like it was the most natural thing in the world.

"When I was twenty-three, my father had a heart attack. Billie came to his funeral. I hadn't seen her for years. She invited Nova and me to her farm. We went the next weekend. She treated us to salami, cheese, bread. She said, 'Your father was a man who lived his values. He was proud that a Black woman owned a farm out here. He spent his dollar and his time at my spot for a reason. He wanted to show his children what making right in this world means.'

"I realized two things that day. The first was that I would spend my life trying to make the world right, just like my dad did. The second was that I did not have the stuff of a father. How could I live up to memories of my dad when I couldn't even grow a beard? What games would I play with my children? Would Billie even be around when my kids were old enough for Sunday morning drives? No, I decided, the capacity for fatherhood was not one of my gifts."

Jeremiah folded his arms. The humidity seemed to cling to his cheeks.

"A decade later, a boy named Kemba Jefferson walked into my history class. He was new to the school. I offered to teach him chess so he wouldn't have to sit alone at lunch. We started a tradition. We played every day. I would ask him about his classes and he would mumble a few words. I would offer the occasional pointer on his strategy. He would nod and internalize the note.

"One day, he won. I was thrilled. I took him out to dinner to celebrate. That started a second tradition for us. Two or three times a week we would go out for a meal. The shy kid from school disappeared at those restaurants. He wanted to explore every cuisine. Japanese, Thai, Nigerian, Peruvian, Brazilian. Interesting, he would say, before devouring a dish. He would flag down waiters and strike up endless conversations. What spices went into that dish? How did you cook that meat? How long did you marinate?

"For Christmas, I got him one Chinese and one Nigerian cookbook. He pored over them for weeks, scribbling notes in the margins. He stuffed them in his already impossibly stuffed backpack. One day I told him he could keep the books at home. They were truly his. He lifted his backpack onto a desk. He carefully unzipped its pockets. He detailed the contents. On top were textbooks and the cookbooks. Then, there was a change of clothes. A toothbrush, a bar of soap, a tiny bottle of shampoo. Copies of books he loved. *Redwall* and *Martin the Warrior.* In a Ziploc baggie, his birth certificate and vaccination record. A few snack bars were crushed into a corner. In another corner, a blue stuffed elephant, no bigger than a hand.

"He said, 'This is everything I need.'

"I said, 'What do you mean?'

"'For when foster care says I have to move. Sometimes they don't give you time to pack.'"

Jeremiah stopped speaking. He took several deep breaths through his nostrils. Tears subsided. From his pocket, he pulled a thick square of carefully folded paper. He unfolded it, then smoothed it over as if he could rid the sheets of their creases. *State of New Jersey. Application for Adoption.* He handed it to Sylvia.

"He died before I could finish the paperwork."

He saw the application tremble in Sylvia's hands.

"I need to find Marbury," he said. "Will you help me, Sylvester?"

She kept her head bent forward. Her body rocked back and forth. She sniffed and wiped her nose with the back of her hand.

Finally, she nodded.

A slip of sympathy worked into his chest. She seemed childlike in her terror. How many hazards did her panicked mind fling at her hourly? Her every physical need had been met and yet she could not escape torment. He wondered how different her life would have been had John Marbury not been her partner. Eyes wide and fixed to the floorboards, she continued rocking back and forth. He realized she would never recover from what she had done. Was that justice, then? He considered it and answered honestly: he did not know. He watched her for a minute more. Here, he thought, was a human destroyed.

A breath of wind stirred him from contemplation. He let his thoughts go. He returned to the task at hand with an ember of compassion in his tone.

"You're doing the right thing," he said. "Telling me is the right thing."

She stopped rocking and rubbed a hand down her thigh. For a moment, Jeremiah thought she would either collapse into her knees or sprint away. Instead, she folded the adoption papers into a neat square and laid them in the palm of her hand. She mouthed words, almost inaudible, to the papers.

"Thirteen Arch Street."

She said it so soft and low Jeremiah knew she spoke true.

12

FIFTEEN MINUTES AFTER LEAVING the safe house, Jeremiah sat in the passenger seat of a black Impala. Malik, driving, banked right and Jeremiah leaned with the car. An ache nestled at the back of his head. He took off his glasses and pinched the bridge of his nose. The ache did not recede.

He considered the revolution he nurtured and wondered if he'd gone mad. He examined Hush Harbor's emergence from an emotional distance. A country weakened by a historic natural disaster and the subsequent economic upheaval. A city taut with racial tension. A collective sufficiently enraged by injustice. Protests and disarray and violent encounters. The contextual pieces fit. Yet, they failed to explain Hush Harbor. He dug for a more personal question. Why had he, in particular, initiated the rebellion? Why not any number of other people who lost loved ones in similar tragedies?

Jeremiah recalled the picture of Marbury in a white robe. Somehow Quinn had managed to pilfer a copy from confidential evidence presented to the grand jury. She'd sent it to Jeremiah the day Marbury and Sanders were exonerated. He stared at it for an hour. He searched his body and sensed a shift coming.

Was this the turning point, then? The moment madness would overcome him? Perhaps he was different than most. He'd felt pressure release in his chest. His thoughts and intuition snapped into alignment. If this was madness, it held no panic. If this was madness, then madness was only logic set against oppression.

In the car, Jeremiah rolled down his window and put his head and arm out. He rolled his hand through the wind and watched the moonlight illuminate the veins in his knuckles.

"Are you okay?" Malik said.

Jeremiah almost laughed. He had not considered what Malik might make of his actions. He cleaned his glasses and put them on.

"I'm fine. Thank you."

"Do you need more cool air?"

"The temperature is perfect."

"Okay."

Jeremiah mentally traced the route to Aggy's Island. They would zig south along Mt. Olive's side streets for another twenty minutes, carefully working their way along an unpatrolled route. A mile before City Center, they would deposit the car at the home of a Hush Harbor sympathizer and cut toward a check-point manned by soldiers loyal to the rebellion. Then, they would take a circuitous path deep into Southwood, leaning into shadows and alleys. They would come to a small town house with a dull blue door and a golden knob, the same town house Jeremiah and Quinn frequented. They would open a coat closet, nudge shoes to the side and remove loose floorboards. Finally, they would drop into the tunnel and make for a town house with a red door and a black knob on Aggy's Island. The journey would take hours.

Jeremiah thought of asking Malik if he was sure of the streets in Mt. Olive. He quickly abandoned the question, deeming it unnecessary. The young man had demonstrated more diligence

than anyone could have asked. He had, undoubtedly, memorized the route.

"Malik," Jeremiah said.

"Yes."

"May I ask you a question?"

"Yeah."

"Do you know who I was seeing tonight?"

Malik pressed his lips together.

"I have an idea."

"Tell me."

"Sylvia Sanders."

"How did you figure that?"

Malik shrugged.

"I'm around you all the time."

"Do you know why I visited her?"

"Not specifically."

"Then generally."

"Information. You're not carrying a gun."

Jeremiah was taken aback. How simply Malik invoked the
possibility of an execution.

"Would you like to know what I found out?"

"Yes. I would."

Jeremiah recounted his conversations with Sylvia in more detail than necessary. Midway through, he realized he needed the
unburdening. He glanced at Malik every so often. The young
man maintained a studious expression. Jeremiah left out just
one portion of the meeting. His history with Kemba. Some
things, he thought, are best said only once a night. When he
concluded, he checked Malik's expression again. Unchanged.

"I'm going to need you in the coming days," Jeremiah said.
"I don't know how yet. But I will."

"Of course."

Jeremiah appreciated the ease with which he fell in line. The
young man in the driver's seat was distinct from the Malik who

arrived at Hush Harbor. Jeremiah considered this for a moment. He thought of the characteristics they shared. A studiousness bordering on obsession. An almost unnatural patience in the face of uncertainty. A tendency toward privacy. If Malik had a revelation, he would not have told Jeremiah. He would simply continue working. The thought perturbed him. Should he not know more about the daily life of the person with whom he spent, by far, the most time?

"I did have a question though," Malik said.

"Please."

"Did she tell you where Marbury is?"

Jeremiah realized he had inadvertently left out the ending. The point of it all. He wondered just how much the concussion affected him.

"Yes. She told me. Arch Street."

"Where is that?"

He remembered the young man was not from Bliss. Malik knew the roads they traveled together, the roads he was asked to know, but little else. Even many of the streets around Hamilton Heights were a mystery to him.

"Three blocks northeast."

"Of us? Right now?"

He paused. "Of Hush Harbor."

Jeremiah stripped carefully. He filled the sink and washed his dirty clothes in soapy water, then hung them to dry on a hook across from his room's only window. He turned on the shower and the bathroom filled with steam. He splashed his face and his tears mixed with the bathwater. He let them come.

He slipped into memory once again: a moonless night during the first week of Hush Harbor's existence. He'd woven through backstreets to see Quinn. He recalled how he ached for her, how that hunger consumed him. They'd dared meet at her apartment. They never made it past her living room. Bodies and no words. Socks hastily pulled off. A table lamp knocked to the carpet. How sweet that frenzy. Their lips searched and their fingers roamed and her breath gathered, hot and rushed, on his neck. How simple it was. The act of not thinking when he was around her.

After they made love, a peace settled over him. His mind reveled in it. Not quite joyous and not quite free but as close as he could get. He let himself slip into sleep. His watch buzzed just as he approached a dream. His mind reeled back to his skull, or wherever minds exist, and he looked around and there he was, on the carpet, with Quinn to his side. He kissed her and sat up, reaching across the floor for his shirt.

"Wait," she said. "Before you go."

She left the living room and returned, clothed, with a small piece of paper. He, too, had dressed. A beat passed between them.

"What's that?" he asked.

"The city is going into full lockdown."

"I know."

"You won't be able to get food."

"We've got stockpiles that will last a few weeks."

"That won't be enough."

He knew she was right. The same thought had worried him endlessly since they occupied Hamilton Heights: What would they eat? Their stock was limited. Rationing would take them only so far. They needed a long-term supply and a means by which to fund it. Reflecting on it, his pride shrank. He had made no progress on this most basic of problems.

Quinn handed him the piece of paper. Ten digits were scrawled on it in blue ink.

"There's no name," he said.

"Funders."

"For Hush Harbor?" He recalled countless calls to a prerecorded voice apologizing for disconnected numbers. "The FBI scared off all our funders already."

"This set is new."

He looked down at the number. "Who are they?"

"They don't have a name. Or at least I don't know it."

"Then how'd you get this?"

"Earl."

"Does he know who they are?"

"It's Earl. He's not going to say which person told him what about who."

Jeremiah pressed a finger to his temple. Earl's secrecy was both intensely frustrating and a primary reason they held complete faith in him. If he had passed on the information, then at least they could be certain the funders were not part of an elaborate government ploy to infiltrate the revolution.

"Who wants to fund a liberation movement?" he asked.

"Philanthropists who sympathize."

"Those are the people the FBI scared away."

"Or companies that can make a profit."

"You think there's a company that looks at Hush Harbor and sees profit?"

"I think anything can be exploited."

"We don't have earning potential."

She shrugged. He laughed and pulled her to him. Already, he missed their closeness. "Are we going to sell merchandise? T-shirts with fists on them? Baseball hats with two *h*'s?"

"Stop being dumb. I'm serious."

"So am I."

Jeremiah considered the source of the funds. His stomach rolled at the thought of working with anonymous outsiders. Hush Harbor's options, though, were limited. How long would the movement survive if he quibbled over ambiguous lifelines? A compromise had to be made.

"They'll help with more than money," Quinn said. "Earl says

these people are more…connected than normal rich people. They can find supplies."

"Food?"

"And arms."

"Arms," he said, quietly, dropping his hands from Quinn's waist. "We don't know anything about these people," he said.

"It's not great."

"No. It's not."

"I don't like it, either."

"I know."

"But you have to survive."

He stared at the foot of carpet between them. Light gray and thick. Only moments earlier they had lain on it together. As though no troubles haunted their city or their future or the lightest of their touches.

"Me or the movement?"

"Both."

"I'm not sure that's possible."

He knew, somehow, that he would become the revolution's sacrifice. First, it would take his principles. Then, his body. In the process, he would lose Quinn and he would lose Nova. He needed to make peace with that certainty. Let himself grieve.

Now, months later, he lifted his face to the showerhead. He scrubbed his body hard enough to redden skin. The physical shock relieved his mood. He turned off the water and noted his clothes were now wrinkle-free.

In his bedroom, he checked the time. A few minutes before 5 a.m. He considered taking a nap before beginning his morning, a patch of rest to recover from his night with Sylvia. His consciousness would slide into sleep easily. Instead, he sat on the edge of the bed next to the window and looked outside. Instinct told him to see as much of life as possible. Time was not his luxury. The sun would soon rise and he wanted to accompany it.

He reached for a small transistor radio on the bedside table and tuned it to NPR just in time for *Morning Edition*. Asha Patel delivered a headline on the West Coast crisis before pivoting to Bliss.

"We have some breaking news," she said. "For the past twenty-four hours, we've been covering the political controversy in Bliss, New Jersey, after leaked audio revealed embattled Mayor Clarence Locke attempting to negotiate with the Hush Harbor rebellion. We just received a press release from the mayor's office indicating that he will resign his position effective immediately. He cites his inability to perform his role due to increased pressure from the state legislature.

"We will get into the how and why of his resignation with a panel of experts in about five minutes. But, first, the immediate and obvious question. Who will assume the mayor's office? The Bliss Constitution stipulates that the city council has the authority to appoint an interim mayor should the elected mayor be unable or unwilling to perform his duties. It seems likely that Police Chief Rex Baker, who, with the exception of Clarence Locke, has been Bliss's most prominent and powerful local official, will be the city council's choice. Sources indicate that council members are looking for a firm hand in this time of crisis."

Jeremiah searched through his pockets before remembering he no longer carried a cell phone. He hurried to his closet and fumbled open the doors, then pulled out a small stool tucked in the corner. Standing atop the stool, he reached toward a large circular watermark on the closet's ceiling. He pushed up on it and a sliver of space opened. He stuck his hand in and worked several clasps. A trapdoor swung free. He reached into the hole and removed a briefcase-sized safe box, then placed it on the bed and hurriedly entered the passcode. The lock stayed shut. "C'mon," he said. He tried the passcode again and this time the top popped free. Two items lay inside. He took out the ancient phone with a long antenna and left the gun. He started dialing Quinn's number. A knock stopped him midway. He cursed and dropped the phone. The knock came again. He returned the phone to the safe box, hid it in the ceiling and answered the door.

"Malik?"

The young man panted. "You need to come with me."

"Why?"

"A prisoner."

"Samuel?"

"Another one."

"Another one?"

"Caught at the northern gate."

"Okay. Show me."

Malik led him to the Jarrell Building. Jeremiah struggled to keep pace with the younger man's rapid steps. When they entered the building, Malik climbed the stairs two at a time. They approached an apartment across the hall from the unit in which Samuel was held. Before they entered, Jeremiah held up a hand. He needed pause. He caught his breath and readied a series of questions. He reminded himself that the prisoner did not matter. Whoever sent him did. He sensed Marbury behind yet another plot. His stomach knotted. As he chased Marbury, Marbury chased him.

He nodded at Malik and they entered the apartment. Two guards greeted them. They gestured at a bedroom in the back. One of the guards produced a key. He unlocked the door and Jeremiah entered. The prisoner took off a baseball cap. Jeremiah halted.

"What…"

Standing next to the window, Quinn shrugged.

"I see why you never invite me over."

She shot him a mischievous smile. He could think only *thank God*. In a split second, he crossed the room and threw his arms around her. They stayed in that embrace for a long time. As though one were a key and one were a lock and the world had blessedly forgotten they were supposed to be apart.

Jeremiah propped himself up on an elbow as sleep scurried away from him. Quinn's eyelids fluttered and fell back into rest. He lay back down, noting how much warmer his bed was with her in it.

He heard a rustle from the front door and quietly rolled out of bed. Unable to resist the temptation, he leaned over and kissed Quinn's cheek. She did not stir. Good, he thought. She needed rest. Her night journey to Hush Harbor must have been grueling. He left the bedroom with reluctant feet.

Under the front door, he found a copy of the *New York Times*. He rubbed his eyes with his knuckles, preparing for bad news. Nothing good ever came from paper shoved under his door.

He read the sticky note on top. *Go to page 4.* Nova's handwriting. He followed the instructions and found another sticky note. *The world is curious.* He read the headline. "An FBI Investigation Asks Who Is Funding the Hush Harbor Rebellion—and Why?"

Jeremiah closed the newspaper. He recalled Nova's warnings over the funders: three weeks into their uprising, standing in Morrison Hall, she had minced no words. "We can't take their money," she'd said. He'd looked past her and at their remaining food. Tucked into a corner of the hall, their inventory would last just a few more days. How would they survive without bread? How would they feed the hundreds more who wanted to join them? They were starving. This, he thought, was why no local or federal force bothered to raid them. They would perish on their own.

In hopes of convincing Nova of its necessity, he had delayed calling the funders for two weeks. Truthfully, he had hoped to further convince himself, too. Staring at dwindling stacks of canned beans, he put questions of right and wrong to the side.

"Technically, we wouldn't be taking their money," he said. "They would just send us what we need. Like food."

"You know what I mean. We can't take help from anonymous donors. Who knows who they are or where their money comes from or what they want from us."

"I hear you."

"And this isn't just about our personal ethics. What if the funders are terrible people and the media or the government finds out? Once that news breaks, we're done. We lose the moral high ground. We lose all credibility."

"I get it."

"Do you?"

"I do. We've had this conversation."

"Good. Then, we're still agreed. We can't take their help."

"No," he said.

"No?"

"We're not agreed."

"You can't be serious, Jeremiah."

He gestured toward the food. "Look."

Her gaze did not budge from him. "I don't need to."

"We can't last."

"We'll be fine. Without their help."

"How? I don't want to call them. We just don't have a choice."

"There is always a choice."

Her stubbornness rankled him. Did she not appreciate the reality plainly in front of them?

"Tell me. Tell me how."

"Not the way you're suggesting."

"That's not good enough."

"There are other options."

"Do you have a secret trust fund somewhere? Did you rob a bank?"

"Did the funders?"

"We didn't start this to starve in the first month."

"We'll figure it out."

"What's the other option?"

She hesitated.

"What's the other option, Nova?" He said it softly and with a truck at the back of his voice.

"I don't know."

"You don't know?"

"That's what I said."

He wished his tongue would stop. But he could no longer control his anger.

"Then don't get in the fucking way."

She clenched her jaw hard enough to break teeth, then turned and walked away, flame on her heels. He spent a minute standing in the rift, wondering if it would close, before hurrying to his room in search of his burner phone and the number Quinn gave him. He made the call.

He and Nova did not speak for ten days. When they did, they made no mention of the argument.

Now, with the newspaper in his hands, his unease with Nova reemerged. He had no wish to linger in it and thought of a distraction. Returning to the living room with the transistor radio, he sat on the couch opposite the window, taking in the late-morning light. He fixed the radio to the nearest jazz station, setting the volume low. A saxophone wept over drums. His feet pulsed against the floor. He imagined himself plucking out the negative thoughts from his mind and floating them away. He did this until Nova was no longer on his mind.

He sorted through his most basic desires. Beyond repairing his relationship with Nova. Beyond finding an ever after with Quinn. He found the only ends that truly mattered.

He wanted John Marbury brought to justice.

He wanted Hush Harbor to thrive.

He fell into a deep sleep.

★ ★ ★

Jeremiah stumbled at the top of the staircase. The tray of food lurched in his hand. A few potato cubes and several peas rolled off. He picked them up and placed them on a napkin. He tried to slow down. The meager dinner would be made more miserable if gravity took half of it. He rounded the corner and spotted Malik idling outside his apartment door.

"I'm sorry to interrupt," Malik said. He was holding an envelope.

"It's no problem."

"From Billie. She said it's urgent."

He lifted the tray and Malik set the envelope on top. He noted a Bliss City flag in the corner. A newspaper article under his door in the morning and a letter in the evening. Two deliveries in one day was two too many.

"Thank you," Jeremiah said.

Malik pointed to Jeremiah's door. "That's Quinn Riley. She worked for Locke."

Jeremiah nodded, impressed. Clearly, Malik had done some homework on their new arrival over the last several hours. "It is."

"She's with us?"

"She is."

"I had no idea."

"That was the whole point." Jeremiah glanced down the hall. "The rest of Hush Harbor knows? That she's here?"

Malik shook his head. "The guards won't tell anyone. They're good at their jobs."

"I don't want to cause a...disturbance."

"I understand."

For the hundredth time, Jeremiah felt gratitude for Malik. The younger man needed no explanation beyond the word *disturbance*. They both knew there were those at Hush Harbor who would not appreciate their leader dating a white woman. Others would never trust anyone from the mayor's inner circle, explanations of espionage be damned. Eventually, Jeremiah would craft a plan to introduce Quinn to Hush Harbor. For the time being, though, he would keep her presence a secret.

"Thank you, Malik. I'll see you tomorrow."

In his bedroom, Jeremiah found Quinn sitting in bed cross-legged, reading the newspaper he had left on the bedside table. She looked up at him and the tray. "Food," she said. "Thank God." She tossed the paper on the floor. He set the tray in front of her and joined her under the sheets.

She popped several potato cubes into her mouth. "I need a shower," she said.

"I wasn't going to say anything..."

She glared at him and laughed. "You know I just had a harrowing night journey?"

"Harrowing?"

She reached for more potato. "Yes."

He leaned over. No matter that she had not yet brushed her teeth and the potato was seasoned with garlic. He kissed her anyway.

"I don't believe you," he said.

"That's rude."

"You're the thing people should fear. Not the other way around."

"I think that's a compliment?"

He took a spoonful of peas and immediately regretted the decision. "I just don't think you scare that easily."

She kissed his shoulder. "It was a long trip though."

"What route did you take?"

He looked off to the side in a half-hearted attempt to hide his competitive undertone. They had long argued about who knew the city better. Who had walked more of its back alleys, who truly connected with its people. Who could more easily catch its pulse.

"I'll never tell."

"You think I wouldn't know?"

"I'm not giving up my secrets."

He gently ran his fingernails up and down her back. "It was okay though? The trip?"

She shrugged. "Long. But uneventful."

"That's good."

She pointed at the envelope on the tray. In between bites, she said, "You gonna open that?"

"I'm procrastinating."

"You shouldn't."

He sighed. "I like being here with you."

"Me, too." She picked up the letter and handed it to him. "Here."

He opened the envelope, slipped out the letter. He thought about putting it back. He steeled himself.

To the Hush Harbor Leadership,
Bliss City demands your immediate surrender. Should you not comply, the Bliss City Police Force along with the National Guard will forcibly enter Hamilton Heights in three days.

Mayor Rex Baker

His heart dropped. He passed the letter to Quinn. After a moment, she set it on the bed. A grave mood enclosed them.

"You think it's a bluff?"

"No."

"You're sure?"

"Rex would drop a nuke on you if he had it."

Jeremiah rubbed his knuckles over his mouth.

"He moves fast."

"He's been planning for this moment."

"Still. Locke was mayor *yesterday.*"

"A day is all it takes to ruin a person."

Jeremiah considered the months spent creating Hush Harbor.

"I'll need to tell our people before they see this announced."

Quinn tilted her head and frowned. "Sometimes I forget this isn't natural for you."

She looked at him with something close to admiration. As though he had a virtue or power that existed only in fables. He waited for her to continue.

"There won't be a public announcement."

"Why not?"

"He's lying."

"I thought you said it wasn't a bluff."

"We don't have three days."

"It says—"

"We have two," she said. "At most."

A moment passed before reality came over him. "He doesn't want us to surrender."

Jeremiah carefully assembled the logic. After the raid, Baker would claim he gave Hush Harbor an out and they refused. The half-truth would be truth enough to convince the world. At best, an argument over the length of the warning would strike the public as a pedantic game of accusations. At worst, no one would ever discover the ploy.

"He wants to be the man that squashed a violent rebellion," said Quinn. "Not the man that accepted a peaceful surrender."

Jeremiah snorted. "Of course. Where's the heroism in peace?"

He looked out the window and attempted to set down his sarcasm. The sun was setting in hues of orange, yellow, red and purple. He wished he and Quinn could vanish into it.

"I wonder if that counts as the end of day one," he said.

"I hope not."

He lifted a finger to the letter. "I don't know what to do about this."

She reached for his hand.

"I think it might be…time."

"Time?"

"To leave. Hamilton Heights."

"You just got here." He tried a smile.

"I mean, for everybody to leave."

He cupped his forehead in his hand. His brain throbbed. The concussion? Stress? Sleeplessness? Regardless, he found it difficult to reason.

"No," he said.

"Jeremiah…"

"It's not over." His voice rose.

"We have to be realistic."

"We didn't make it this far by being realistic."

Her sight landed on the newspaper next to the bed. His followed. "Yes. We did."

Frustration coiled up his throat. "Receiving help was about survival."

"So is leaving."

"It's not the same."

"Why not?"

"I don't want to argue about this with you." He wanted to shout and instead the words came out as a whisper.

She pulled the covers off, sidled to the edge of the mattress. She flicked her hand up and down, silently continuing the argument. "Fine," she said. She started toward the bathroom and lingered at the door. She turned.

"You need to survive."

"What?"

"That's my point. I'm not going to argue. But you, Jeremiah Prince, need to survive."

"I'm not trying to die."

"That's not good enough. Promise me."

"I can't promise that."

"Yes, you can."

"There are a million things I can't control—"

"Control that one thing." She mixed a glare with a plea. "You're all I have."

He dropped his head. How he wished the world could be that simple. A yes or no answer to life and death. He wanted to submit to that hope. He lifted his head. He gave in to the woman he loved.

"I promise," he said.

A pause.

"Okay, then," she said.

"Okay?"

"Yes."

She drew herself up to full height. She squinted and bit down on her teeth and walked into the bathroom. Moments later, he heard the shower running.

He urged himself up and wedged the envelope with Baker's letter into his pocket. In the bathroom, he told Quinn he needed to go for a walk, needed time to think. He left the room hastily and spent the next hour roaming from one building to another, ascending and descending staircases until an approximation of wakefulness returned to him.

He settled at Kemba's memorial and admired the roses. The slight differences in their shade, some a drop darker and others a tad lighter. He said a prayer and then could not remember what he said.

He examined the previous forty-eight hours. An attempted bombing. A visit to Sanders. Locke's resignation. Quinn's arrival. Then, Baker's letter, essentially a countdown notice. Any of those events would have been disruption enough. Taken together, they represented a seismic shift in his reality. Now, each passing minute deposited a pinch of dread in his gut. He faced God's honest truth: nothing was in his control.

Worse. Hush Harbor had two days, at most, until Baker attacked.

Worse still. He had no plan.

Panic slowly twisted in him. Maybe they should leave Hamilton Heights. The idea had crossed his mind daily: at some point, the risk of staying might outweigh the revolution's ideals. Maybe that point had arrived. He could not defend Hush Harbor against a full-out assault. His people would either die or spend the rest of their lives in prison. More souls lost to the state. The government would make an example of them. Torture and capital punishment carried out in the name of justice. How many of his people would he see branded traitors and killed? Or would he be the first person sentenced to death?

He considered the alternative. A retreat. Some revolutionaries might eventually slide back into normal life. Others, more prominent or vocal, would lead lives on the run. He, of course, would be in the latter group. But would that be so terrible? Perhaps he and Quinn could cross a border or two and squirrel away on a farm in Bolivia or Ecuador or Venezuela. Places where relations with the American government were strained. Someday they might make it across the Atlantic. He had long wanted to visit Senegal and Ethiopia and Rwanda, places conveniently without extradition treaties. They could settle on the outskirts of Addis Ababa. Learn Amharic. Work a farm. Raise children. That would be a life well worth living.

He heard footsteps and turned to see Malik approaching. Jeremiah welcomed the company. He had come to rely on Malik. And now, more than ever, he craved dependability.

"I saw you walking," Malik said.

"I needed the air. The last couple of days... Eventful."

"I thought you might need me for something."

Jeremiah smiled at the sharpness of Malik's senses. Perhaps he did need him. He pulled the letter from his pocket and handed it over. Malik took a moment to read it. He folded it carefully and passed it back. Jeremiah spoke with unusual apprehension.

"I'm thinking...we need to retreat."

"Retreat?"

"Leave. Hamilton Heights."

Malik scratched the side of his neck. Jeremiah waited for a response.

"You know about my parents."

Nova had gathered Malik's life story and shared it with Jeremiah before introducing them. Jeremiah had never mentioned it, never steered their conversation toward that pain. But, clearly, Malik figured Jeremiah knew something of his past.

"Yes," Jeremiah said.

"Then you know why I'm here. How much this place means to me."

"I do."

Malik swayed an inch left, an inch right. He came to center. "Stay, go. Retreat, advance. Doesn't matter. We can leave Hamilton Heights. But we can't ever stop fighting. Hush Harbor is a vision, not a place. It represents a world where a five-year-old doesn't wait at the door for hours for his falsely accused parents to come home. A world where a fourteen-year-old wearing headphones isn't gunned down for reaching into his pocket. A world where their killers aren't left free because they have badges." A cool rage spun off Malik. "That vision has enemies."

Jeremiah's own fury stirred. He focused.

"We can retreat," Malik said. "As long as we also attack."

Jeremiah shifted his weight from one foot to the other. "Also attack," he repeated. "Yes."

They spoke for an hour more, arranging their enemies as if on a chessboard. Methodically, they played out scenario after scenario. Each ended with Marbury free and Hamilton Heights trampled under Baker's forces. They cycled through the scenarios again. The same results. They pushed beyond the limits of their mental chessboard. Beyond Bliss. After all, a local rebellion was never the end of Hush Harbor's ambitions. They wondered if the loss of Hamilton Heights could mean the beginning of Hush Harbor elsewhere. Many elsewheres. Weapons had already been sent to sympathizers in cities across the country. There were fires prepped and ready. They only needed a match.

What if leaving Hamilton Heights offered opportunity for a different sort of conflict? Cautiously, Jeremiah voiced the question. Malik pulled out his notebook, scribbled down a series of thoughts. If the revolutionaries left Hamilton Heights, what harm could there be in a direct assault on the Originists? A counterattack would prove impossible. There would be no central Hush Harbor to raid or shoot or bomb.

Jeremiah patted his pocket. The letter sat in it like a curse. They crafted a desperate plan, holding to the faint hope that a more direct attack would inspire other cities to rise in rebellion. Neither of them could tell if or how that might happen. But they knew they could meet a simpler aim: signal, to the Originists and to the government and to the country at large, that oppression would be met with force.

Briefly, Jeremiah considered that their plan might bring about Marbury's death. He neither intended to kill the former police officer nor opposed that outcome. And what about the potential deaths of other Originists? Would they rest so easily on his conscience? He let the question go unexamined. There were costs to their revolution, more than he could count. What use was ruminating over ethical dilemmas when the present was so urgent, so complex? He set aside his need for an absolute right and looked to the sky and prayed that whoever tallied sins and deeds would find in his favor.

13

JEREMIAH RUSHED AWAY FROM Kemba's memorial. He and Malik had arranged to meet again in an hour. First, though, he needed to have a conversation with his sister.

In Morrison Hall, he found her sitting on a folding chair across from her mural. He observed her from the doorway. Her braids, coiled on her head like a crown, swayed when she shifted her gaze from one spot to the next. Her face carried a softness Jeremiah recognized from their childhood. He often mistook it for timidity. This, he had learned, was among his many errors.

He grabbed a chair and unfolded it next to her. She continued her contemplation of the mural. He sensed she would acknowledge him in her own time. He would show patience with her, he would be kind.

"You see the horizon line?" she said.

"Yes."

"It's tilted. They're running uphill."

"Was that your intention?"

"No."

Jeremiah followed the line closely from end to end. He saw

the barely perceptible incline. Perhaps, he thought, he could bond with her over the mural. Use it to warm their relationship.

"The sun," he said. "I can't figure out if it's dawn or dusk."

"It's both."

"Both?"

"Paintings can live in this or that time."

He tried to digest Nova's reasoning. It gave him little peace. He liked a thing to begin and end discretely.

"Where are they?" he asked.

"I'm not entirely sure."

He tried another question, hoping to find a point on which they might resonate.

"Where are they running to?"

"I don't know."

"Are they running to or away from something?"

"Neither."

"I don't know what that means."

"They're just running, Jeremiah."

"But *why*?"

"That's what children do when they want to fly."

Jeremiah's cheeks puffed as he blew out a long stream of air. Could she not answer his questions directly? He stared at the mural in silent irritation. He noticed that the soles of the children's feet hovered half an inch above the ground. He wanted to ask if that meant they were already in flight but worried over Nova's response. It would just be more evidence that he and his sister lived galaxies apart.

"I hope they can."

As if a spell had been broken, she snapped her head to him.

"I came to check in on you last night."

"I was out."

"Evidently."

He tapped the side of his chair. "I have a plan now."

"Do I want to know?"

He determined to state it directly. No time for roundabout communication.

"You have to leave Hush Harbor."

She rolled her eyes. "I knew you'd say something stupid."

"Everyone has to leave."

He handed her Baker's letter. She read it. Her face hardened. She folded it until it was a tiny square in her palm. She flicked her finger and sent it twirling to the wall. It landed beneath the mural.

"We don't respond to threats."

"Nova…"

"How do you know he's not bluffing?"

"He wants a battle."

"Then we protect ourselves. Self-defense."

"He's serious."

"So am I."

"It'll be bloodbath."

"We don't respond to threats."

Jeremiah's frustration set in. His sister's willful naivete bothered him more than he could say.

"Don't be impractical."

She snorted. "Don't give in so easy."

Jeremiah opened his mouth and caught his retort just before it escaped. He steadied himself. Slowly, he thought. Patience, kindness.

He watched Nova chew on her upper lip. Hard enough to break skin. He recognized their shared habit from when they were young. A sign of consternation, of fear. Instinct kicked in, and he wanted to put an arm around her, say something comforting. Set aside the role of revolutionary and be her brother again. But he could not quite figure how. He reached for a subject, any subject, to connect them.

"Quinn's here," he said, abruptly.

Nova's eyebrows lifted. "Quinn's at Hush Harbor?"

"She came last night. The guards stopped her at the northern gate."

"Is she okay?"

Jeremiah heard concern in her tone.

"She's fine. All things considered."

"Where's she now?"

"My apartment. You should visit."

"I will." Nova hinted at a smile and picked up an old joke.
"You know, she's never liked you as much as she likes me."

He laughed. Instinctively, he placed a hand on hers.

"I love you very much," he said.

She squeezed his hand back and the tenderness of it softened
him.

"Think about it," he said. "Evacuating. Please."

Nova let go and stood. She unwound her braids and pulled
them back into a ponytail.

"Fine. But don't expect me to change my mind."

14

THE WEAPONS CAME WITH instruction manuals. This surprised Jeremiah. Perhaps, he mused, they came from a particularly thoughtful arms manufacturer. He and Malik searched through a basement filled with them.

In less than an hour, they found a suitable bomb. It was far smaller than Jeremiah expected. The size of a microwave. Remote detonated, it came with a small clicker. He read its guide closely. How could something intended to kill dozens of people be easier to use than a cell phone? Set it in the desired location. Pull a red tab to activate its radio. Click the remote from anywhere within half a mile. He gave himself a moment to grieve for humanity. All its progress and for what? A small device that made it exceedingly simple to kill.

He tucked it under his arm and then adjusted it on his hip. He hated how snugly it fit. He tried to ignore it and looked at Malik. A realization came to him.

"I never thanked you," he said. "For saving us from the bombing."

"It was nothing."

Jeremiah shook his head at the enormous understatement. "How did you know? That he had a bomb."

"A bunch of little things that added up."

"Like?"

"I would have recognized him if he was part of Hush Harbor. He was a clean-shaven frat kid, and the white guys here look like out-of-practice lumberjacks. Then he started glancing at you. Moving closer. There was something in the way he walked, his energy. Like he didn't want to scare you away. I thought, why is he wearing a jacket? It was hot out. Someone in the crowd bumped him and his body turned sideways. From that angle, you could see a weird protrusion from his chest. We looked at each other for a second. And, then, I just knew."

Jeremiah recognized the mix of logic and intuition that sparked most courageous acts. He considered how to properly thank Malik. Not just for his obvious heroism. For his daily devotion to the revolution's mundane details, for his thoughtfulness, for what was a genuine friendship. Absently, he drummed his fingers on the device and then remembered what it was. He put his hand in his pocket. His fingers touched a small wooden rook from a favorite chessboard his father had given him as a boy. The piece had become something of a good luck charm to him.

"I want you to have this," he said, handing it to Malik.

"What is it?"

"A rook."

"I mean, what's it for?"

"Luck. And to say thank you."

Malik stared at it in his palm. His eyes softened and he closed his fingers around it.

"Thank you," Malik said.

"It's nothing."

"Still."

Together, they left the basement. They kept to shadows and avoided passersby. Jeremiah did not want to explain, or lie about, the thing in the crook of his arm. They made for Hamilton Heights' northernmost gate and rushed out.

A block east, Jeremiah glanced at his watch. Only two hours had passed since his conversation with Nova. How could that possibly be? Time ticked at double speed over the last couple of days. He reflected on the pace of their decision-making. Had it been too fast as well? Yes, undoubtedly, it had. But what choice did they have? If the attempted bombing was not warning enough, Baker's letter surely was. Soon, their world would collapse.

He led them past two intersections and then turned left. He pointed at a three-story building.

"Marbury's location," he said quietly, "13 Arch Street."

"The warehouse?" Malik asked.

"Garment factory. Former. And, yes, that one."

Jeremiah assessed the structure in the lamplight. Boards on the arched windows sagged. Golf ball–sized holes pocked old brick. Paint, once red, had left only a weather-beaten umber on the walls. He watched a small thing with a tail scurry across the front door. He ventured developers might say, *The building has good bones*. A nice way of saying its flesh had decayed.

"It doesn't seem...secure," Malik said. "We could raid it. Try to detain some of them. Get more information."

Jeremiah had considered the option and found too many uncertainties: How many people were in Marbury's Originist cell? What rooms did they occupy? How many were armed and how well-trained were they? A larger Hush Harbor cohort would have to supplement him and Malik if they were to avoid a fruitless suicide mission.

"Too risky for just the two of us," he said.

"We could bring more."

"I'm not chancing more Hush Harbor lives."

"Okay."

Jeremiah sensed a hint of disagreement. "Okay?"

Malik nodded. "Yes."

Jeremiah gestured for Malik to circle the building clockwise. He would go the other way. He counted their luck: equally tall buildings surrounded the factory. They could hide in their shadows.

"Take your time," he said. "No sounds. Stay out of the light."

The two walked in opposite directions. From across the street, Jeremiah glanced at the windows and wondered if John Marbury or some other Originist was keeping watch. He darted away from the light and concentrated on making his footfalls as soft as possible. He studied the base of the building, looking for a hole or well-covered patch of grass. He found none. He took a lazy step. A twig cracked beneath his foot. He stopped and suppressed the desire to curse, waited for a long minute and then another. No cries of alarm, no factory doors opening. He resumed his deliberate pace.

Rounding a corner, he saw Malik a dozen yards away. The young man pointed. A white drainage pipe ran down the side of the wall. Beneath it, a small divot interrupted flat land. Jeremiah looked to the right and to the left. The street remained empty and dark. His heart hammered. He crossed quickly. At the drainage pipe, he stuck a hand into the divot. Damp earth enfolded it. He dug out handfuls. Down and toward the building. He set the device in the hole, covered it up with dirt. His heart climbed to his throat. He forced himself to remember Kemba's murder. To remember the attempted suicide bombing. To imagine Baker's forces invading Hush Harbor. He backed away from the explosive. He crossed the street, quickly, and resisted the urge to look over his shoulder.

When he reached Malik, he realized he had skipped a step.

"I forgot to pull it," he whispered. "The red tab. To activate the radio."

He was about to cross the street again when intuition halted him. He stared at the spot that cradled the bomb. Maybe his forgetfulness was a blessing. What the hell was he doing there anyway? Who was this person planting explosives under buildings? He took off his glasses and rubbed his eyes. He needed a moment to think. He heard the patter of footsteps and spotted Malik halfway to the building. How had he gotten there so fast? He reached the drainage pipe and hunched over the divot and dug out the device. His hand gave a small jerk. He placed the bomb in the hole and layered earth on top.

He approached Jeremiah with the tab held between his thumb and index finger.

"It's done," he said.

Malik tucked the tab into his pocket.

"It's done," Jeremiah repeated.

He sensed weight in the words. A burden without blessing. For the first time since Hush Harbor's inception, he did not know if he could bear it.

PART FOUR

Nova

15

NOVA SAT NEXT TO ZAHRA, paying hardly any mind to the prayer circle. After her conversation with Jeremiah, she had thought to visit Quinn but reconsidered. If her friend shared Jeremiah's views on evacuation, their conversation would surely devolve into a heated debate. She wanted, even needed, their first interaction in months to be joyful. And how could it be when she was already so agitated? She decided to stick to her original evening plan: joining the hundred or so worshippers who met weekly in the central courtyard to pray beneath the stars.

Nova's attention returned to the circle when Zahra stood. Her friend flipped open a thin book. Nova anticipated a poem and smiled at the warmth of a memory: during her first week of law school, Zahra had wedged a poetry collection into her textbook and read for the better portion of the lecture. After class, Nova had introduced herself and Zahra grinned as though they had shared some harmless mischief. Already, Nova felt they had.

"You were reading something during class."

"The contracts textbook?"

"I think it might've been something else."

Zahra held up a shushing finger and laughed. "You caught me."

"What was it?"

Zahra pulled the collection from her backpack. "Do you read poetry?"

"Not as much as I should."

"Take this." Zahra handed her the collection. *My American Kundiman* by Patrick Rosal. "I've got plenty."

Over the following months, the two folded into each other's lives. Zahra eagerly tugged Nova away from textbooks whenever the hours she spent in theater standby lines were rewarded with a pair of tickets. Nova nudged Zahra back to their studies, back to the law school library, back to torts. Once, Zahra showed her a nearly perfect midterm exam score and Nova could hardly believe it. When had Zahra studied? In the standby line? More excellent grades followed and soon Nova felt silly cajoling Zahra into endless studying when, clearly, the younger woman had little need for it. She finally joined her on a weekend of art gallery visits. At a Faith Ringgold exhibition, she let slip that she painted. Zahra looked at her sharply.

"You paint?"

"Yes."

"How could you not tell me this?"

"I'm trying to get you, get us, to focus on school."

"Show me."

"Show you what?"

"Your paintings."

"Now?"

Zahra marched to the exit. Nova watched her and wondered if this was how Jeremiah felt when she set her mind on an objectionable course.

Thirty minutes later, at her apartment, Nova opened her bedroom closet. Stacks of art supplies crowded it.

"Lord," Zahra said. "Where do you keep your clothes?"

Nova laughed, pointing at plastic tubs beneath the bed. She slipped a small canvas out of the closet and rested it on her desk.

She watched Zahra take in the image: a mother cradling her sleeping newborn, lips delicately placed on the child's head. Tufts of baby hair swirled around the mother's cheeks. The newborn's lips puckered as though sending a kiss in return. Zahra's eyes softened, pulled inward.

"It looks real," Zahra said.

"It's based on a picture of me and my mom."

"That comes through." Zahra swallowed a slight tremble in her voice. She turned her head to the side. "Do you have others?"

Nova sensed an unease in Zahra. She let it go undiscussed, trusting time would reveal its source. She brought out more paintings from the closet.

Now, at Hush Harbor, Nova again sensed Zahra's disquiet. As always, Zahra projected ease and fooled most: a useful skill for someone who held so many secrets. But Nova saw the tells—a subtle dip of her chin, a knitting of the eyebrows. If they had been in law school, Nova might have nudged Zahra into a meal or a movie or a moment to be still, together. She tended to Zahra and Zahra to her. At Hush Harbor, though, their friendship took on a more transactional tone. An exchange of instructions and information. And though Nova sorely missed their prior relationship, she did not regret its transformation. Without Zahra as her source, she would not know Jeremiah was smuggling arms across Bliss. Across the country. She would not know he was preparing for all-out war.

Zahra placed a hand beneath her collarbone and prepared to read. Nova listened closely and the poem's familiarity surprised her. Words clicked into her as a bone might snap into its joint: *your rebellious heart constructed of lard and salt, your / life labored but long. You are built of what should kill you.*

Nova tried to recall the poet's name and tripped on a memory instead: her final Sunday at church. No more than five or six, she'd sat on her mother's lap in a garden while the pastor had preached inside.

"Remember what I'm about to tell you," her mother had said.
"Okay."

"Always follow the prayer. Not those doing the praying."

Nova did not understand her meaning. But she pressed no
further, content to sit on her mother's lap in the sun. She admired her earrings, which reminded her of roots. A golden
vertical line broke off into several diverging squiggles a quarter of an inch below her mother's ear. Nova reached for them.
She tapped them and they rocked back and forth. Did they
make a sound when swung? Like wind channeled through an
instrument. Maybe she would hear it if she listened intently.
She thought to ask her mother how to juice music from the
roots. Then she thought how much sweeter it would be if she
discovered the trick herself.

A sudden absence of rhythm pulled Nova from memory.
Zahra closed the book, sat back down. Nova regretted not listening to the poem's conclusion. A moment passed before Zahra
handed her a pen and the poetry collection, opened to the back
page, with a note scribbled in it.

You okay?

Nova thought she should be asking Zahra that exact question. She wrote back.

I'm okay. Worried. How about you?

Fine. Worried about?

Nova could not think of how to respond. She watched another woman stand and ask for prayers for her father, who had
turned eighty several days ago. She explained that his health
had been deteriorating when she'd left Baltimore for Hush Harbor. When she finished, a young man asked for prayers for his
baby sister. She, too, had her birthday the prior week. Another
worshipper stood and then another. One by one, they asked
for prayers for their loved ones. Nova listened closely, catalog-
ing their lost days. Their sacrifices. Sacrifices that should not
be wasted.

She wrote back: *Jeremiah doing stupid things.*

Quickly, a reply. *Do you want to talk about it?*

Nova considered the suggestion. She was frustrated with Jeremiah. The bombing Hush Harbor had suffered. Quinn's sudden appearance. She reminded herself that Zahra would be keenly interested in Quinn's arrival as well. She imagined telling her and grew weary. How would that conversation end? With an explanation of why they could not see Quinn just yet? Or with them traipsing to Jeremiah's room to pay their mutual friend a visit, only to have the moment crash into argument? She decided against telling Zahra, which made her feel guilty, but she promised she would later, when the time was right.

Actually, there's something I need to do.

She started to stand but Zahra tapped her knee.

Can I come with you?

Zahra, she knew, was trying to look after her. She found that kindness endearing. Nova nodded and the two slipped away from the prayer circle. She led them to the cafeteria's kitchen where she filled a bowl with sweet potatoes and grabbed a fork. Food in hand, they walked to the Jarrell Building in silence. Nova paused at the end of the third-floor hallway. She tilted her head toward an apartment door.

"The suicide bomber," she said. "His name is Samuel. He's in there."

Zahra glanced at the bowl. "That's for him?"

"Yes."

"Why? It's way past dinner. I'm sure someone brought him food."

"He's a prisoner. I think he'd appreciate extra."

"He'd appreciate extra?" she asked, indignant.

"We are always just. We are always humane. We are always kind."

"He tried to kill us."

"He was stopped."

"So?"

"He's locked up. Indefinitely. What other punishment do you want?"

Nova could almost hear Zahra's heart wrestling with the question. Did she want him dead? Wiped off the earth? His remains sent on a rocket ship to outer space? Nova let her have a minute before speaking again.

"His behavior does not determine ours. We need to remember that, Zahra."

Nova knocked on the door and a guard opened. They entered a living room with sparse furniture. Another guard, resting on the couch, recognized Nova and hastily jumped to his feet. He brought his hand to his forehead as if in salute. Nova waved him off.

"I told you," she said. "I'm not a general. We don't do that here."

The guard put his hand down but stayed at attention. Nova mouthed *ex-army* to Zahra.

"I'm going to visit Samuel now," Nova said.

The guards hustled to the bedroom door.

"No," she said. "He's handcuffed to the bed frame, right?"

"Yes, ma'am," the ex-army guard said.

"Then that'll be enough. You don't need to tie him up."

The guards passed a look and begrudgingly moved out of the way. Nova gestured for Zahra to stay with them.

Samuel lay on the bed, facing the wall. A wrist, handcuffed to the bed frame, was his pillow. She could not tell if he was asleep or awake. She sensed the latter. She placed the food in front of the bed. Samuel stirred as she sat in a wooden chair across the room. He flipped over. His red eyes fixed on her. She noticed how dry his lips were. He breathed heavily. She could smell him: putrid sweat, a scent of rot. He swung his feet off the bed. His free arm reached for the bowl until he caught its edge with his fingertips. He tugged it close enough to grip and pulled it to his lap, then bowed his head.

For a long moment, Nova thought he was deep in prayer. She wondered what kind of prayers suicide bombers offer. Did they question their faith and seek assuredness? Did they feel bits of their soul agitating and ajar? Or had they been completely washed in hate? She wondered if it were possible to lose the soul. For it to drift away like a balloon.

Under his breath, Samuel began to sing. Nova leaned forward.

"Ring around the Rosa's. A pocket full of posies. Ashes, ashes. We all fall down."

Head down, he giggled. He sang the rhyme several more times. On the third, Nova almost interrupted him, irritated by his mispronunciation of *rosies*.

Finally, he raised his head. He took a forkful of sweet potato and ate it slowly. He squeezed his eyes shut as if relishing the taste.

"Except it won't be the plague for you. Or for me. So, thank you." His gratitude took her aback and galvanized her. However long it took, she would find the humanity in him. "You're the first person to bring me a fork."

Then he smirked, and she realized her mistake. In one swift movement, he stabbed the underside of his sneaker and twisted. The bottom came off. A pill dropped to the floor and he picked it up and she heard herself yelling for the guards. The door swung open and slammed against the wall just as he finished swallowing. Her gut tightened and she pointed at him and shouted, "Get it out," and then, "The pill," and somehow the guards understood. They wrestled Samuel down to the bed before one of them realized mattresses are too soft for the force they needed. The ex-army guard fumbled with a set of keys while the other pinned down Samuel's jerking body. By the time they unlocked the handcuffs, Samuel's body was limp. They tossed him to the ground and he landed with a thud. They took turns straddling him and pressing their palms down on his chest and calling one, two, three. They watched his lips for signs of a pill miraculously bubbling up. His face went blank. They kept pushing. His lips parted. His head bobbled. A second later, his eyes went out.

It took an hour to find shovels. Another to think of a spot hidden enough. They made their way to the backside of the easternmost building, well out of sight. They took turns digging. Horrid intuition struck Nova when the grave was complete. She tried to dismiss it, but it clawed at her until she gave in. She leaned over Samuel's body and rifled through his pockets. She found nothing. She took off the shoe he had not touched. She asked the guards if they had something sharp. One handed her a pocketknife. The other trained his flashlight on her hands. She stabbed the shoe's underside and twisted, just as Samuel had done. A key and several slips of paper lay inside. She scraped them out. One slip read, *It is joy to the just to do judgment: but destruction shall be to the workers of iniquity. Proverbs 21:15.* The second slip listed seven people. They all had the same surname. The last line read, *David Samuel Zebulon.* She read the notes twice over. She tucked the key and the papers in her pocket. She put the shoe back on Samuel's foot. With the help of Zahra and the guards, she buried the corpse.

A few minutes later, Nova and Zahra exited Hamilton Heights from its northern gate. Though Aggy's Island was barricaded off from police and government soldiers, Nova stuck to shadows. Only inside Hamilton Heights, heavily patrolled and surrounded by compatriots, were they completely safe.

She led Zahra through a series of winding alleys, recalling the landmarks. A friend's mother owned the now shuttered Chinese restaurant two blocks east. The bodega three blocks west carried the best summer popsicles at the lowest prices. A right at the next corner would lead to MLK Park, a place to see or be seen. A left would lead to Angelou Public Library. At each turn, Nova recalled friends who lived in this or that apartment. She wondered where they were now.

"You know you didn't need to come with me," she said to Zahra.

"I wanted to."

"You're a good friend."

"I'm a curious friend."

Nova laughed under her breath. She had presumed Zahra was there only to support her. Now she dismissed that silly assumption. Nova had witnessed her pursue important truths before. She recalled an exam review session at the end of their first semester at law school. Zahra had spent it glued to her phone, flipping through the social media profiles of a college-aged woman with a nose ring and cornrow braids. Later, at dinner out with friends, she'd barely spoken and had taken lulls in the conversation as opportunities to scroll. When the table broke into a heated debate over prenatal genetic screening, Zahra remained fixed to her screen. Nova leaned toward her until their shoulders touched. Zahra's head snapped up as though waking from a nightmare. Quickly, she turned over her phone.

"Sorry. Distracted."

"No need to apologize."

Zahra scanned the rest of the table, still loudly engrossed in their argument. She turned back to her phone and pulled up an image. The woman whose social media profiles she had fixated on during the exam review session. She spoke softly so only Nova could hear.

"A friend. Audrey."

"Okay."

"Or, was a friend."

"Was?"

"She passed a few days ago. Her first year in college."

"I'm so sorry." Nova set a hand on Zahra's. "Was she sick?"

"Suicide."

Zahra said the word quickly and not quite to Nova. Her shoulders tightened, curled inward. She tapped the side of the phone. Her voice found an edge.

"Can't be the whole story."

Returning to the present, Nova appraised Zahra and sensed a similar agitation in her friend. She knew not to ask directly. She needed only to make space. A warm starlight infused the night with gentleness.

"I'm not sure anymore," Zahra said.

"I'm sorry?"

"You, Jeremiah, the guards, the cooks, the teachers… Everyone seems so certain."

"Of?"

"Of what we're doing. Hush Harbor."

"You're not?"

"I think we're trapped."

Nova empathized. The same thought came to her a dozen times per day. But it was only a thought. Easily swatted aside or argued away. She knew, though, that her methods of mental discipline were of little use to other people. She searched for a different tack. One with greater compassion.

"You know, we should be graduating soon," Nova said.

"Law school?"

"Yeah. Do you miss it?"

"Not even a little."

"Why did we go in the first place?"

They smiled at each other.

"It was a safer bet than a career in theater," Zahra said.

"Most things are safer bets than a career in theater. But I remember you telling me why you chose law school in particular."

Zahra sighed. "I thought I could use a law degree to promote justice."

"I thought the same."

"I should've been an actor."

Nova let the conversation ebb, wondering if she had chosen the right strategy. Pointing out the tension between law and justice was too vague to assuage doubts about Hush Harbor. She searched for another approach and returned to the memory she had set down only moments ago: the night she learned of Audrey. She recalled anxiously waiting for their dinner to end. When the bill had been paid, they'd said goodbye to their friends and steered through a busy street. The pedestrian crowd thinned a block away from Nova's apartment. Zahra placed a hand over her mouth, squeezed her cheeks to her lips. She pointed a finger outward as if about to speak and then stopped herself. She tried again.

"I don't know how to talk about this."

"About Audrey?"

"Yeah."

"That's okay. We don't need to talk about it if you don't want to."

Zahra rubbed her arms though the weather was warm. "We weren't that close. I kept tabs on her. An occasional message, like happy birthday or congratulations. We had a phone call when she got into Cornell."

"Did you grow up with her?"

"You could say that," Zahra said. "In my kindergarten play, I was an oak tree. My costume was a nightmare. Scratchy and hot and smelly. A million kids wore it before me and I'm pretty sure it never got washed. By the end of our rehearsals, my skin itched like a bad rash and my forehead was covered with sweat and my feet ached from standing the whole time. But, holy shit, I loved being on that stage. I had no lines, no special moments, no spotlight. Didn't matter. I had twenty minutes when I could pretend to be something other than me and the whole world would play along." She looked down at her shoes. "Audrey and I lived in the same foster home for two years."

Nova was surprised. Surely she and Zahra had spoken about their families, their upbringings? Or were they so absorbed in their present lives, their textbooks and paintings and plays, that they had skipped over the past? She could not recall a single conversation about parents or siblings. She wondered if that was not accidental.

"I didn't know."

"I wouldn't have let you." Zahra looked up, rested her eyes on Nova. "It's easier to play along if you don't know anything to begin with."

They walked the few remaining steps to the apartment in silence. Nova recognized that Zahra had placed a trust in her, and she was wrestling with her response. *That must have been so hard. There's nothing to be ashamed about. Your journey from there to here is remarkable.* None satisfied. Instead, she reached for and held Zahra's hand.

Sitting on Nova's couch, Zahra pulled up chains of emails between her and Cornell's campus security, Ithaca's police department, the Tompkins County District Attorney's Office. Then, Instagram and Facebook messages to Audrey's friends, classmates, high school teachers.

"I asked everyone if there had been something off," Zahra said.

"And?"

"They thought she was doing great."

Zahra clicked on a thread between her and a friend from high school. She pointed at one message in particular. She was the second you. Zahra 2.0. College girl. What the fuck happened for her to kill herself?

"The campus security," Nova said. "They gave you nothing?"

"They told me to talk to the police."

"And the police...?"

"Even less helpful than the campus security."

"What about the DA's office?"

Zahra shook her head. "Stock reply. Not investigating at this time."

Nova laid her hands on her lap. Fidgeted. "Did you tell any of them you're her foster family?"

"No."

"Maybe that would help?"

"It won't. We aren't real fa…" She let the sentence trail away. Her breath halted. Her eyes welled. She closed the laptop slowly and laid it on the floor. Her chest trembled and a tear escaped her control. "Some of us are born with family and die with family. Some of us don't."

The words sank into Nova. They deposited weight onto her bones. She could hardly move. She watched Zahra tug her knees to her chest and wrap her arms around her shins. The movement reminded her of a child. She saw it now, so plainly. The fear. She could not imagine its currents or its depths but she sensed it ran to the heart. Always, with questions: who loves us, who are we permitted to love.

Nova wrapped her arms around Zahra and felt Zahra's body stiffen. Then, she let her head fall on Nova's shoulder and began to cry unbidden.

"To hell with what the law says. We'll be sisters."

Nova returned to the present. Newly resolved, she ushered them through a parking lot to a strip mall. She stopped at a small shuttered storefront between a pizza shop and a pharmacy, both out of business. A red sign on the door read Rosa's Laundry Service.

"We're here," she said.

She pressed her ear to the door. No sounds came. She looked at Zahra.

"You're sure this is what he meant?" Zahra asked.

"No."

"But you're sure he meant *something*?"

"I'm sure. You should have heard him. He was taunting me."

"Okay." Zahra rolled her neck. It cracked several times. "It's a long shot. You're either right or we just took a nice walk."

Nova set the key in the lock and turned. It gave way.

"It worked," Nova said.

She had not thought about what might be on the other side of the door, just of finding it. Now doubt crept through her. Were they walking into an Originist den? Had she made another enormous mistake?

"Open it," Zahra said.

"I have no idea what's in there."

"Then open it quietly."

"It's a stupid risk."

"So is this whole fucking revolution."

Zahra opened the door before Nova could stop her. She stepped inside and Nova followed hesitantly. The space was dark and silent, no bigger than a corner bodega. Nova made out the outlines of a cash register at the front and two rows of shelves stretching to the back. She returned to the entrance and reached for the light switch. Fluorescent bulbs crackled on. She blinked rapidly. The brightness almost hurt.

When her sight adjusted, she cataloged the room. Top shelves carefully stocked with boxes of ammunition. Middle shelves lined with tidily wrapped cords and duct tape and packages the size of microwaves. She walked to the aisle and read the label on one of the packages. Blast Radius: 150 feet. She knelt to examine a bottom shelf lined with white buckets labeled Quicklime. She knew the purpose of quicklime. She backed out of the aisle and noticed several stacks of large boxes behind the cash register. Similar stacks lined the front of the room. One on top had been opened. She peeked inside: guns.

"Look," Zahra said.

Nova's shoulders jumped at the sound. She turned and saw Zahra at the end of an aisle. Three lengthy tension rods spanned the width of the back wall: one at the ceiling, one just above their heads and one at their shoulders. Long black bags dangled from hangers on each rod. At first, Nova thought they were garment bags.

"Are those…"

"I think so."

"Body bags." Zahra pointed all the way to the right. "They have different sizes. Smaller ones."

Nova looked at bags no more than three feet tall. Her heart collapsed into her stomach.

"Why would you need…" Zahra started. Nova was grateful she did not complete the question. She did not want to answer. It seemed there were enough bags for every soul at Hush Harbor.

"They unpacked these," Zahra said.

"I don't follow."

"They left everything else in boxes. But they unpacked these and hung them up."

Nova digested the observation.

"Why would they do that?" Zahra asked.

Nova turned her back to the body bags.

"Why do any of us put anything on display?" she said. "We like what it says about us."

Nova removed a shoebox from underneath her bed. She knew she should sleep, make use of the final hours of a long night, but incessant questions pestered her: How responsible was she for the boy's death? How many more Originists would spend their final hours at the weapons bunker before attacking Hush Harbor? How many of the body bags, the small ones, would have their purpose fulfilled?

Why hadn't she just brought Samuel a goddamn spoon?

She sat cross-legged with her back to the bed and placed the shoebox on the floor in front of her. Its contents were her final attempt to find center.

She opened it and smiled weakly at a thin paintbrush. Her very first. Her father gave it to her when she could barely hold a crayon. She removed it and set it aside. Next, she studied a watercolor painting of her family. Four stick figures, shaded bright green and blue and yellow, held hands. She read a slanted *J* and barely legible *N* in the corner. She recalled painting with Jeremiah when they were children. She pulled *Children of Blood and Bone* from the box and flipped through it. As teenagers, she and Quinn had read the novel a dozen times. The weight and thickness of the pages brought her joy. She drew a sheet of lined paper out of the box. It contained bits of praise a favorite college art professor had once given her and which she, late at night, scribbled down so as not to forget: *You are on your way to brilliance. In a day and a half you did what other students couldn't learn in a year.* She laid the paper down with her other memories.

The only remaining item in the box was her mother's golden earrings. She placed an index finger on one and traced its shape. In a hospital bed a couple of years prior, her mother had taken them off and cupped them in her palm. As though estimating their weight. She'd gestured for Nova and opened her daughter's hands and set the earrings in them.

"Take these," she said.

"Mom?"

"I don't think I'll need them anymore."

"Mom."

"Come on, Nova. You know just like I do."

Nova sat on the edge of the hospital bed. Dark splotches dotted her mother's face. Her eyes were sunken. Her thinning hair frizzed. Nova clasped her mother's hand gently, afraid she might crack a bone.

"I do," she said.

"You like the earrings, yes?"

"I like them."

"You used to play with them when you were a child."

Nova remembered tapping the earrings and watching them sway. They delighted her when she was younger. After all these years, she harbored a question.

"Mom?"

"Yes."

"Why did we stop going to church?"

Nova's mother smiled. "That was some two decades ago."

"I'd like to know."

Her mother pushed herself into a sitting position.

"The pastor talked garbage every week."

Nova almost laughed. "What did he say?"

"Everything happens for a reason."

"You don't believe that? That everything happens for a reason."

"Not the divine reasons the pastor peddled. 'It's all God's plan.' 'Thank the Lord for your troubles.' Silly platitude after silly platitude."

"They're comforting."

"The world does not need comfort at the expense of truth." Her mother looked at her with more ferocity than Nova thought possible from a person in a hospital bed. "Where there is suffering, there is oppression. Where there is oppression, there is cruelty. Where there is cruelty, there are human beings. We do not have an issue with God. We have an issue with the soul of humankind."

Her mother's burst of energy dissipated just as quickly as it had arrived. Her arms trembled and slid downward. Her head fell against the pillow. She shivered and struggled for breath. Nova pulled a blanket over her.

"Do you need water?" Nova asked. "Juice?"

Her mother shook her head. Her speech grew halted.

"Did I ever tell you. Why. I became a nurse? Labor and delivery nurse?"

"I don't think so."

"So much debris. In this life. So many ways we are cheated. And spat on. And told we are less than. For the handful of souls. Whose mothers trusted me. I helped make their first journey. Noble." She smiled. "And you, my sweet girl. How are you going. To make justice?"

Nova froze. "I don't know."

Her mother pointed at a small pile of books on the food cart and told Nova to take the first one.

"The first page. Out loud. And stand."

Nova opened the book and stood next to the bed and read.

"The second stanza," her mother said. "Again. Slowly."

Nova widened her stance a touch and read the stanza aloud a second time. The first line caught her attention: *Where's that girl going?* The last line gave her pause: *And still, whispers / about the disappeared, whole souls lost in the passage.*

Nova's mother repeated the line softly.

"Where are you going, my love?" she said.

"I don't know, Mom."

"Don't you think. It's time. You figured it out?"

Just then, her brother walked in with several paper ice cream cups. Sensing the tension in the room, he paused. Nova could tell he thought about moonwalking out but their mother's eyes caught him. He lifted the ice cream cups.

"Chocolate," he said.

"That's good," said their mother. "Set mine down. I'll have it a little later. I'm tired now."

"It'll melt."

"Then it'll be. Like a chocolate milkshake. Nothing wrong with that."

Their mother turned to her side and fell asleep before either Nova or Jeremiah could say another word. They stood for a minute, one with ice cream and the other with a book of poems. They watched their dying mother nap. Jeremiah switched off the lights and closed the window curtain halfway. He came to Nova's side and whispered.

"Ice cream?"

"Sure."

He gestured at the book of poems.

"Mom," she said.

"She wanted you to find purpose?"

Nova looked at him with suspicion. "How'd you know that?"

"She did the same to me."

"She's on a kick."

"Last words. She's making them count."

Neither bothered to take a seat. They ate their ice cream in silence. Their mother's breath fluttered up and down. Nova was grateful her brother was there.

"I'm glad you moved back," she said.

He wrapped his arm around her and she set her head on his shoulder.

"So am I."

"You know who else is glad?"

"Who?"

"Quinn."

"How do you know that?"

"She told me."

"She told you she's happy I'm back?"

"Apparently you made an impression at some dinner. You should call her."

"Maybe I will."

"The more people you get to know here, the less you'll miss Chapel Hill."

"You think I miss it that much?"

"You've got the Dean Dome as your phone's screensaver."

"It was nice down there. But it's more important that I'm here with Mom. And you." He paused, measuring his words. "I want to be here for Mom and for you."

They watched their mother rest for another thirty minutes. The next day, she passed away in her sleep.

On her bedroom floor at Hush Harbor, Nova placed each item but the earrings back in the box. A sudden flash of memory brought her the name Patricia Smith. The poet whose work she read to her mother. The same poet, she now realized, whom Zahra had read at the prayer circle. She put on the earrings.

16

NOVA GATHERED THE TODDLER in her arms. "Up, up," Amos squealed in her ear. His legs squeezed around her waist as she lifted him. "Hug, Auntie, hug me." He flopped on her chest and she wrapped an arm around his back. "See?" he said, as though to tell her this was the proper way to greet somebody.

"I see," she said, peppering the top of his head with kisses. "Amos, do you know how to count to ten?"

In a whisper, he counted to ten.

"See?"

"Yes. You made such a good effort learning those numbers. I have another question."

The boy looked at her wide-eyed.

"How many kisses should Auntie give you? One? Or ten?"

Amos gifted Nova with a delighted shriek. Nova deposited kisses on his forehead and nose and chin. She marveled at the size and softness of his cheeks.

"Ten," she said.

Arms at his sides, Amos raised his palms upward. "All done?"

"All done, sweetie."

"All done, Auntie."

Amos squirmed out of her embrace and raced from the door-way to a bedroom. Billie watched him go with mild concern. "Bring your blocks back in here," she told her grandson. She turned to Nova and the two embraced and for a moment Nova forgot they were at Hush Harbor. She forgot that she had not slept the previous night. That she had snuck a corpse across Hamilton Heights. That she had found a bunker that foretold horrors. And that this early morning visit was for little else but comfort.

Billie led her to a small couch and then left to make tea. When she returned, she handed Nova a mug and sat.

"Tell me, then," Billie said, with a look of concern.

She was the closest thing to an aunt or grandmother that Nova ever had. Truthfully, they had not grown close till her father passed. Billie invited Jeremiah and Nova to her farm fol-lowing their father's funeral. After their visit, Nova promised herself that she would visit monthly—and she kept that prom-ise. She and Billie spent many Sunday mornings eating bread and cheese, sitting at a picnic table overlooking the farm. Some-times they said little, sometimes they said lots. Billie liked to explain how to grow crops, flowers, trees. Nova liked to chat about how to nurture new types of society. Not so different, Nova once said. Exactly the same, Billie responded. Patience, care, work. And pray the weather is right.

"What's wrong, Nova?" Billie said.

She wondered how Billie so readily intuited something amiss with her. Then again, she was not exactly a beacon of joy. She prepared an evasive answer before Amos came running out of his bedroom with a toy maraca.

"Look, Auntie, look," he said. "I shake."

He shook the maraca and waited for applause. Nova clapped and he returned to his bedroom pleased.

"He's big," Nova said. She recalled the day she showed up at the farm to find Billie in her store with a two-year-old by her side. Billie shrugged and said her son and the child's mother were not able to take care of the boy as they should. Nova did not know Billie had children, let alone a grandchild. She gathered that Billie had little inclination to delve into the details of her family life and so she asked nothing at all. Instead, she pulled bread and cheese from the shelf and walked outside with Billie, Amos waddling alongside them. They ate at the picnic table as if all was normal, Nova handing Amos bits of food.

Now sitting on Billic's couch at Hamilton Heights, a deluge of worries flooded her. She thought of the child's joy, then of the peril confronting Hush Harbor. She remembered her conviction that she could somehow appeal to Samuel, find his humanity. God, she thought. Her arrogance. She remembered shoveling. How small the grave looked. How much smaller a child's grave would look. The image devastated her. She remembered the body bags; maybe there would not even be graves. Her insides shrank, and she felt like disappearing. A terrible acid flushed through her stomach. Was that guilt? She recalled Jeremiah's words. *They're coming.* He was right. The Originists had already sent a bomber. Rex Baker had given them a countdown. If nothing else, the stockpile had been proof of their intentions: their enemies were preparing for war.

What was she doing, gambling with the lives of her people? Gambling with Amos's life?

She realized she had no choice. Then and there, she came to her decision.

"We have to leave Hush Harbor," she said. "It's not safe anymore."

The evacuation plan cemented in her mind so quickly it startled her. She wondered if a part of her had been planning it all along.

"Families will leave before individuals. I want you to be part of the first group. It leaves tonight. Take whatever you can carry. I'm going to find supply bags and put them in Morrison Hall.

We'll have several people in your group whose sole purpose will be to help carry the children when they get tired. The trip will take several hours."

Billie gazed at Nova for a long while.

"Nova," she said.

"Yes?"

"Are you sure?"

"I'm sure." A tremble in her voice.

"You've thought this through?"

She looked away. "We need to get everyone to safe houses. People can stay for however long they want. But you should think about ways to get even farther."

"Nova. Look at me, child." A tender command.

Nova listened to Amos giggle in the bedroom. Toys clattered on the floor. He said, "Uh-oh." Nova looked at the bedroom door and then at Billie.

"You should start packing," she said, a tear coming down her cheek. "Please, Billie. Please start packing."

Nova paused at Jeremiah's office door. She had brought Zahra with her and regretted the decision now. Conversations between her and her brother often veered personal. Then again, perhaps Zahra's presence would provide a buffer. Relieve them of their sibling bickering, all that misused effort.

Nova opened the door without knocking. Jeremiah and Malik were studying several maps strewn over the desk. Malik looked up at Zahra with a tender expression and she hid an embarrassed smile under her palm. Nova wondered when the thing so clearly between them had started. With equal surprise, she wondered how she had missed it.

"You're right," she said to Jeremiah.

Jeremiah sat and took off his glasses. "Not usually."

"We need to evacuate."

He lifted his eyebrows. "You changed your mind."

She hesitated. She could not entirely dismiss her discomfort at giving in to her older brother's plan. She sensed he was hiding something. Still, she recounted her previous night in full, speaking dispassionately, as though reading out a list of chores. He did not react when she detailed Samuel's death or the discovery of the bunker. She admired his stoicism. She feared it, too: the things he could bury inside. When she finished, he leaned forward.

"It's time, then," he said.

"It's time." She looked askance and subdued her uncertainty. No time to linger on doubt. She moved on to the next decision point on her checklist. "And the bunker."

"What about it?"

"We need to destroy it. Or confiscate the weapons."

He interlaced his fingers and tapped his thumbs. "We can't do that."

"Why not?"

"Who supplied the space? Who transported the weapons? Who bought them?"

"I don't know."

"Neither do I. That's a problem."

"It's probably the Originists. Or someone who supports them."

"And what if that someone is close to our new mayor?"

Nova followed the thread. A spooked mayor might launch an immediate attack on Hush Harbor, unknowingly preventing their evacuation. They could not risk upsetting a chessboard so precariously arranged.

"I understand."

They stared at each other in uneasy agreement. Zahra broke the silence.

"I'm sorry. What's going on?"

Now it was Jeremiah's turn to share details. He slid Rex Baker's letter across the desk. When Zahra finished reading, she stared at the ground and chewed on her lower lip. Nova wondered how much time she should give her to digest.

"We need to evacuate," Nova said.

"Everyone?" Zahra said.

"Everyone."

"That's hundreds of people."

"It is."

"We can't just march through the streets."

"Unfortunately."

"The tunnels?"

"I think so. In small groups."

"How many people per group?"

"Maybe fifteen or twenty?"

Zahra squinted. "That's more than two dozen groups."

"Yes."

"It'll take weeks."

Jeremiah interjected. "We only have a day. Two, maximum."

Zahra rolled her lips together. She twisted her mouth to the side. She and Malik exchanged a sad look. "You're worried," Nova said.

"You know I don't really like it here."

"I know."

"I struggle with this place every day. But I stay anyway. Because I know, in my gut, it's important. Us being here together is important. When we leave, where do we go? One place? Many? Do we stay together? Do we scatter?"

Nova followed the question to its root. Did abandoning their physical location, the place they named Hush Harbor, also mean abandoning Hush Harbor the movement? She searched for an answer. Jeremiah spoke before she could find one.

"You know there's no place large enough for everyone," he said.

"So, we scatter," said Zahra.

"We find safety."

"It's a good reason."

"But not good enough?"

"I don't think anyone is so sure of good enough anymore."

"We're trying to survive."

"I get it. I just want to make sure we're okay with what we're giving up."

"It's not the end."

"Maybe."

"Hush Harbor, the idea, will continue."

Zahra tapped her lips, clearly unconvinced.

Nova thought of their first week at the Hamilton Heights projects. She'd found abandoned cleaning supplies in one of the basements. She and Jeremiah and their small handful of companions, Zahra among them, had set about mopping hallways. Nova used cutlery to scrape mold from ceilings and the tops of walls. Sometimes the forks left scratches. As though a crazed animal had tried digging from the ceiling through to the roof. Jeremiah and Zahra cleared spiderwebs from corners with broom handles. Nova encouraged gentleness in their removal.

The spiders were the project buildings' only tenants. Nova recalled the local housing authority shuttering Hamilton Heights several years prior. They cited concerns over unhealthy living conditions and decrepit buildings. They scattered its residents throughout the city and occasionally into neighboring suburbs. Nova wondered what kind of choices those families were given. A few months after the closing, a developer announced it had bought the property and intended to build condominiums. Fortunately, the developer tripped over plans and permits and had not yet broken ground. An empty Hamilton Heights was protected only by spiders, a wire chain fence and several locked gates.

As they cleaned, Nova cataloged the rooms. She took note of apartments suited to families or the elderly and those better for young individuals. She outlined how new recruits might flow from a dormitory-style living space to more permanent accommodations when their roles had been settled. She imagined a variety of living quarters organized by daily patterns. The early risers, like cooks and guards, in one building. Teachers and those charged with maintaining the buildings and courtyards in another. Smugglers might need their own space, marked by transience. Recruiters, likely sent out to cities across the Eastern seaboard, would need only temporary spaces at all.

As Nova's ideas solidified, her mind drifted from the practical to the conceptual. She thought of the uprising as both a revolution and a sanctuary. She knew the young would come, moths drawn to a titillating new flame. Their energy would drive the movement. But she also knew they would need the maturity that came with age and the seriousness exercised in raising children. The revolution could not conceive of a new world without taking all of that world's willing participants into account. Hamilton Heights, then, would be both a center for brazen youth and a sanctuary for families and elders who believed in a different kind of being. Several families from Aggy's Island, hemmed in by the barricades, had already trickled into Hamilton Heights. They sought community and safe haven. She was certain that more would follow.

She finished inventorying the rooms in one building and moved on to the next. Outside, she wiped dirt from a metal sign that solemnly stated Building A. Another idea struck her. New names were required. The housing project's generic labels expressed only bureaucratic logic. She wanted them to capture a sense of hope and history. She hurried to her room and came back with paper, tape and a marker. She wrote out The Walker Building and taped it on the front door. Inside, she found the Main Hall and rechristened it Morrison Hall. She quickly wrote out names for four of the remaining eight buildings. Basquiat, Jarrell, Parks, Mingus. She stopped herself there, thinking others should generate names, too. She roamed the complex until she discovered Jeremiah and Zahra scrubbing down a particularly dirty hallway. She explained her plan and Jeremiah offered Simone and Baldwin. Zahra offered Ringgold and Lamar.

"What about Hamilton Heights?" Zahra asked.

"What about it?" said Nova.

"What should we call it?"

Nova's imagination had not yet wandered to that scale. What they called Hamilton Heights might imply a name for themselves. She wanted nothing of the classic political party or rebellion group designations. No unions or associations or alliances. They ought to represent an idea that spoke to human nature more than it indicated a political aim. She knew there was an ontology behind their actions. They needed a name that would give it life. The three spent several minutes in thought. Finally, Jeremiah offered an idea.

"Hush Harbor," he said.

Zahra nodded several times. "Like the places enslaved people would worship?"

Nova considered the term. At a hush harbor, slaves could pray to whomever or whatever they wished. They could shout and dance and speak in languages unknown to their foreign masters. They could create a world spiritually distinct from the ones in which they toiled. Yes, Nova thought. It was a perfect name. An ode to the past and the future. At their newly baptized hush harbor, greed and malice and the stink of rotten hearts would remain outside the projects' gates. They would live as though in prayer, hopeful and unsure of their mark, but free, or at least as free as destiny would allow.

"Yes," Nova said. "Like the places slaves would worship."

They decided to put the name to the rest of their companions.

Now, months later, Nova thought she should gently remind Zahra of Hush Harbor's origins.

"The idea of a hush harbor never belonged to us alone," she said.

Zahra crossed her arms and bowed her head.

"Yes," she said. "You're right."

Another uncomfortable silence descended over the room. This time, Malik stepped forward. He flipped his notebook to a blank page and jotted down a heading. He said, in almost a whisper, "We need to plan the evacuation. The details. We need to start now."

A light rain grayed Hush Harbor's yards. Nova walked in the direction of Jeremiah's apartment. She had spent the day informing her fellow revolutionaries of the impending evacuation. After all they had sacrificed for Hush Harbor, she felt compelled to deliver the news herself, to look each of them in the eye. She repeated the same lines whether her audience was a group of two or twenty: *They were in imminent danger. The revolution needed to survive and they were the revolution, even without a physical location to call home. Therefore, they needed to leave.* Some cried, some protested, some remained in stunned silence. Nova cajoled when necessary but mostly assuaged fears. One discussion at a time, Hush Harbor's residents fell in line.

The conversations had exhausted her.

She heard muffled footfalls as she entered Jeremiah's building. She kept the door open and a thin figure wearing a backpack scurried inside. The figure pulled back her hood and drew down a fluffy scarf that covered the lower half of her face.

"Where do you keep the umbrellas?" Quinn said.

Nova's mouth fell halfway open. "Oh my God," she said. She took a step forward and collected Quinn in an embrace. Her blond hair had grown dark at the roots and her eyes were edged with crow's feet. She looked almost dangerously thin. Nova wondered if Quinn saw similar changes in her. "I've been meaning to come see you. I can't believe you're here."

"Neither can I. You look good."

"You, too."

"You're lying."

"So are you."

Quinn held her hand. "I missed you."

"I'm so sorry I didn't come earlier—"

"Please. You've got more important things to do." Quinn slung the backpack from her shoulder. "Besides, I wanted to get out. It took rain, a hoodie and this scarf for Jeremiah to finally be okay with me leaving the room. And then he had the audacity to send me with an errand."

She handed the backpack to Nova. Nova opened it and found white envelopes overflowing with cash.

"He wanted you to divide it between the groups that are leaving. So that they have something to get started with."

Nova zipped up the backpack and placed it on the ground. She could not be sure, but she figured the cash came from Hush Harbor's anonymous funders. She knew that she would, as suggested, deliver the envelopes to each group. She also knew that their evacuation plan required this sort of contingency. The groups would be disconnected from each other and from Jeremiah. Surviving would prove an almost impossible task without capital. Yet she resented the money and its source for existing. She shoved the backpack even farther.

She leaned against the wall and let herself slide down to the floor. How long had it been since she'd slept? She pressed the back of her skull to the wall, enjoying the discomfort: it reminded her that she still had some measure of control, some ability to cause or ease distress.

Quinn, too, lowered herself to the floor. "I also wanted to tell you something."

Nova dropped her head. How many more revelations could she take? She fortified herself against whatever was coming.

"Okay," she said.

"Jeremiah's not leaving. Not with the evacuation groups."

A flush of exasperation came over her. In less than a day,

her certainty regarding the world and her place in it had vanished. She knew only this: she wanted no more graves, least of all her brother's. She had intuited that Jeremiah's personal exit plan was not so straightforward. She could not imagine him departing Hamilton Heights easily. Still, hearing his intentions out loud maddened her. How quickly she had gone from the evacuation's opponent to its greatest supporter.

"He asked you to tell me?"

"No."

Nova bit her lower lip. "He wasn't going to tell me till the last minute. Or not at all."

"I thought you deserved to know."

"Do you know his plan?"

"Not entirely. My part in it is small."

"You have a part?"

"I send out a picture."

"Of Marbury? In the robe?"

"Yes."

"When?"

Quinn stared at the wall and said nothing. Nova nodded.

"He's going to retaliate," Nova said.

"Yes. But I don't know how."

Nova exhaled slowly. Why did her brother keep so many secrets? She shook her head and reminded herself that she was friends with Quinn long before her brother came back to Bliss. She changed course.

"Are you coming with us?"

"Leaving?"

"Yes. Leaving."

"I am."

"Even without Jeremiah?"

Quinn hesitated. She picked at her jeans. "We're planning to meet. After this is all over."

"Like a rendezvous?" Nova laughed. The notion struck her

as absurd and romantic and even a bit delightful. It drew her, for a moment, away from Hamilton Heights.

"I guess like a rendezvous, yeah," said Quinn.

Nova rubbed Quinn's knee. She did not want to puncture her friend's optimism but recognized her overly buoyant hope. If Jeremiah did not evacuate with the rest of Hush Harbor, he would likely not make it out alive or free or even the same person.

"People love Jeremiah for the same reason he's dangerous. He does not do half measures."

Quinn spoke quietly. "I love him for that."

"So do I. But he's still wrong."

"We have to play the game, Nova."

"We can't create a just world through unjust means," Nova said.

"The means don't matter in the real world."

"I don't want to live in the real world," Nova replied. "I want a different world."

"I don't follow."

"Jeremiah thinks he can make justice by attacking power."

"You don't think that?"

"I think we need to rewrite the definition of *power*." Nova reached for a simple analogy. Silly enough to take some weight off their conversation. "If Jeremiah wants to slice the apple differently, I want to eat an orange."

Quinn crossed her arms. They spent a moment in contemplation. Nova fantasized about an alternate life in which she graduated and joined a firm and grunted through a dozen years until she made partner. How blessedly simple that would be. She could have bought a loft apartment with a view and frequented a local café on the corner. The baristas would know her name and her order and on what mornings a croissant would do her good. Gently, they would ask if she wanted pastry. She would grieve when the landlord hiked their rent and their doors shut-

tered. A larger coffee chain would swoop in. Perhaps, in the
irony of wealth, her firm would represent the larger chain in
an acquisition or lawsuit. She would spend a week or two ruminating over the ethics of it all and then wake one morning
to a clear conscience. She would get to know the new baristas.
They would be nice, too, but she would guard her loyalties and
reminisce with neighbors about the original café. In her day-
dream, she wondered if she should get a dog. That life seemed
far more attractive to her now than it did a year prior.

"I understand," said Quinn.

"Do you?"

"I think so."

"But you don't agree?"

Quinn opened and closed her mouth. She took a second more.
"It doesn't matter if I agree or not."

"Of course it does."

With knitted eyebrows, Quinn spoke solemnly. "When Jeremiah leaves Hamilton Heights, you'll be long gone. You'll
be in touch with the rest of Hush Harbor. Your people. You'll
be comforting them, you'll be guiding them, you'll be leading them. This revolution will be yours alone. What matters is
what you think."

Nova tapped her head against the wall. Hard enough to hurt.
"That's not how it works. The revolution doesn't belong to any
individual."

"Maybe. But it has to be led by one."

Amos rode in a carrier on Nova's back as she trudged through
the tunnel. She looked at the group. Their movements seemed
lethargic, their boots sticking in the mud. They all stooped just
a tad. As though defeated or, at the least, in mourning.

She attempted a deep breath and quickly shut her mouth
against the tunnel's stench. Not quite sewage, but certainly rot.
She blew the smell out of her nose. She wanted to close her

eyes and settle herself but she dared not lose what little sight she had. What if she bumped into Billie, walking beside her, and woke Amos?

She tried focusing on the spot created by a flashlight ahead. Her vision sluggishly obeyed. The light did not come in sharp rays but in gauzy waves. That was it, Nova thought. They moved as if walking through water. Her heart eased. Tension dropped from her body and her hips swayed with her steps.

She reached for Billie's hand.

"When do you have to go back?" Billie asked.

"Soon. The next group is scheduled to leave an hour after you all left."

"You'll walk with them, too?"

"For a bit, yes."

"We're going to miss you."

"We'll see each other soon."

Billie curled an arm around Nova's waist, below Amos. "I'm not sure we will."

Billie spoke honestly, in ways Nova herself had tried to avoid. Now, with the reality spoken, she found little use in evasion.

"Neither am I," she said.

They trekked through the mud for another minute. Amos lifted his face from one of Nova's shoulder blades and placed it on the other. She imagined the boy's sweat-stained cheek cooling. She hoped he felt that slight relief.

A dozen yards in front of them, Nova saw heads turn left and right. When she and Billie reached the same spot, a flashlight revealed another tunnel, much smaller, that bypassed the one they traversed. Before Hush Harbor, other secret-makers had found the tunnels and worked underpasses from the larger artery. Nova loved this untold past. How many generations had joined small channels to the tunnel? How many purposes were drawn into their design? Who had dug them and who had maintained them and who had kept them clandestine for so many years? Lost histories were lived in the tunnels.

Nova loosened the carrier and rested Amos's bottom on her forearm. She shimmied him around to her torso and kissed his head. Billie took over the carrier and Nova tenderly eased him onto Billie's back. Billie moved side to side, testing the carrier's hold. Nothing slackened.

The most normal of things, Nova thought. How to keep a child asleep. How to carry a child. How to make sure a child is safe.

Grief panged at her chest. They would be fine. She was sure of it. But she would miss them dearly. She hugged Billie.

"Tell Amos his auntie loves him," Nova said.

"I will," said Billie.

Nova reached into her pocket and pulled out a small flashlight. She flipped it on. She made her way back down the tunnel.

17

ON THE FINAL EVENING of the evacuation, Nova stood outside of Jeremiah's office door. She counted the number of remaining groups: fewer than a handful. Soon, she and Zahra would permanently depart. She wondered if she should update her brother. Surely, he received information from one of the many people involved in the evacuation. She wondered if he wanted to hear from her directly. But if he did, wouldn't he seek her out? She wanted to see him intensely. She itched to tell him, again and again and again, how wrong he was on so many things. How he never should have accepted anonymous funds, money whose source could be anyone with any motive. How he never should have kept secrets from her. How his impulse to attack was understandable but an error nonetheless. She longed to tell him that she had no better answers than he did. But could they not, together, find courage in that uncertainty? Could they not train their sight on glimmers of hope? She burned to say that a revolution is born of creativity and spirit before it becomes violent. Their creativity was not yet exhausted. Their prayers were strong. She wanted, desperately, to ask him to come with them. To leave Hush Harbor. To abandon whatever retribution he had planned. This thing she was somehow sure would kill or imprison or forever alter him. She longed to ask him to live. She needed her brother, too.

She raised her hand to knock on his door, but stopped herself. She remembered the afternoon she'd helped him start on the adoption paperwork, remembered his joy. He had told her he never thought he'd be a father.

He'd introduced her to Kemba that night. They went out to a Thai restaurant. The boy, shy, averted his gaze. Aware of his passion for food, she asked for his recommendation. He raised his eyebrows, apparently surprised that anyone other than Jeremiah would seek his opinion. He thought for ten seconds. He asked her if she liked spicy food. Sweet or savory or sour. Light or heavy. She leaned toward him, drawn by a softness in his voice. They hunched over a menu. He pointed at several dishes she had never tried. Eventually, he said, "I think you'll like the *khao soi* the most."

After they placed the order, Kemba smiled at her for the first time. She smiled back and instinctively squeezed his shoulder.

"It better be good," she said.

"I think you'll like it."

She sensed a small trust form between them. She watched him adjust his cutlery. Although she could not recall her brother ever doing the same, the act reminded her of Jeremiah. The care Kemba took, the patience. He straightened his fork as if it were the final addition to a great work of art.

"You're a lawyer?" he asked.

"Not yet. But in a few years. I'm in law school."

"I think I might want to be a lawyer one day."

"Really?"

"Yeah."

"I think that's a great idea. But I'm biased. What makes you want to be a lawyer?"

"I don't totally understand it yet, but I think the law is about right and wrong." Kemba scrunched his face inward and Nova saw both child and young man in him. She could tell that he had directed all his brainpower to decoding his reality. "It's not just rules. The rules come from somewhere."

"That's very insightful. Where do you think they come from?"

"Us? I mean, all of the people in this country."

"In theory. Yes."

"But not really?"

"Some people get a lot more say than others."

"Rich people. White people."

Nova laughed. Jeremiah, too, chuckled at Kemba's blunt sincerity. She saw pride in her brother's expression.

"Yes," she said. "Rich people. White people. Have you heard the term *privilege*?"

Kemba nodded. "Basically, if someone has privilege, it means they get to have or do things that other people don't. Usually, for no good reason. It's unfair."

"We could even say it's unjust."

"Unjust." Kemba spoke the word as if his tongue were trying out a strange and pleasantly textured food. "So, people who have privilege make the rules for everyone. They make the law."

Nova wondered how complicated the thought needed to be. How much did he need to know, right then, about white supremacy and institutional racism and mass incarceration and implicit bias and microaggressions and violent boundaries? Perhaps more interestingly, how much could he explain on his own? He had, undoubtedly, experienced racism in its myriad forms. Young and Black and poor, he already knew America. Why not give him the language of resistance?

"In more ways than one," she said. She brought their conversation to constitutional law and the country's original sins. She spent an ample moment discussing the hypocrisy of both the founding fathers and the nation's founding documents. Then, she worked through the Missouri Compromise and Jim Crow and "separate but equal" and the civil rights movement and Black Lives Matter. In every era, she described violence. The whipping and chaining and hanging. The suffocations, the tarrings, the live burials. The beatings. The shootings. The things Black bodies suffered so white ones might feel secure. She peppered her discussion with revolutionary figures, twining narratives of resistance around a history of perverted law. At some point, their meals arrived and they ate and ordered dessert. She found the *khao soi* excellent and told Kemba so. He smiled, the second time that night, and asked her about Malcolm X. She continued her lecture. She paused often, sure her audience was satiated and ready to move on to less weighty topics. Each time, Kemba nudged her forward with a question. *What if Nat Turner had escaped? What if Hayes hadn't sold out Black America? What if the FBI had never figured out how to spy on the Black Panther Party?* She glanced at Jeremiah more than once. Who was this quiet youth with good questions and stellar meal recommendations? Whose precious few words hinted at brilliance? Whose tone was as soft as kindness? She wondered how many hours he and her brother had spent in a similar fashion. How easy it must have been to love Kemba.

Now, outside of Jeremiah's office, she gently opened the door. Jeremiah sat behind the desk. She thought about making her case. She wavered. He rose and set his glasses down. She noticed how his hand trembled more than usual, saw confusion in his eyes. She saw him clearly for the first time in months. Too much grief, fury, exhaustion. The remnants of a lynching inside him. He walked to her. Slowly and broken. She embraced him. He leaned his weight on her. She leaned back. One cried and then the other and they did not know who was first.

"I can't go," he said.

Of course not. She saw it now, so obvious. Whatever plan he had was only logic wrapped around a far deeper impulse. He needed to feel whatever Kemba felt in the seconds before the trigger pulled. The fear. The despair. Her brother could not heal from trauma without walking into it. He could not abandon Kemba to the horror of that moment. He needed to stare down the guns. He needed to join the boy who would have been his son.

And how could she ask him to do otherwise? How could she ask him to remain in tortured limbo? He would stay at Hush Harbor until the police arrived and stormed up the stairs. Until he felt their footsteps corner him.

"I know," she said.

She could not stomach the thought of goodbye. She lowered her head, gathered strength. One by one, she pulled her fingers from his back. She let their embrace go. She stepped to the side and tried not to think.

"Try," she said.

He shot her a confused look. "Try what?"

"To stay alive."

He swallowed. "I will."

"I love you."

"I love you, too."

18

NOVA POINTED HER FLASHLIGHT at the tunnel's muddy ground and stared straight ahead. Her backpack tugged against her shoulders. An ache refused to leave her feet. She reminded herself to stop pushing her body and instead sway through this lightless place.

She had taken a final glimpse of Hush Harbor an hour prior. She happened to observe Malik on a lonely patrol. He stopped between buildings and looked toward Bliss's skyline as though expecting a missile at any moment. His restlessness reminded Nova that he was only a few years past adolescence. Not yet comfortable with the broadness of his shoulders or the strength in his arms. He spoke into a two-way radio. Only Jeremiah would be on the other end. The sight saddened her.

She knew she should say goodbye. But she couldn't muster the energy to face him. To quell the remorse burning through her. His life was at risk because she had paired him with Jeremiah, and now she badly wished to save him. She knew how patronizing the thought was. That she might save another human being who thought and walked and talked and made his own choices just as she made her own choices. She wished it none-

theless. She could not summon the willpower to hear him refuse evacuation. She reprimanded herself for a lack of resolve.
Still, she left that goodbye unsaid.

In the tunnel, Nova observed her friends. Together, they were
the last three people to leave Hush Harbor. She watched Zahra
run a hand across her head. Quinn pulled her baseball cap low.
She worried that her secrecy over Quinn's presence had encouraged Zahra's already lively doubt. She imagined details of their
first meeting, a meeting she had encouraged Quinn to seek
out, in hopes it would ease her conscience. Had Zahra frozen in
shock? Did they embrace? How long did their conversation last?
Most importantly: Was the joy of seeing an old friend enough
to sweep away inquiries as to when she arrived and who knew?

Walking next to Zahra now, she recognized only determination. Quinn radiated the same resolve. As though the tunnel's
gloom had swamped their individual emotion and replaced it
with a collective willpower. At the same moment, all three adjusted the guns strapped to their lower backs. Nova grimaced.
She conceded the necessity of weapons and prayed they would
not need to use them.

She settled her attention on the hurt in her feet. She guessed
that she had trekked a couple dozen miles over the past day
and a half. No one had suggested she accompany groups out of
Hamilton Heights and into their new uncertain futures. Intuitively, though, she understood the comfort her presence would
provide. Now a sharp pain laced the balls of her feet and a dull
throb kept her heels company. She tried taking steps with her
toes pointed inward. The pain remained. She directed her toes
outward and smiled when she realized her gait had turned into
a waddle. If only for the little silliness it provided, she kept step-
ping in that manner.

In need of the respite of happy memories, she recalled an
afternoon spent at a Bliss public library looking for books for
Amos. She had combed through the children's section for pic-

ture books featuring Black girls. She'd stopped and read through *Ada Twist, Scientist*. She tucked the book in a large tote bag and went in search of more. She found *I Am Enough*. She read it twice and put it in her bag. She searched for another hour and plucked *Amazing Grace* and *Serafina's Promise* from the shelves.

Satisfied with her small collection, she sat on the floor and read through the books again. On the third and fourth reads, she imagined how the characters might speak. Ada Twist had a higher pitched voice than Serafina and Grace. Grace held her vowels for a millisecond longer than the other two. Serafina spoke with greater rhythm. Nova contemplated the narrator in *I Am Enough* and was unable to place her sound. She concluded that she could be anyone so long as she spoke with conviction.

In the tunnel, Nova told herself the stories from those children's books. She filled in what she could not recollect with sturdy sentences that fit. As though words were bricks and she were repairing a home. On her second retelling, she tried to give her sentences more meaning. On her third, she took liberty with the original work. She felt joy in the re-creation. She spent a minute finding the right synonym for *laugh*. She spent another trying to understand how Grace might demonstrate love. She empathized with the thrill of Ada's genius. She held Serafina's hand and found boundless kindness in it. The girls stepped out of their stories and talked to each other and floated around her. She felt an urge to tell other people about them. She wondered if this was how fables were born. She wondered if this was why fables were needed. To walk with through long, dark tunnels with uncertain endings.

She reached for Zahra. Just as she touched her arm, she noticed a light flicker up ahead. Her shoulders tensed.

"Did you see that?" Zahra said.

"Yes."

"Are we expecting anyone?" Quinn asked.

"No."

The light flashed again. Nova knew the intersection they'd uncovered with Billie and Amos lay ahead. A perfect spot for someone to lie in wait. She guessed they were only twenty or thirty yards from it.

They nodded in unison. Quinn and Zahra reached for their guns. Reluctantly, Nova unholstered hers as well. They approached, hearts pounding. They crouched down low. She understood the instinct and forced her way free of it. If they met someone hostile, crouching would hardly help in this small space. If they met someone friendly, there would be no need to crouch. Either way, she wished to meet whatever futures awaited with her back unbent. She straightened. She noticed Zahra and Quinn do the same.

They arrived at the intersection and stood as if awaiting a green light. Nova peered to the left. A beam hit her eyes, blotting her vision. A moment passed before she saw a stooped figure half a dozen yards away. He held his hands crossed in front of his face, a flashlight in one and a gun in the other. His posture struck Nova as unnatural. As though he were an actor ill-suited to the role of a soldier.

He lowered his hands, pointed the gun toward them from his hip. He sucked in air and red patches on his face expanded and contracted. Sweat clung to his forehead. His eyes darted from Nova to Zahra to Quinn and back again. One of their flashlights caught the side of his face and Nova caught a glimpse of his irises. Hazel. She knew those eyes. She imagined him without the beard and without the red patches distorting his skin. She imagined him with thirty extra pounds. An energy, almost violent, tore into her veins.

"John Marbury," she said.

He grinned.

"In the flesh," he said. "Nova Prince, I'm at your service."

He took a bow in mockery. Quinn took a step forward. Nova put a hand on her wrist to stop her from taking another.

"Apologies," he said. "For my appearance, of course."

He pointed the flashlight at his clothes. Soaked in sweat, his shirt was midway between green and brown. Several tears in his jeans bared his knees. He pointed the flashlight at Nova. He sucked his teeth.

"Then again," he said. "Not like you dressed up, either."

Nova said nothing. She watched him labor for breath. He sneezed and sniffed and rubbed his nose on a sleeve.

"Excuse me," he said. He jutted his jaw and scowled. "What? No 'God bless you'? You don't even have to put the 'God' in there. Just 'bless you' would be enough for manners."

"What are you doing here?"

He stuck his tongue between his teeth and bit. "Waiting."

"For?"

"A word with your brother. But I've been down here two days. So, you'll have to do."

"You're waiting to talk with Jeremiah?"

He grinned again and shrugged before lifting his gun several inches.

"Maybe something a little more than talk."

Nova ignored the threat. She already understood the end Marbury plotted for her brother. Instead, she thought of him watching as she shuttled people out of Hamilton Heights. Thought of his bloodshot eyes scouring bodies. She held back a shiver and considered the cause of his waiting. What had prompted him to hole up like a rodent in a sewer system? What had prompted him to stay? Two days was too long in the tunnels. No wonder it seemed as though he had caught the plague.

"What happened two days ago?"

"Oh, you know the answer to that. Think." He tapped the barrel against his forehead. His smile vanished. "I don't take kindly to attempts on my life."

Nova considered asking what he meant. She watched him gnaw his lower lip. He desperately wanted to speak. Did he have a fever or something worse? She felt Quinn vibrating with anger and prayed her friend could remain calm. Marbury could not stand for as long as they could. They would not have to say a thing for this man to drivel on.

"Did you hear me?" he said. "I'm onto you."

"I heard you."

"You think you're so smart."

"Truly, I don't."

"I've been onto you every step of the way. I knew you'd come for me."

"We're not here for you."

"How stupid do you think I am?"

"I don't think you're stupid."

"I saw him."

She loitered in the silence.

"I saw your brother and his friend. Spying on my cell. Looking for me. Then I saw him digging a hole and putting something in it right under my building. What do you say to that?"

She held her tongue.

"You think I don't know what he put in that hole?"

She pieced together his meaning. She knew Jeremiah's plan would involve an act of violence. She could not say she was surprised.

"That wasn't *my* plan."

He snorted.

"Of course not. You people never take responsibility. Even when you're caught. To tell you the truth, I'm not even mad. It makes sense to me. Try to kill the enemy. We're all animals."

"I don't believe that's true."

"The thing is, except for the part where I'm supposed to die, I actually like your plan. I see the logic in it." He wiggled the gun in front of his face as if tracing lines between imaginary bullet points. "You're backed into a corner. Only so long until the government strangles you. Turns off the water. Waits for winter and cuts off your heat. Or just comes barging right in. It's going to happen. You know it. I know it. You're going to lose the battle. Why not start a war?" He laid the barrel of the gun flat against the side of his mouth and mocked a whisper. "Here's the thing… I want a war, too." He giggled. "Only way to sort this race problem once and for all. That's why I sent the boy Samuel. Thought bombing Hush Harbor would kick it off. If I had known we wanted the same thing, I would've avoided that fuss and talked to you to begin with."

He spread his arms out wide and a high-pitched laugh scratched out of his throat. It died quickly. He tried another. The sound disturbed Nova. The laugh became a cough and Nova heard something rattle in him. He held his stomach and bent over and spat several times. When he stood again, tears covered his face. He wiped them with a sleeve.

"Don't worry about me," he said. "I'm strong as an ox."

Nova doubted this. He was sick and alone. She paused. Why alone? She pointed the flashlight over his shoulder.

"Where are the rest of you?"

"The rest?"

"Your people. Your cell."

"May God bless their sacrifice."

"What?"

"But, from a purely pragmatic standpoint… Is it really that great of a loss? They were all talk and talk and talk." He bobbed his head and widened his eyes and mimicked a chatty mouth with his free hand. "No action. Even when they followed me to Aggy's Island, none of them except Samuel ever wanted to put real skin in the game. I'm the only person that ever does anything about the problem."

Nova forced her mind to detach. Quinn rustled at her side, eager to join the fray. Nova pressed three fingers toward the ground as though pumping a brake. Quinn caught the signal and stilled. Nova wanted information, not a debate.

"They don't know about the bomb."

"Not exactly."

"And you left them there?"

"It's a tragedy, what you're about to do to them."

"They're going to—"

"That's the point, sweetheart. Body counts equal outrage."

Nova caught his meaning. Bombing an empty building caught attention but little outrage. Bombing a building with two dozen Originists in it would awaken white nationalists across the country.

"That's disgusting."

"Precious. Coming from one of the people who planned it."

"I didn't plan it."

"Of course not. Happened all on its own."

Nova stopped herself from arguing further. What use was there in convincing Marbury of her innocence? Still, her arteries pressed against her skin as though muscling a message from her heart to the world.

"I do not think or feel or live the way you are thinking and feeling and living."

She read confusion on his face. Then, his lips jerked into a slanted smile.

"Somebody does."

She considered it. Her brother, who would not let their people starve even if it meant compromising his morality. Her brother, who insisted she leave with their people when violence was imminent. Her brother, who would likely die for the cause in which he believed. Her brother, who did all of this because he loved a boy as his son.

"No," she said.

Marbury waved the gun in the air.

"Enough. Doesn't matter. The end will be a war and that is what you planned out and that is what I want, anyway. And, not to mention, that's what our generous funders want, too."

The gun slipped in Nova's grip. She caught it just before it rolled off her fingers.

"Our funders?"

Marbury's cheek twitched.

"You didn't know?"

He took a step forward. A strand of saliva dangled from his open mouth. He spoke slowly, savoring the moment.

"You and me are in the same bed, sister. Baze Defense Solutions. An arms manufacturer. Your weapons come from them. Our weapons come from them. They even set us up with a nice little storage bunker nearby. You should come for a visit sometime." A chill gripped Nova. He cackled. "You really didn't know. Your money comes from them. Our money comes from them. Your food, our food. Goddamn, we even use the same tunnels to get our goodies."

The revelation rocked her as though it were a physical force. She felt a fall pull at her back. She curled her toes inward and clung to balance. She slowed her breath, drove her feet into the ground. She shut her eyes and counted down from ten. Second by long second, she nudged herself back to center.

"Did you hear me?" Marbury said.

She continued counting down. She reached zero. She did not know if or how to accept Marbury's word. A joint funder. An arms manufacturer. Of course, she thought. Who would profit more from a war than the people who sold weapons? She cycled through the same question over and over and over: How could she expect justice to come from this world of terrible compromise?

She could not. She knew this, she always had.

Her body found balance.

She opened her eyes and turned her attention, wholly, to Marbury. She studied his face. As though she were observing phenomena in a lab. He squirmed. He rubbed his nose and furrowed his brows.

"Why the hell are you looking at me like that?"

She said nothing. He looked to Zahra and Quinn.

"I think your leader's gone dumb or insane."

Nova heard Quinn grunt quietly, as though swallowing words. With effort, they kept their silence. Marbury trembled. His face reddened.

"You're all insane. I try to have one rational conversation and I get this bullshit. I should know better though. It's always the same with you people. I say here is two and two, and you say five. I say this is how you jump, and you lie down." He gave a short whistle. "I shouldn't be mad though. It's not really your fault. You're made that way. The wiring is different. You shouldn't be blamed for the abilities that you just don't have." He squinted, pointed the gun's barrel at them as though pointing his finger. "The thing is, though, that you do know your place in the world. God gave you that knowledge. In your heart of hearts, you understand the natural order. You know that it's good and right and the way things are meant to be. But you push back against it. You push and you push and you push and you just won't quit. You want control. It's like coming home to your dog, and all of a sudden he decides that you're sleeping on his mat in the living room. It's not natural. It's not the way God wanted it."

An almost scientific detachment came over Nova. His words fell at her feet. He suppressed a cough and his cheeks puffed. He ran a hand over his head and Nova noticed strands of thin hair fall off. He made a kind of sense to her. Something inside him was misaligned. She thought of what he had done and she could see him doing it.

"You killed Kemba," she said.

He glared. He opened his mouth to say something and the cough he had shoved down burst. It rattled his lungs and battered his throat. He bent over and spat up thick phlegm. It dripped from his lower lip. He wheezed. Nova kept her gaze on him. She again contemplated what she saw. A decaying man. Hemmed in by ideas about his own body. A body that failed him now.

Nova slung her backpack off her shoulder. She unzipped it and dug a hand into the corner. She pulled out a bottle of ibuprofen. She put on her backpack and set the bottle down. "I don't want your pills," he said.

"Then leave them for the next sick person to come by here."

"You think you're a fucking witch doctor."

Nova thought about this. Would life as a witch doctor be so bad? She could spend her days drawing from centuries-old healing traditions. She would learn about herbs and spices and tonics. She would sharpen her perception of the human condition. She would see physical maladies in relation to their spiritual struggles. She would pray. She would dispense poetry and children's books and novels. She would call them preventative medicine. She would rub lavender-scented oil onto the soles of newborns. Perhaps, she thought, her fingers were best used as balms.

"It's not a bad option."

"I've got a flu. Not the plague."

Nova considered. "You have something God alone can cure."

She crossed the intersecting tunnels. She did not bother to look back. He started to holler and a series of coughs overcame him. Zahra and Quinn walked a few steps behind her. Her gun felt hot in her hand. In ten or fifteen minutes, with an ailing Marbury well behind them, she could holster it.

"Pathetic," Quinn said.

Nova closed her eyes. Marbury collected his ragged breath.

"What the hell did you say?"

Quinn turned around. "I said you're pathetic."

Rage, almost gleeful, broke into his expression. "I recognize you."

Quinn stayed silent.

"A baseball cap can't hide a traitor."

She took the cap off and tossed it to the floor. "Who the hell is hiding?"

"You should." Menace in his voice.

"Go to hell."

"Your father would be ashamed."

"Fuck my father."

"Nigger-loving bitch." Then, so quietly Nova almost missed it, he said, "I'll take care of you first."

The words flared in her mind. Lightning before the thunderclap. Had the others heard the threat, too? She spun and Marbury's flashlight burned her sight. She saw only outlines: his fumbling with a gun and the others standing stock-still. In a split second, she raised her own and conceded to instinct and aimed into the blinding light. She pulled twice. The shots split her eardrum. Recoil shoved her shoulders back. Marbury dropped the flashlight. She heard a grunt. She blinked and made out his kneeling figure. He staggered up. He held his shoulder and put all his weight on his right leg. He swayed to the side. She looked at his hands. Empty now. His gun a little in front of him, a little off to the right. He took a half step forward before toppling to a knee. He reached beside him. A terrible confusion swallowed her. Would he make her shoot again? She raised her gun an inch. His hand slithered closer to his weapon. Her third shot rang out. The bullet found its mark. Marbury crumpled.

They walked in a silent daze. Marbury's body lay seconds or minutes or hours behind them. They had not buried him. They had not spoken about that decision. They had not spoken at all. One of them had lifted a foot and taken a step and trudged on. Nova could not remember who.

They came upon a second intersection. Quinn stopped and hugged Zahra. The two exchanged quiet words and embraced again. Then, Quinn came to Nova.

"This is my exit," Quinn said.

Nova was confused. "You're leaving us?"

"I'm going to our meeting spot. Me and Jeremiah."

Nova recollected their earlier conversation. Quinn and Jeremiah had a rendezvous. It seemed sweet and silly then. Now she felt, what? Abandoned? She wished she could give voice to the feeling.

Quinn met Nova's eyes. "You did the right thing. Zahra and I froze."

Nova could say nothing in return.

"He would have killed us. There was no choice."

Nova gave her a slight nod. They held hands. An anxious energy passed between their fingers. Nova struggled to find the right words. Words that might make better meaning of pulled triggers and consequences.

Quinn tightened her hold. "I love you. And thank you."

Nova watched her walk away. Why had Quinn thanked her? For shooting Marbury? For potentially saving their lives? For not pointing out the obvious: events would have unfolded differently if Quinn had only held silent a minute longer?

She followed Zahra through the tunnel. She tried to shake her swirl of emotions. Guilt at leaving her brother at Hamilton Heights. Fear of the future. Shame for Marbury's death. She examined that last one, replaying the shooting in her mind. Marbury verbally threatened them. He raised his weapon first. She shot in self-defense. Nova went over the scene twice more. The same narrative unfolded. And, still, she felt shame.

Why?

She focused on the moment between the second and third shot. Marbury already wounded. His gun at his feet. He reached for it, she told herself. That third shot followed the pattern. A necessary act. She placed a hand on her stomach. A desire flickered deep in her gut. She encouraged it to rise. Finally, the fact she did not wish to recognize: she wanted Marbury dead. Her third shot was not only in self-defense. It was an execution.

She lifted that realization to the center of her consciousness. Slowly, her daze ebbed. She saw herself clearly: neither saint nor devil. A person, only a person, reaching for justice. She had instincts both righteous and horrid. She would falter more often than not. But at least she would continue on the path toward it. She knew the same was true of Zahra and Quinn. Of her brother. He, too, must have wanted Marbury's death. Enough to risk his own life. If only he had known Marbury was onto his scheme.

And, now, what if he knew his enemy lay lifeless in the tunnel? Would his rage subside and, finally, give his conscience room to speak? Would he heed its warnings and confront the person he had become and, with only a moment to spare, call off the bombing?

Nova grabbed Zahra's elbow. "We have to go back."

"What?" Zahra asked.

"We have to go back to Hamilton Heights."

"We can't go back there."

"Jeremiah might leave. Malik, too. If we tell them Marbury is dead, they might leave."

Zahra bent her head and ran her hand over it. "No."

"No?"

"I'm not going back."

"But Jeremiah... Malik—"

"They made their choices."

"We can still save them."

"God, Nova."

"There's still time."

"You just killed a man."

Nova went breathless. Zahra swallowed. Her sentence hung between them. She pressed her hands to her temples as if putting up blinders.

"I'm not this person," said Zahra. "I don't want to be this person."

"Zahra—"

"Listen, please. I could handle when they were shooting at us. I don't want to find out if I can handle shooting at them."

Zahra began to tremble. She wiped tears from her eyes before they could escape. She took several deep breaths to collect herself.

"Please understand."

Nova found she did.

"I understand."

She wished she could embrace her friend, her sister. But the ground between them had ruptured and she did not know how to traverse the rift. Or if Zahra would want it crossed. She backed away. She thought she saw a tear and then another roll down Zahra's cheeks. She could not tell with darkness packed between them.

PART FIVE

Malik

19

MALIK TAPPED HUSH HARBOR'S westernmost gate. His skin warmed as the morning gained heat. He would leave Hamilton Heights as soon as Jeremiah was ready. Safely outside, they would detonate the explosive as they watched the government invade their home. Perhaps he should have been nervous: Jeremiah's final act, emptying his office of evidence that could compromise the revolution, was taking more time than anticipated. Jeremiah insisted on completing the task alone as a final goodbye to the place he loved. Malik glanced at his watch every so often but felt no anxiety about time. Their plan would succeed. Come what may, they would see justice done.

As he waited for Jeremiah, he looked across the complex and took in its emptiness. He patted his pocket, inside which rested Jeremiah's wooden rook. The other pocket held his notebook and a poem Zahra had gifted him. On their final night together, she had carefully torn it from its book, folded it once and placed it in his palm.

"Don't read it now," she'd said.

"Why not?"

"Read it in a lonely moment. When you need it."

He'd kissed her and they sat on the bed together. She rested her head on his shoulder. He gathered his nerve.

"Jeremiah and I," he said. "We're not—"

She waved a hand. She made the same gesture the last time he tried to tell her he was not evacuating. This time, he forged on.

"I'm not leaving Hamilton Heights," he said. "Not yet."

She did not respond. He prepared to detail the plan he had created with Jeremiah. Defend its logic. He did not want to argue on this, their last night together. But he owed her honesty. She surprised him before he could speak again.

"The reason you're staying. It's important?"

"It is."

"Worth risking your life?"

"Yes."

"And it's something you'd rather not tell me about. I can feel it."

He bit his lower lip. "You're right. I don't want to tell you about it. It's something…violent. And cruel. And necessary."

She lifted her head from his shoulder. "Okay."

Both of them looked straight ahead. He started on the specifics. "The plan is to—"

"You don't need to tell me."

He leaned an inch back. "You don't want to know?"

"No."

"Even after I told you it's cruel?"

"Especially after that."

She cupped his chin in her palm and turned it toward her. Tenderness shone in her face. Light as a feather, she kissed him. She lingered on his lips and touched her forehead to his. "We all have our own choices to make. Based on our own lives."

He knew she was referring to his parents. She placed a hand on his chest. His heart battered his ribs.

"This isn't a goodbye," he said.

She smiled at him sadly. "Okay."

Now, alone at Hush Harbor, he reached for the page she had given him. At the top, she had written *Lucille Clifton*. He read the poem's first line: *won't you celebrate with me*. A faint sound floated over him. He paid it no mind and kept reading. He lingered on the final lines. *Come celebrate / with me that everyday / something has tried to kill me / and has failed*. The sound grew louder before he could reflect on the poem's meaning. He looked through the gate's metal bars, but the morning sun momentarily blinded him. When his vision came back, he saw helicopters break over the horizon. He went still. The helicopter blades clawed upward like insects rending the sky. He jammed the poem into his pocket and adrenaline, sudden and hot, swept his body. His legs jolted forward. He sprinted across the empty courtyard and struggled to unclip his two-way radio. He held it to his lips.

"Jeremiah," he said. "They're here."

He panted. No answer.

"Jeremiah," he said again. "Can you hear me?"

Only static came through.

He rushed into the Baldwin Building and took the stairs two at a time. He reached the fourth floor. Smoke filled the hallway. It streamed out of Jeremiah's office. He approached the room. Fires burned inside of several metal bins, incinerating the paper inside: rolled-up maps and envelopes and manila folders filled with names, dates, routes. Jeremiah had destroyed any evidence that could hurt Hush Harbor or those who fought for it. Malik backed out of the room and shook the smoke from his shoulders and climbed up two more flights of stairs. He ran down another hallway and heard movement when he arrived at Jeremiah's apartment. He followed the sounds to a bedroom at the back. On the bed, he saw the remote belonging to the explosive they planted at the factory. Next to it lay Jeremiah's two-way radio. Jeremiah stood over the bed, looking down.

"Jeremiah," he said. "They're here."

Despair clouded Jeremiah's eyes. He picked up the remote and weighed it in his hand.

"We have to do it now," Malik said.

Jeremiah rubbed the top of the remote with his thumb. He grazed its only button.

"How many people do you think are in there?" he asked.

"The factory?"

"A dozen? Two? Three?"

"It doesn't matter."

Jeremiah looked at him. "Why not?"

"This is a war."

"That's the problem, then. I just realized it."

"Realized what?"

"I'm a teacher. Not a general."

Malik opened his mouth to protest and then caught the sight of helicopters in the window. How many of them were there? They dotted the sky as though an infestation. Urgency filled him. How could Jeremiah vacillate at this final moment?

"You have to push the button."

Jeremiah stared at the remote. Slowly, he set it on the bed. He crossed the room and stood in front of Malik. He cupped the young man's face in his palms. He spoke with love.

"I can't do this."

"We—"

"This is not us."

"Jeremiah—"

"We're not killers."

"They attacked us first." Anger simmered in the words.

"It's not our right. To sentence people to death."

"It's not theirs, either."

"We can't become like them."

"We're nothing like them." A growl in his tone.

"Then we can't press that button."

"This is different than what they do."

"How is our murder different, Malik?"

Malik grew frustrated. All this quibbling when their plan was near completion. He pulled Jeremiah's hands from his face. "It's justice. The movement needs it, we need it, I need—" He stopped himself short. A beat passed.

"I'll do it."

He brushed by Jeremiah, nipping his shoulder. Before he reached the bed, Jeremiah grabbed his elbow. He bristled at the touch and shook him off.

"You can't," Jeremiah said.

Rage rushed through him.

"This isn't your choice," he said.

"Back away." Steel in Jeremiah's voice.

"No."

Jeremiah took a step forward. "Malik."

Malik straightened his back. He squared his shoulders. Jeremiah did the same. How had they come to this? The room collapsed into the space between them. Neither gave an inch.

Jeremiah lunged for the remote and Malik grabbed his arm, spinning him away. Jeremiah caught himself against the bed. He turned around quickly and rushed at Malik headfirst. His shoulder slammed into Malik's stomach. They crashed to the floor. Malik gasped for air and his back spasmed in pain. He rolled over and pushed himself halfway up. Jeremiah tugged at his ankles and, instinctively, Malik kicked out. His sole caught Jeremiah square in the face and he heard a gruesome crack. As though Jeremiah's nose or jaw or both had shattered. Malik jumped to his feet and grabbed the remote off the bed and looked down. Jeremiah's eyes glazed over, rolled back. He coughed and spat blood. He tried standing and wobbled and then knelt on one knee. He lifted his gaze.

"You can't do this," Jeremiah said. "You shouldn't."

"They deserve it."

"It's not about them. You do this, what do you become?"

A steady whir descended over them. The noise grew until it seemed to come from inside the building. Was that one chopper or a dozen? The sound sunk beneath them and Malik knew the soldiers were landing.

He pushed the button.

Nothing happened. Less than a handful of blocks away, the sound of the explosion should have reached them. He pushed the button again. Nothing. He examined the remote and found a knob on the back. An on-and-off switch. Before he could flip it, Jeremiah sprang toward him. He sidestepped and Jeremiah stumbled. He did not wait for their next tussle. He ran into the living room, looking over his shoulder. Jeremiah ran after him, legs unsteady. Malik got halfway down the hallway before he heard a loud thud. He glanced back. He saw Jeremiah slumped on the floor just outside his apartment. Red stained a spot, eye-level, on the doorframe. Had Jeremiah slammed into it hard enough to leave blood? Malik stopped at the top of the stairs. Jeremiah struggled from the floor to a sitting position. His head flopped back against the wall.

Malik faltered. An instinct told him to run back to Jeremiah. Check on him. A stronger instinct told him to run away. To settle a score with history. His fury carried him down the stairs. He exited the building through the rear entrance and sprinted for the nearest gate, where the sound of blades and wheels and feet echoed around him. He thought he saw Nova running toward the building he had just left but ignored the illusion. He raced out of Hush Harbor and sprinted east. The garment factory came into view. He stopped a block away from it. The remote almost slipped out of his palm. He flipped the on switch.

He pressed the button.

The blast jarred his senses and the earth rumbled and a wave of heat flowed over him. He covered his head as debris crashed into him. Dust enwrapped his body and he made the mistake of inhaling. He tried to cough out the dirt and only took more in.

His lungs fought for breath as he staggered away from the inter-section. He faltered onto his knees. Gradually, the air cleared. He looked to the sky and saw a plume of smoke above the spot the factory once stood.

The world went silent. As though he had stumbled into the eye of a hurricane. Then, gunfire interrupted. He looked around him. More shots came. He ducked. Several seconds passed and the noise died. He lifted his head, saw no one. He noticed static. The sound was coming from the two-way radio in his pocket. He set it down and turned it off. He pulled out the wooden rook and placed it on the road. He started to run again. He started to weep.

Malik hid behind garbage dumpsters and in back alleys and beneath abandoned cars for hours. Government soldiers, newly arrived, crawled over Aggy's Island. When the sounds of their footsteps came too close, he stopped his breath. The soldiers did not know the island as he did. They had memorized maps, he had learned shadows. At some point, intuition took over, or maybe survival instinct. His feet turned north. He slipped from one hidden corner to another. Eventually, he found the row house with the dull red door and black knob. He thought maybe there was a bed in it. If not, a floor would do just fine. Any spot he could lie down.

THE PRINCES

Hope

Bravery

Harmony

20

NOVA'S WATCH READ 3:17. She thought another day in thick darkness would guarantee safety. Her leg tingled. Soon, she knew, the numbness would give way to cramps. That might last an hour or two or ten before her leg went numb again. She had wept, silently and often, at the start. So had her brother. Now, though, she could not afford to cry. She needed to conserve energy. The thought of the next twenty-four hours broke her patience. She shook her brother. He rustled and went still. She shook him again.

"We're going now," she said. "I'll drop first. Wait thirty seconds. Then you."

He mumbled something inaudible under his breath.

"Did you hear me?"

She thought she saw him nod. She reached to her side and unhooked a ring of clasps. She made a fist and banged at the circle's center. The trapdoor fell open. A rush of air came from below. She gulped it down. She waited for several more minutes. No other sound came. No boots, no doors, no voices. She moved her feet to the hole. Inch by inch, she slid out. With only her forearms still in the ceiling, she let herself drop. Her legs buckled against the ground. A searing pain tore through her back and spread into her limbs. She curled on the floor, let the pain smolder. She rolled away from where she had landed and looked up.

Her memory flashed an image of her brother half-conscious and leaning against the wall outside his door. His jaw had hung to the side, unnaturally twisted. Blood had covered the bottom of his face. His nose had dripped. She'd raced toward him, knelt, her stomach filled with dread. She held his face tenderly.

"Jeremiah." It had been both a plea and a command.

He opened his eyes. The slightest relief came to her.

"I need you to focus," she said. "Stand on three."

She wrapped his arm around her shoulder, then counted to three and stood. She began walking down the hall and he grumbled something and slowed.

"We have to go now," she said. "The soldiers are already here."

He fought for breath. "Not this way. My room."

She wavered.

"Trust," he said.

She walked them to his room. He pointed at the closet. She opened it and they squeezed in and he pointed up. She made out a large watermark.

Now, two days later, she waited for him to drop out of the ceiling. Would she have to climb back in and pull him down? She waited some more. Just as she determined to hiss his name, he tumbled out. His shoulder hit the floor with a crack. It missed her by an inch. He flopped from his side to his back. A heap of limbs not quite alive. But not dead, either.

Jeremiah rotated his ankles and stretched his neck, testing his joints. He heard a faucet. How long ago had his sister dragged herself to the bathroom? How long had they been in the ceiling? His head swam. His nose ached. He opened his mouth and hurt stabbed through his jaw. He decided not to open it again.

He crawled out of the closet.

Bullet holes pocked the wall. He almost smiled thinking that the soldiers had shot at their own shadows. He dragged himself across the bedroom and his sister opened the bathroom door and helped him in. He opened the tap and water came out. A miracle, he thought. He drank it by the mouthful. The moisture burned dry tissue in his throat. His sister handed him a bar of soap and left the room. He stripped down. Every bend caused a fresh agony. He washed himself. His skin, flaky and covered in small cuts, flamed. When he finished, he put his dirty clothes back on.

He tried to recollect how Nova had saved him. He caught fragments of it, but pain had already overcome him by the time she arrived. He did remember what came before. His fight with Malik. His hand flew to his collarbone as if holding in his heart. Had Malik done it in the end? Had he detonated the bomb? Jeremiah buried his face in his palms. How could he have let their disagreement come to blows? Was Malik another boy he had lost? Grief trembled through him, feverish and hungry. He shook his head. No, he told himself. If he let the hurt come now, it would break his bones.

Nova checked the time again. Her watch read 4:15. She opened the bathroom door and found Jeremiah leaning over the sink. He dipped his face in handfuls of water.

"We should go now," she said. "Before it gets light."

He shut off the faucet. Silently, they left the bathroom and exited the apartment. She walked near the walls in case her legs bowed. The stairs tested her ankles. Her tendons curled like pieces of cardboard. Still, she moved much faster than her brother. He labored as though moving through a hurricane. She slackened her pace.

On the ground floor, she looked side to side. The hallway was empty. She crept to the back door and peered out its glass window, then pushed it open enough to squeeze through. She and

Jeremiah rounded the building, avoiding the central courtyard. She did not know if they were lucky or if the night shielded them or if the government truly had set no patrol for Hamilton Heights. She did not dwell on the reason no soldiers spotted them.

They came to a small, unmanned gate. When she placed a hand on it, the metal sent a chill through her palm.

"Nova."

The voice came from the other side of the gate. She and Jeremiah halted. A soldier held the gate open. She read the name sewn into the soldier's uniform. *P. Schwab.* One of theirs. She hurried through the gate. The soldier scanned their surroundings, leaned in. He hissed street names and patrol times.

"Fucking miracle. You're both still here and still alive and I'm the one on duty," he said. "Go. Now."

She mouthed *thank you* and did not know if it was meant for him or God or the island's guardian angels. She tugged at her brother's elbow.

His feet hurt, but he tried to match Nova's strides. Adrenaline pumped through his joints. They broke into a half jog. They heard the sound of a car and hid in an alley against a brick building. The sound passed.

They started walking down another backstreet, and he wondered if Quinn had followed through on their plan, if she was waiting in the safe house for him. He smiled and then the thought turned sour. What if she had been caught? He felt a rising panic. He brought his attention back to the street. He knew his stamina would wane in minutes. He needed to focus. He saw daybreak ahead.

Several hours later, Nova stood in front of the row house with the dull red door. Jeremiah trailed her by a dozen yards. She thought he might collapse at any moment. She had thought this for the last hour. When he finally caught up to her, she placed a hand under his elbow.

"This is the one?" she asked.

"This is it."

He kneeled down, jiggled a loose brick and slid it out. He scooped a key from its hollowed center.

"Here," he said. He gave her the key. She noticed his hand trembling. "My hand… It won't stop. I don't think I can open the door."

A consequence, so small, of their trauma. It caught her off guard. She turned her head and blinked away tears, told herself to hold back the feeling. They were not safe just yet. She slid the key into a black knob and opened the door.

Inside the row house, Jeremiah noticed Nova's shoulders drop. He felt the full weight of his exhaustion. Were they safe now? Were they okay?

Nova heard a television playing at the back of the house. She signaled for Jeremiah to stay put. He seemed in a daze. She walked toward the noise, stopping outside the living room. The door was ajar. She glanced in and saw the back of a couch with two heads facing the television. She drew her gun and pushed the door open with her toe. It made no sound.

She readied to clear her throat. To call the room's attention. Then, the screen filled with an image of Hamilton Heights. A pair of newscasters marveled at how quickly it had emptied out. They played a clip of Interim Mayor Rex Baker's press conference. He stood at a podium in front of several American flags, sweat glistening on his brow. Stark light drenched the room. He pushed his chin out, called on a reporter.

"Do you have any idea where they went? Or how they escaped?" the reporter asked.

Baker set his hands on the podium's edges. "We've got noth-ing to share with you about that."

He pointed to a second reporter.

"Does this mean that the Hush Harbor movement is still active?"

"I'm not going to speculate."

"What about their leadership? Do you have any information on the Princes?"

"Nothing to share."

"What about John Marbury?" called a reporter from the back row. "Was he at the bombing of the Originists' cell on Aggy's Island?"

"We're still working to gather all of the facts."

The questions came faster now.

"Were you aware of the group's location?"

"We were aware of what we needed to be aware of."

"Have you seen the image of Marbury wearing a white robe?"

"I have."

"Are you worried about the impression it gives the public?"

"What impression?"

Cameras flashed. The room tensed.

"Is the Bliss City government allied with white nationalist groups?"

Baker's face twitched.

"That's ridiculous."

"Bliss exonerated John Marbury. Then it raided Hush Har-bor at the same time the Originists were bombed. Was that just coincidence?"

"Those things have nothing to do with each other."

"Are you protecting white nationalists?"

"Enough. Press conference over."

Baker stomped away from the microphone.

The program returned to the newscasters. They showed the picture of John Marbury again. They explained that it had enflamed the country. Who had known white nationalists were tied, directly, to Kemba's death? Had Marbury acted impulsively in killing Kemba or was he part of a scheme orchestrated to provoke further violence? Had the Originists tried to start a war? Images of various protests flashed across the screen. In some, police stayed behind barricades. In others, they used batons and tear gas against the crowds.

Then, the broadcast turned to footage of counterprotests. Thousands carrying white supremacist signs. They shouted, "Marbury lives." One interviewee claimed that biased media only wanted Americans to believe Marbury was dead to damage the Originist cause. The newscasters attempted to dispel the misinformation. They stressed that Marbury had not been heard from in days, that he and a dozen others likely died in the bombing of the Originist hideout on Aggy's Island. A political commentator noted that some Originists now claimed to be the victims of Hush Harbor aggression. "I can't entirely disagree," the commentator said. "They did just murder a whole cell of Originists."

Then, the newscasters began inventorying violent incidents between protestors and counterprotestors. Places where the sides had met. Brawls and gunfire and hundreds wounded. They asked themselves if the protesting white supremacists were organized. They wondered if Hush Harbor's network had been national. If the Originists were nationwide as well.

One of the newscasters pressed on her earpiece. She held up a finger, interrupting her co-anchor. She looked down at the desk, distressed.

"Various groups have delivered declarations of independence to mayor's offices in Atlanta, Baltimore, Philadelphia, Chicago, Houston, Hartford and at least five other cities. The groups claim to be local branches of Hush Harbor. Our teams on the ground are working to confirm details."

Nova's stomach dropped. Hush Harbors across the country.

A month ago, she would have welcomed this. Now questions derailed her optimism. How would they feed themselves? How many weapons did they have? How would they learn how to aim and breathe and shoot true?

Did they know how many lines they would need to cross to survive?

She stared at the television. She no longer heard the news-casters. She no longer registered the screen. She saw ruin, only ruin, snaking into the future.

Jeremiah limped into the living room. He watched the news segment over Nova's shoulder. Hush Harbors across the country. A nationwide revolution. Armed and defiant. What he had wanted.

And yet no joy came to him. No elation, no satisfaction. Only grief. He ran a hand over his chest. A gale of dizziness broke over him. His vision flicked in and out and his mind warned of collapse. He begged his body to push a bit further. He took several steps forward and stood next to Nova. He reached for her hand.

Finally, he noticed the couch. The two people sitting at the ends turned simultaneously. He watched them stand. He watched their eyes widen and their faces flush with relief. Quinn and Malik. He thought hallucination had taken hold of him. He shook his head. How to believe this was real? How to believe they were alive? How to believe they were here and so was Nova and so was he? These small mercies. He could not bear them. His breath came in staccato bursts, and he dropped to his knees, and he laid his forehead on the ground. He felt hands on his back. Warmth. He cried out but no noise came. Only a gasp. Only a flicker of hope. And, then, the sound of his loved ones, gently ushering him alive.

★ ★ ★ ★ ★

ACKNOWLEDGMENTS

THANK YOU TO:

God, above all, for too many blessings to count.

My two beautiful children, Ella and Taraz, who deepen and enrich every facet of my life, including my writing.

My wife, Candace, who sacrificed sleep and sanity for this novel. I could not have asked for a more loving, curious and perceptive partner.

My parents, Ladan and Anthony, who continue to teach me how to live in this world. The older I grow, the more I realize how much your love, guidance and example shaped the core of who I am today.

My sister and brother-in-law, Shayda and Andrew, who are beloved mentors and my closest friends. I am so grateful that we get to share our lives with each other.

My Mamanjoon, for her laughter, love and rebellious spirit, traits that she passed down to my mother, my uncle and my generation.

My grandma, Juanita, for so diligently and courageously raising three boys, including my father, in a world that didn't want them.

My mother-in-law, Ann, for infusing my life with just the right mix of vibrancy and compassion.

My ancestors, especially Aggy, Richard and Hudson Vance, who survived slavery. I pray you have peace.

My best friend, Chris, for being among the inspirations for the novel and reading through more drafts than I can recall.

My cousins, Erica and Zhaleh, for their thoughtful readership and consistent support.

My agent, Caroline, who is likely a genius and definitely a real one. Also, thank you to everyone at what has long been my dream literary home, Frances Goldin Literary Agency, for their continual support.

My editor, John, who is a brilliant writer, a wise editor and a warm partner in this work. Also, thank you to everyone at Hanover Square Press and the whole publishing team (Eden, Justine, Sophie, Brianna and so many more) who have shaped this wonderful process.

My writing professors and mentors, Lauren, Lisa and Pat, for so expertly channeling my passion and sometimes frenetic energy into the joyous craft of writing.

My friend Shannon Delaney, who used one of her many formidable talents to make me look good in the jacket cover photo.

Everyone, everyone, everyone who has encouraged me along the way, including but not limited to: Antonio B., Ayo C., Charlotte E.S., Chris A., Chris M., David B., Ian S., Jacob C., Justin V., Lee E.C., Myra A., Peter S., Ryan S., Soyica C. and Suzanne P., as well as:

All my English teachers.

All the poets I wrote with and for in college.

All the writers I workshopped with in graduate school.

All the writers I have read and loved.